I KICK AND I FLY

RUCHIRA GUPTA

SCHOLASTIC PRESS / NEW YORK

All rights reserved. Published by Scholastic Press, an imprint of Scholastic Inc.,
Publishers since 1920. SCHOLASTIC and associated logos are trademarks and/or
registered trademarks of Scholastic Inc.

Library of Congress Cataloging-in-Publication Data available

ISBN 978-1-338-82509-1

10 9 8 7 6 5 4 3 2 1   23 24 25 26 27

Printed in the U.S.A.   37

First edition, April 2023

Book design by Christopher Stengel

To all the Heeras of the world,
because I know you will fly . . .

PART I

There would be no bright
stars without dim stars.

~Bruce Lee

CHAPTER ONE

Forbesganj, Bihar, India

My stomach growls as I walk through the wrought-iron gates into school.

Today is Monday. I'm always hungriest after the weekend at home.

The main gate of the school opens off a tarred road lined with tall eucalyptus trees. I breathe in their tangy, sour smell. The faded pink of our L-shaped, two-story school building greets me with a brief, reassuring familiarity.

The low wall is very gray now, though at some point I'd like to think that it too had been pink. It wraps around the entire compound, marking our patch as separate from the green rice fields that surround us on three sides.

I feel the other kids' eyes on me as I cross the courtyard. Maybe because their clothes are washed and starched every day and mine aren't. Maybe they can hear my stomach's hungry growl. Maybe they know that food is why I really come to school.

Last night, Mai found some potato peels and boiled them with a little salt. She forages the garbage near the railway tracks for leftovers because Baba takes her earnings to gamble.

I think of him, big and tall, despite his limp. He twirls his flowing black mustache as he walks around with a swagger in his lungi sarong, red plastic sunglasses, and a bandanna tied around his neck. Looking at him, you wouldn't think that our family is starving.

But, in our lane, when everyone is cold, dirty, and hungry, we are hungrier, dirtier, and colder than everyone else.

I breathe deeply and remind myself that I can feel confident, because today, I look more like the other children. I'm not barefoot. I have on a pair of white canvas shoes that I found near the railway tracks. I stare down at the bindis I've stuck over the torn parts, where I've painted little flower petals of blue and black around them with eyeliner pencils.

Still, the nerves find their way to my chest. Whenever I get anxious about class, about the other kids, I think of the breeze over the green rice fields and the white birds that nest there.

I arrive at the two buildings at the end of the courtyard. The hostel for orphaned and vulnerable girls is on one side and the school building on the other. All the rooms of the L-shaped school building open onto a long wraparound veranda. The doors are never shut, even in the monsoon season, and there is always a breeze, even when there is no electricity to power the ceiling fans.

Parrots, sparrows, crows, and even squirrels all nest in the old mango, semal cotton, and guava trees here. And in a corner of the courtyard, just near the swings, is a mud stretch where the hostel girls exercise in white pants and jackets every day. I watch them practice their high kicks as I walk to class.

The kids point and whisper at me as I walk into the school building, but I don't stop or look at anyone. I keep walking down the long corridor and into class. I prefer the days that they don't notice me. It's better than the alternative. The heady smell of steaming rice wafts in from the school kitchen and my eyes blur from the hunger.

"Pretty shoes," says Manish as I walk in. I blush with pleasure and sit next to him.

Perhaps he's back to being my friend again like the old days. Before Rosy went away.

It's been a while since I let myself think of her. Her long black hair, just like mine. Her dimpled round cheeks and upturned eyes. Our teacher always mixed us up, even though I'm much darker than her and am always dressed in the same black salwar kameez, patched up in many places. I wonder if Manish misses his sister as much as I miss my best friend.

I don't know how or when Manish became the most popular kid in school. Maybe because he's a good student, or because he's strong and powerfully built. The girls clamor for his attention and the boys cling to him as if his confidence might rub off on them. Or maybe because his father is a police officer, the famous Suraj Sharma, and Manish comes to school in the police van. In the monsoon season, he gives the school principal a lift too.

I place my schoolbooks on the desk and turn to him with a smile. He points at my painted shoes. "They don't really hide your dirty feet. You can still see that they're old and torn."

Everyone bursts out laughing.

Math class begins. Our teacher, Sunil Sir, sits on a big chair behind a wooden desk. He's neatly dressed, as usual. His large bony body conceals his gentle and patient nature. I take my stubby pencil and dirty notebook out of my worn cloth satchel and begin to listen.

I'm so hungry I can't hear a word. If anyone bothered to check, they would see just how completely lost I really am. I copy the problem set on the board and then write borderline nonsense. Or maybe it does make sense, and I just can't tell. I can't stop thinking about the rice and daal boiling in the kitchen.

My stomach performs a big, famished rumble as soon as the bell rings.

Manish hears. "Don't worry, Heera, it's lunchtime now," he says mockingly. And again, everyone starts laughing. Of course they know food is why I come to school.

I focus my eyes away from my classmates and toward the trees outside. One day I'll get used to the hunger and hopelessness like Mai.

Manish gets up from the wooden bench we share and walks to one near the door. He sits down like royalty with his feet up on a desk in front of him and his back resting on a table behind him. A few of the boys gather around him. He says something and they all laugh. I know they're up to something, but I have to get past them to get to the mess hall.

When I make my way through the narrow aisle between the tables, my gaze is fixed toward the door. I'm almost there when I trip over something—a foot perhaps—and the ground falls out from under me.

My arms shoot out to break my fall, but I'm too late. I'm flat on my face. A spot of blood leaks from my nose as I get up off the floor.

Without wiping it, I run from the laughter. My toes push apart the already-torn canvas of my shoes.

I take my mat and spread it on the floor of the mess hall. As I cross my legs to sit, I sneak a look at my toes peeping out of the torn shoes. Are my feet really dirty? I look more closely. They're cracked and coated with filth. I thought my brown skin hid the dirt, but it doesn't really work that way, I suppose. I curl my toes into my shoes and tuck my feet under me.

And then the food arrives. Whole spices, cauliflower, and chunks of potatoes almost melt into the roasted moong daal that has been boiled with rice and arhar daal. The khichdi glistens with the spoonful of ghee topping it. I can think of nothing else as I swallow great, big, hungry mouthfuls. We are almost done eating by the time they bring around the boiled eggs. One perfect, gleaming oval hits my steel plate and rolls around. Eggs are only served twice a week, and they have always been my favorite food. I can practically taste the egg's rich, heavy, buttery flavor.

I keep my eye on it as I finish the rest of my food. I know it won't disappear, but I don't dare to look away. The kids around me don't seem to notice when I slip the egg into my bag.

What if I were to leave now and bring Mai the egg for lunch? My full stomach is a heavy burden to bear. But as I quietly file out, Manish suddenly appears at my elbow with two other boys who I don't know as well.

"Oh, hello, Heera," Manish says with a smirk. "What's in the bag?"

I hold on to my bag tightly.

"What do you do when you aren't at school?" asks one of the boys with him before I can respond.

"I bet I know what she does when she isn't here," says another boy. He walks forward and stands beside Manish. They don't live far from our lane lined with small brothel rooms behind the huts. They know.

"Why does she come to school, anyway? We know what she'll end up doing. You don't need to read and write to do that," the first boy says, as if I'm not even here.

"Yeah, like that cousin of hers, Mira. Bet she spends all day *reading*," taunts the other boy.

Their laughter echoes through my brain. My cheeks are on fire and my heart begins to race. Shame creeps onto my skin, heating my face from the inside.

And then Manish grabs my bag, and I know immediately what he's going to do. I try to snatch it back, but he's already reached inside. His smile is an awful thing across his face.

"Heera laid an egg! Heera laid an egg!" he sings as he pulls out the egg and holds it above his head.

I run after him as he strides down the corridor. It's as though I'm back in front of my family's tiny hut just a few days ago, chasing down the pig that stole my little sister Chotu's only good shirt. That didn't end well, and neither will this.

I don't even know my next move; I act on impulse and kick Manish hard in his butt. And as he tumbles to the floor, I reach out and yank the egg out of his hand.

Miraculously, it is intact. I put it into my pocket, and before he can get up, I let my fist fly, hitting him straight in the face. I watch, as though in slow motion. Blood flies out of his mouth. I lean down and pick up a tooth off the ground, and he looks at me with horror as he reaches up to his face. The shouts around me grow louder, crying for punishment. The crowd wants retribution for Manish and his broken tooth.

I return the tooth but keep the egg.

The principal is not in his office after Manish has finished dragging me through the hallways. As we wait outside, he continues to taunt me. "You're not gonna get away with this. I will make sure you never come to school again. You Nats are all thieves and prostitutes. You'll never change."

It's nothing I haven't heard before. But I can't seem to quell the anger stirring inside me before my reflexes kick in and I spit at his feet.

The principal comes around the corner at that very moment. "What is going on?" he asks angrily, waving his walking stick.

"Manish tripped me and pulled my bag, sir," I stammer.

Manish shows him the broken tooth.

The principal looks at me furiously, his bald head glimmering. "As it is, the other parents object to admitting children like you to this school."

I hang my head, staring at the floor just in time to see a mouse scuttling by.

"Please come to my office," the principal says. He doesn't say a word to Manish.

Manish returns to class as I walk into the principal's chamber.

"I'm sorry," I mumble, my head still down as I slowly enter.

"I'm afraid I can't keep you in school any longer. Your father can come and take all your certificates. But you will have to find admission in some other school," the principal says in a firm voice as I stand in front of his desk.

"Please, sir . . ." I attempt to explain what happened, but he pulls out a file and begins to make notes as if I'm not there.

"No explanations necessary. There's no room for discussion under the circumstances. Just leave," the principal repeats in a voice that brooks no ifs, ands, or buts.

I wait silently for a few moments, hoping he will give me an opening. But after an agonizing minute of standing there, invisible, I walk out, tormented by the principal's words.

I begin to shake uncontrollably.

My arms and legs feel too heavy to walk home. I don't want to face Mai's tears and Baba's fists. But it's too late for that. Much too late. Baba will tell her he was right: We Nat tribes are not meant for school. Mai will lose face to Baba after all her sacrifices to make sure I could attend.

What will I eat?

I walk past the empty schoolyard, my feet pinching in my hand-me-down shoes. The other children are all still in class, including Salman, my model older brother—always so calm and studious. He's able to crack a joke to defuse a fight. But me? I fight too easily. I lose my temper in a minute.

I reach the referral hospital. I can see our dirt lane, smell the rotten food dumped by the food carts as I cross the railway tracks. My stomach growls automatically while my senses revolt. My insides know that the smell means food.

I leave the pigs to it this time. Tomorrow, when the hunger rises like a serpent in my stomach, biting my insides, when even the swallowing of my saliva won't still the cramps, I will come back.

My eyes sting and I realize the tears have already come.

I straighten my shoulders and walk to our makeshift plastic home propped against one solid wall. My future is a hazy, unknowable thing, full of menacing shadows. My actions could very well seal the fate for my younger sisters, Chotu and Sania, as well.

Perhaps Chotu might fulfill my mother's dreams. She is a plucky five-year-old. Her thin, spiny body conceals a determined spirit. Perhaps my brother, Salman, will calm Baba down. He'll crack a joke, and everyone will forget that they have to share their portion of food with me. Perhaps Baba will be happy that he was right. Perhaps he will leave for the liquor shop without beating me or yelling at Mai.

Perhaps Mira Di has sent some milk over for Sania, the baby.

Perhaps I will be able to sell my canvas shoes to the garbage recycling uncle at the head of our lane.

Perhaps I will accustom myself to the constant hunger like Mai. Now that I am old enough—fourteen going on fifteen.

Perhaps, perhaps, perhaps . . .

But perhaps, now that I am not in school, it will be easier for Baba to sell me. I can quell the pangs of hunger, but I cannot quell the fear of what awaits me if Baba and Ravi Lala push aside Mai's wishes.

CHAPTER TWO

Chotu coughs from inside our hut as I stand outside, my feet still bolted to the ground. I finally stop thinking about school when I realize that she's been sick for a full week now. With her short curly hair, tiny brown body, and black night-sky eyes, she is the favorite child of our lane. Her whining can outdo the Bollywood songs that play on mikes. But these days she hardly makes a sound except to cough.

It started the day the rain came down. Great heavy drops poured onto our tarpaulin sheet roof. We put our small collection of pots, pans, bottles, and cans where we could. The sound of the water was frightening. *Dhup-dhup dhup-dhup.* Louder and heavier by the second. There was no corner to hide in the large makeshift room we call a home—made from plastic sheets strung up in a gap between two other huts, covered by some torn tarpaulin. The plastic sheets flapped mercilessly. We sat, shivering, in the center of our hut while the water pooled around us. It soaked the plastic sheet on the floor that protected us from the cold damp earth.

A huge hole opened up in the roof as the rain tore through the tarpaulin and the water fell like a cannonball. Mai sat with Chotu on her lap, cradling her from the cold. Salman and I huddled together around Sania, the spirited toddler looking so much smaller in that moment. Our bodies were soaked. The water rose in the lane and mixed with the muddy water inside our house. Unknown pieces of garbage floated around us. The other squats made of brick walls with a cement floor were more protected. Their tin and straw and bamboo-thatched roofs shielded them.

We somehow kept Sania and Chotu above the water on our laps, but we couldn't protect them from the water that poured down when the tarpaulin gave way. Baba was missing, as usual. We stayed awake all night.

I could still smell the overpowering stench the following morning when the rain finally stopped—the yucky water with garbage and excrement would take time to recede. Luckily, the railway platform was dry. So we gathered our few meager possessions and went there. We washed the pots, pans, mats, clothes, textbooks, and ourselves in the hand pump.

As we sat and dried out, I saw Mai wipe a tear. Her five-foot frame has almost disappeared into her wispy cotton sari. Her hair is nearly fully gray, though she's barely thirty. It's still long, always tied up in a bun to keep it out of the way.

The little sugar and oil we owned had washed away. There was no garbage along the tracks to scavenge from. It was all just one large pool of water. And Chotu's body was burning with a fever that she must have caught during the night.

The water is gone but Chotu's fever remains. Mai has not taken Chotu to the referral hospital. "What is the point?" she said. "I can't afford the medicine that the doctor saheb will ask me to buy anyway." She took Chotu to the bhagat, the sorcerer in our lane, instead. He said that Chotu was possessed by a demon and took five rupees from my mother to exorcise the spirit.

The bhagat had a dholak drum that he started playing. Chotu started whining. The bhagat started swaying. This was a sign of a spirit's arrival in the sorcerer's body. The spirit gave its name and asked Mai about the disease. Mai described the symptoms. He took out a banana and fed Chotu a spoonful. As Chotu stopped crying, the dhagat said the spirit had been appeased. He tied a black thread around Chotu's left arm and sent us on our way.

As I hear Chotu cough, I know she's not cured. I boil with rage at the five wasted rupees, at Mai's dependence on the sorcerer, at the price of medicine, at the boys who don't want me in school, at the principal who listens to them, at all the injustices in my life, at the shoes that are of no use.

I will tell Mai what happened at school, but not now. Maybe later, when Chotu gets better.

I pause just as I'm about to step inside.

Chotu has stopped coughing.

I can hear Mira Di's sobbing more clearly from next door in the back room of my uncle's shack and suddenly I can't bring myself to move.

A customer walks out with a swagger. He tightens his belt and I wonder if he's beaten her with it. Two other men are already lined up outside their hut. Chacha, my uncle, comes out and nods toward Chachi, my aunt, who is sitting on a bench outside their door. She takes money from the man next in line and he goes to the back room.

The fear that lurks in the dark recesses of my heart uncoils. It pursues me like a shadow whenever I lose hope. Along the lane, behind each hut made of bamboo, thatch, straw, and brick, there is a back room with a narrow door, a small window with iron bars, and a large wooden bed. On one of those beds is my cousin, Mira Di. She is a prostitute, and one day, if Baba has his way, I will be one too—one of the ghost-like girls sitting on benches outside the seventy or so shacks that line both sides of our lane. They sit in a pool of light in bright, tight clothes and red lipstick. The light comes from lanterns that hang above each bench, giving our area the name Lalten Bazaar, but mostly it is known as Girls Bazaar.

Salman and I have often waited outside these huts, hoping to collect tips from the clients who asked us to fetch the local liquor, tharra, or the more expensive Ingleesh. The girls sometimes ask for other things like a white powder in a little packet known as pudiya or the tobacco called zarda and khaini. Sometimes they ask for paan masala. We get the powder from shops that call themselves dispensaries, manned by people who call themselves doctors.

I twirl Rosy's bracelet on my wrist. The one she gave me before she left. Suddenly, I feel I will go mad with all this noise. The crying and the sobbing mingle with the sound of the quarreling children, the speakers blaring Bollywood item songs, the screaming vendors, the drunken brawls and customers haggling over the price of a girl.

I think of Mira Di, the textbooks she bought Salman and me with the money she hides from Chacha. Of Mai and the daily wages she hands over to Baba to keep him satisfied whenever he wants alcohol, so that he will not be tempted to reach out for me.

I can't go into our shack. I can't bear to see Mai's face just yet.

I walk to the railway platform. I will watch the trains come and go. I will watch laughing families, people in clean clothes, busy porters and vendors, and forget about my day.

The lane is not long, but every inch is occupied with filth—more broken glass bottles, discarded food, tinfoil, used condoms, plastic soda bottles, discarded sanitary pads, medicine wraps, beedi, and ciga- rette butts per square inch than a dumping ground. Rats and pigs vie with dogs for the dregs of grime they can eat.

I cross the road and stay in the shadows. I pass the gambling joint. Luckily, Baba is not there. It's just a few benches, a couple of carrom tables, and some straw mats for the men playing cards. Men leer at me, shouting obscene comments as I walk past while they gather around a makeshift roulette wheel on the floor.

My stomach rumbles as I smell pakoras frying in the tin shack café on the other side of the road. Jamila Bua greets me with a motherly smile. She often has a sweet for Chotu and Sania tied inside a knot at the end of her sari. The old lady fries her famous pakoras in a huge pan resting on some bricks over an open wood fire. She says she makes the strongest tea in the world. Her big aluminum pot brews it all day and all night on the same makeshift brick oven.

The pawnshop is a brick room with an iron shutter that's pulled down and bolted with heavy locks in the mornings. Outside, the pawnshop uncle sits on a folding chair in a loose shirt and pajamas. He is square and fat and only gets up if someone has gold to sell. Mira Di has seen him pull gold from someone's teeth with an iron plier. She says he lends money at an exorbitant interest. That if you're in his clutches, you'll never get out. I know that he also recycles discarded things.

I look down at my shoes. They've caused enough problems today. If I hadn't worn these shoes, the kids wouldn't have laughed at me, and I wouldn't have gotten angry. Manish wouldn't have gotten under my skin. I wouldn't have broken his tooth. I wouldn't have to worry about my next meal.

My whole family has always been barefoot. Everyone except Salman—the blue-eyed boy of the family and our future hope—and my father. Mira Di buys Salman laced black leather shoes with her earnings every two years. My father wears sandals made from used car tires. My mother is barefoot, as are my two younger sisters. She walks on the hot tar road and works in the fields without any slippers. She says her soles have hardened over the years. She ignores her bleeding feet, simply washes them in water and rubs them with some aloe vera leaves without a murmur.

I am the first one in our family to wear laced canvas shoes and I'm sure fate has punished me for my presumption. If I sell the shoes, perhaps my luck will turn. I take them off and walk to the pawn uncle.

He takes one look from his chair and utters the word *garbage*.

I feel tears threaten my eyes. But then I decide that the shoes have value to me.

I put them back on defiantly. But as I lace them tight, I can feel someone looking at me from the only two-storied house in the red-light area. Standing on the second-floor balcony above the pawnshop is a man with a lungi wrapped around his waist and a gold chain gleaming on his bare chest. I know at once who he is without looking him in the face. Ravi Lala picks at his teeth. His eyes focus on me speculatively. His henna-dyed orange beard glints in the setting sun.

From his perch, he makes sure that everyone knows he controls the red-light area. He knows what's going on in every family, in every mud hut. He knows when babies are born, when girls reach puberty, when a baby girl is abandoned at the referral hospital across the road, which nurse will sell her, and which brothel owner will buy her. He knows. And as a part of Ravi Lala's gang, Baba and Chacha do what they're told.

He looks at me now as he has since the moment we came to Girls Bazaar seven years ago. Now I am a girl of just the right age. *Ripe, fresh meat, a new commodity, naya maal* are terms used for girls like us. We starve because he wants us to starve. The police do not protect us when we are attacked because he wants it that way. That's what Mira Di says. So that he can buy me on the cheap from my father and sell me to the dance companies in the fair.

And I realize that even if my shoes were of value, there is no point.

They might have paid for one more meal, but then what? The Mela, our annual traveling fair, is coming to town in a few weeks. The best time to auction a girl. The dance companies that accompany the fair buy the girls and sell them to enough "clients" to recover their investment within days.

Men come from far and wide to sell and buy their produce. The harvest of Girls Bazaar is us girls. My shoes alone could never be worth enough to save me from my fate.

I can't hear Chotu coughing as I walk into our hut after nightfall, hanging my schoolbag from a rusty nail that juts out from the bamboo poles of the neighboring hut.

"Salman has taken the girls with him to the highway," Mai says.

I picture him studying under the streetlight. Here, the burning coal collected from the railway tracks, which my mother is cooking on, does not throw out enough light to read by—though it dispels the darkness somewhat.

Mai balances a pot on a stove made of three bricks that enclose the coal. She boils half a fistful of rice with water filled to the brim. When the rice is ready, she will drain out the water into a different bowl and divide it into six used cans that we have collected from near the tracks. The hot drink of rice water will fill our stomachs nicely along with a bite each of the salted rice.

I take out the egg from my bag and give it to Mai with a smile. She immediately cuts it in four. I wait for her to eat a quarter, but she wants to wait for the children.

We are alone. This is the best time to break the news.

I sit next to her and hide my face in her sari.

"Mai." I take a deep breath. "The principal has told me not to come back to school."

Her eyes lock onto mine. "Heera, why? What's happened?"

It all comes out so fast. "I hit a boy. Manish and his friends tripped me, then stole my egg, so I broke his tooth and spat on him. The principal caught us and now I'm kicked out of school." My tears begin to roll.

Mai holds me tight and starts crying too. "What will we do with you?"

We both know what this means.

I sob harder.

"We will find a way," Mai says. "You will go to school in the morning as usual. Go and apologize to the principal. If he does not listen, we will talk to Mira Di. We will figure something out."

She cradles me in her arms as she thinks. I try to envision her calculations. To Mai, keeping me in school will buy enough time for her brothers, my uncles, to find me a good husband. They are pehelwans—champion wrestlers who travel far and wide to take part in competitions—and will surely find me a "suitable boy," according to Mai. But Mira Di believes that I can have a future unlike hers. She thinks that with an education, I can get a job. That the caste system is changing.

But I want neither. I've seen my uncles' strength with my own eyes. Salman and I wrestle each other and our friends all the time. I'm quite good at it. I want my uncles' strength, not their help.

Mai gets me a glass of water. I sip it slowly.

"Tonight, we will not tell your father anything. Nor the other children," she says.

Salman and the children share the egg when they come back, and Sania's cry of glee when she gets her quarter almost makes my fight with Manish worth it. I play a bit with Sania and Chotu before our little household slowly falls asleep.

Baba returns much later. I can see him talking to Mai, silhouetted in the light of his beedi stub. My father is pointing at me and saying it is time. My mother says no, a little longer. Maybe we'll find a good boy for her. My father shouts at her, saying she is crazy if she thinks they'll find a match for a girl from Girls Bazaar with no dowry.

Sania, Chotu, and Salman wake up and Chotu begins to cough. Sania whines that she is hungry. I cover my ears with my elbows to block out the sound of the quarreling and the crying. Salman picks up his books, takes the children, and goes back to the highway. Tall and gangly, Salman seems to wobble as he walks. Unlike my father, he keeps to himself but is always by our side if we need him. I listen to Baba whisper to Mai that Mira knows her duty to her family. That it's time I too did something for this family. Our hut still doesn't have walls. Chotu is sick. And Ravi Lala says he can get a good price for me when the Mela comes.

I think of the night before Rosy left. We had both cried because the Mela was in town and she would miss everything—the rides, the magic shows, the fortune-teller, the sweets, the circus, the jugglers, and the storytellers. A bamboo fence enclosed a big, tented city that came up in the Mela ground acres every winter. Suddenly rows of stalls and kiosks bustling with goods and cattle sprang up along neatly designed alleys inside this makeshift city. It housed hundreds of wonders. You needed to buy a ticket to get in, but Rosy and I simply slipped under the flapping canvases of the stalls. We used to love a motorcycle show called Maut Ka Kuan—Well of Death. Heroic cyclists would drive their bikes over the longest yawning gaps, toward impossibly far away sandpits. I used to hold my breath and shake in fear when the cyclist revved his engine and drove off a wooden plank into thin air.

Since then, I have learned to fear something much more ominous at the fair—stalls owned by dancing companies, where girls like me are bought and sold. I've heard their cries and screams when the Mela comes to town.

I pretend to be fast asleep while my mother goes to find Salman and the children.

If Baba listens to Ravi Lala, I will certainly be sold this time, especially now that I'm not even in school. My father saved my mother from the Mela in the past. For a long time, I thought he would do the same for me and my younger sisters. But now there seems to be no other option. Tomorrow I will go to school and beg.

CHAPTER THREE

Mai is already up by the time I wake to the sound of roosters crowing. She has boiled the water and mixed some sugar in it for Sania. She goes about her tasks silently. Salman, Sania, Chotu, and I each get a spoonful of the dumped rice biryani that she found near the tracks last night.

Baba is still snoring.

"Get ready," Mai orders Salman and me.

We walk to the railway platform to wash up and, at last, I have the chance to tell Salman what has happened.

"It's just not fair," I say to Salman in frustration. I swing my braid behind me and say with all the emphasis I can muster, "Even if I can somehow convince the principal to let me back in, I'm not any good at school."

Salman smiles and squeezes my shoulder. He's much less impetuous than I am.

"What other option do you have, Heera?" he asks, pulling his left ear.

He's worried. He always tugs his ears when he's nervous.

I've thought about what I want to do all night through. I hold up my hand and count out all the answers on my fingers. "Simple. I will run away from home. Join our uncles in Nepal. Become a wrestling champion. A pehelwan. Win prize money too. Then I'll come back and beat the hell out of Manish," I respond with a grin.

As usual, Salman tries to use logic. "How will you reach Nepal? Kathmandu is nearly two hundred and fifty miles away and you have no money. And you're a girl. You can't walk down this street without being harassed. Plus, you know girls aren't allowed to become pehelwans."

His words sink in. "This isn't fair," I manage to say again.

Salman sighs with relief. He knows me well enough to realize that he's talked me out of running away. That I never really intended to run away to begin with.

I feel my skin begin to prick with anger. I'm a better wrestler than Salman, but I can never become a champion wrestler. All I can do is get married or become a prostitute. Just because I'm a girl.

"Just go to school like Mai said and apologize to the principal. Go early before the other children arrive. No one will notice," Salman advises.

I'm lucky to have Salman in my life. He makes the male species look better. He says he wants to be a physicist like Galileo Galilei and study the stars or mathematics, but they don't teach advanced science in his high school because they can't afford a lab. At some point, someone just decided that poor children don't need to know advanced science.

Mira Di always says that Salman is different from other boys. "Not like my brother, Shaukat. He will save you from this place."

I remember Shaukat when he was Salman's age, when his father pulled him out of school and told him to join the line as a pimp. Now he finds clients for Mira Di and the other girls who use the back rooms.

"Promise me you won't end up like Shaukat," I said to Salman as we picked coal that had fallen from the railway engines. I had just seen Mira Di beaten by one of her clients for the first time.

"Gross, why would I do that?" he replied, brushing his hand against his cheek. A long sooty mark crisscrossed his face.

"So, you will fight for me if they try to sell me off?" I asked him as we walked to the water pump on the platform.

"Yes, I promise," he said, splashing some water on his face, feet, and hair.

"Even if that means standing up to Baba?"

"Yes, even then."

Now Salman and I pick up our books. I put on my canvas shoes and lace them tight. I've decided to wear them to school and not be ashamed. We walk back quietly, preoccupied with our own thoughts. Mai has already left for the fields with Chotu. Sania is with Jamila Bua until Mira Di wakes up. Baba is nowhere to be seen.

At the corner of the referral hospital, Salman gives me a gentle push in the direction of my school as he turns toward his own.

It takes all my inner strength to walk back into the school with my head held high. Luckily, no one is there. I pass the girls from the orphans' hostel practicing near the swings in their white pants and jackets, trying not to get distracted by their movements.

When I reach the principal's room, he's not there. I'm told to wait on the bench outside. How am I supposed to explain to him why school is so important to me? Not just important, *vital*. I don't have a parent or elder with me. I'm just a fourteen-year-old in a torn salwar kameez.

Hunger pangs begin to gnaw at my stomach.

I touch Rosy's bracelet for luck, wishing she were here.

The last time I saw her, she was dressed in a red salwar kameez, red ribbons tied around her two ponytails. She tied her bracelet with its little pink hearts around my wrist and asked me to wear it every day while she was away in Nepal. Her dad was only supposed to send her and her mother there for a few weeks. "He is always yelling these days," Rosy whispered, wiping a tear. "My mother woke up with a black eye this morning. It will be better in Nepal. At least he won't be with us."

Later that night, we had snuck into the cowshed behind her home to get out of the rain and away from the prying eyes of her father. We heard Rosy's mother cry: "How can you do this to your own daughter?"

There was a loud sound, like a *thwack*, followed by sobs.

I looked at Rosy, her blank expression.

Rosy never came back. Nor did her mother.

I finger the pink hearts on my bracelet when it dawns on me: Rosy knew she wasn't coming back.

Manish changed after that. The three of us used to be friends until then. It didn't used to matter that I came from the red-light area or that my cousin was a prostitute. Now he takes every opportunity he can to hurt me.

Suddenly I'm aware of the time passing by the second. I don't want the other children to see me. I imagine their comments. Their dirty smirks. Their hoots of laughter.

I look out at the road from the window in the corridor just as Manish's father drops him off in the police car. The car comes to a stop at the school gate and the sweat begins to leak from my pores. Manish steps out, giving a hand to someone else once his feet are planted. I imagine his father coming to complain about me, putting a nail in the coffin. And then I see that it's the principal Manish is helping out of the car.

My heart drops. There is no point in waiting. There is no point in speaking with the principal. He will only choose Manish's side again.

I want to cry, but all I can do is walk.

I walk to the guava tree in the courtyard where the girls are exercising in their white uniforms. I sit, leaning against the tree, and watch them to give my mind a rest.

There are maybe twenty of them. They stand in two lines, facing one another. All the girls have one foot slightly in front of the other, fists up, as if they're protecting their faces, their knees relaxed.

A bronze-skinned woman in her twenties, dressed in black pants and a white T-shirt, with round, wire-rimmed glasses shouts out: "Begin!" She's only five foot something, but her air of confidence and drill sergeant demeanor make her look taller.

The girls immediately widen their legs a bit farther apart, bend their knees a bit deeper, snap out their wrists, and make their fingers into a claw shape. These girls aren't just exercising. They're fighting. They're laughing. They're chatting. It doesn't look like kushti, but there is kicking and boxing. There is structure and there are rules.

One girl blocks another girl's kick. In a series of quick moves, the first girl overthrows the other with a flick of the wrist. But these girls are not big and brawny like my uncle. They are thin and small. And they are *girls*.

I look more closely. I recognize the drill sergeant, the woman in black pants and white T-shirt shouting out the instructions. Her name is Rini Di, the hostel owner who visits Mira Di from time to time.

I watch, fascinated, as girls on one side suddenly come out of their squats and into a side kick aimed for the stomach of their opponent. The girls facing them are equally quick. They block their opponents by grabbing their arm, lunging at them with their right foot straight out in front.

They repeat different kinds of kicks without actually hurting each other, and I breathe a sigh of relief. The girls know how to protect themselves. They keep their arms bent near their faces. They rotate their hips to whichever side is threatened. They move as fast as the wind, with both speed and balance. I think of my younger uncle, who I call Chote Mama—so light on his feet despite his weight.

Baba took me and Salman to a match once. We sat around a square dirt floor about fourteen feet long on each side. "That's the akhara, the wrestling area," Baba explained to Salman and me. The competition managers spread some buttermilk, oil, and red ocher color on the floor.

The air was filled with energy that felt like the electric current from the pole I had once touched on the highway.

My uncle walked inside the ring followed by a brawny man dressed in square cloth underwear. "That's a langoti, perfect for wrestling." I could hear the excitement in my father's voice as he explained each thing to us. The bodies of the pehelwans were glistening with mustard oil.

The audience cheered. Chote Mama and his opponent picked up some dirt from the floor and sprinkled it on themselves and each other. Baba enlightened us: "They are blessing themselves with the earth."

The match began and my uncle and his opponent tried to pin each other's shoulders and hips to the ground simultaneously. Both were strong but their bodies were slippery. There were cheers of excitement among the onlookers every time my uncle took down his opponent. After a minute or so, his opponent would get up and the crowd would roar in excitement. But he was no match for my uncle.

Mama kept him down for most of the match. There were brief seconds when we thought he would slip out, but my uncle would just get him down again. And at last came the moment when my uncle had his opponent's shoulder and hip on the ground. The referee counted to ten. Chote Mama had won. The match only lasted forty-five minutes, but the prize was ten thousand rupees. I ate mutton and chicken to my heart's content for the first time in my life that night. Before they left, my uncles gave us all sorts of goodies: a toffee called chhurpi made from yak's milk that I chewed on all day long, colored beads for my mother, and Raksi, a Nepali rice wine, for my father.

Now, as I look at the girls sparring with each other, kicking and boxing, I feel that same thrill come back. I feel the electric current. I glanced at them often enough when walking into school in the past without really noticing them. Without noticing Rini Di.

Baba and Chacha disapprove of everything she stands for. They've warned Mira Di and Mai that their interactions with Rini Di will come to no good. That "she is not of our world. Her life is her life. Don't let her put ideas into your heads."

Mira Di has told me about their conversations. About the stories that Rini Di tells. "She has opened my eyes to so many things. She tells me women are powerful. That they can earn their own living and don't have to depend on men. All they need is an education and guts."

I once saw her march on the streets with students from the Forbesganj College. They held a meeting in the Mela ground near us, demanding the punishment of some men who had raped and murdered a girl on a bus in Delhi. The Mela ground was full when she was speaking. Her voice was strong and full of passion.

She spoke about freedom. That no one has any right to a woman's body. That women should have the freedom to go out, night or day, to wear what they want, marry whom they want, study what they want, and have the livelihood they desire. That no one owns them. They have the right to a life without fear.

She thundered from the makeshift stage while the students clapped.

The energy was electric.

Baba and Chacha and all the men in our lane stood, listening.

I remember Chacha's sneer. "Who does she think she is? This is India. Women belong to their fathers and husbands. She has no idea about our culture."

Baba and other men from the gambling joint had nodded in assent. I had never seen such unity among the quarrelsome men of Girls Bazaar. They had not allowed Mai or any of the women to go to the rally, even though the Mela ground was just a stone's throw away.

I had been mesmerized then and I'm mesmerized now.

The tightness in my chest releases its grip.

I loiter until Rini Di's exercise group breaks and everyone begins to disperse. Some of the girls walk to the hostel, but others walk to school. I spot a familiar curly brown head of hair in the crowd of girls and realize it's Sadaf. But I stiffen when I see that she's with Razia.

If I try to talk to Razia, she'll only ignore me. But Sadaf has been kind to me, especially since Rosy left—the only one who holds a place for me next to her on the bench in class. The only one who doesn't laugh at Manish's pranks. I've often walked by her house on my way to school just to have the chance to walk through the nice neighborhood—the paved roads, neat gardens, walled houses. It's not too far from my hut in the Girls Bazaar, but it feels like an entirely different world.

My hand is waving at her before my nerves get the better of me.

Sadaf jogs over and greets me with a smile. "Heera! Are you okay? I didn't see you in class after lunch yesterday."

I watch her brow furrow as I explain what happened.

"They're bullies. I see how they treat you. They get away with everything," she fumes.

Suddenly, I feel as if I have an ally. Before I can help myself, I flood my friend with a volley of questions. "What sport is this? Is it a game?

How can I learn it? Can I join her classes? Now that I am expelled from school—"

"Whoa! Slow down," Sadaf laughs. "It's kung fu. It was practiced for centuries in China. Now it's popular all over."

"Do you think I can join and train under her?" I ask again.

"You'll have to ask Rini Di," Sadaf responds.

I nod, hopeful that Mira Di will be able to help me sort that out.

As I say my goodbyes and turn to leave, I'm stunned to discover that Razia is running after me, her flowered cotton salwar kameez flowing behind her. She holds out a bag. Inside is a book and six hard-boiled eggs.

I look at the book. *Bruce Lee: Artist of Life.* Flipping through the pages, I see a photo of a man dressed in white, his fist up, poised for a kick.

"From Rini Di for you," she says, smiling shyly.

My heart stops. Rini Di noticed me. And she's made the standoffish Razia notice me too. I stare up at her. She must be the tallest girl in our class.

I smile as I thank her.

I savor the moment as I look at the book again, opening it up to a random page.

> There is no such thing as defeat until you admit one to yourself, but not until then.

CHAPTER FOUR

Everyone looks so carefree as I run home that night. The vendors carry on with their business. The twinkling lamps in each shop radiate an inviting light. A woman sings inside her home. The children on the swings near the playground wave. I wave back.

It is twilight. The sun and the moon are both out in the purple-blue sky. The wind is still. The air is not freezing yet. I pull my cotton dupatta scarf tight around me as I cross in front of Ravi Lala's home, but he is not there. My feet are dry and I am warm. It's been a good day.

I storm into the hut, out of breath and bursting with pride at the precious cargo in my hands. Manish and his teeth could go jump into a lake for all I care. Today I have food for my family, a present from Rini Di, and most importantly, a plan.

"Mai!" I yell, but as soon as I do, I know something's wrong.

Chotu is not coughing. The air is heavy.

My mother is huddled in a corner of the hut, cradling Chotu in her arms. A sense of unease creeps through me. As I walk toward her, she looks up at me, her face ashen. "I'm going to the hospital. Go and fetch your father and tell him to come there."

"What's wrong, Mai?"

"Just go!" Her voice is hoarse. She looks as white as a sheet.

Before I know it, she charges off with Chotu.

Something that I cannot name pushes my heart from all sides. I feel suffocated.

Sania plays with a pair of spoons, sitting on an old sari on the ground. She has wet herself; I'm not sure when. I quickly change her dress and roll up the sari.

I sling Sania onto my hip and head to the liquor shack, knowing I'll find my father there. He sits on a stool watching a few of his friends play cards on the mat spread out on the dirt road, a steel tumbler in his hand. It is empty.

He's angry I'm here; I can see it in his eyes. I hold down my panic and speak before he can object. "Mai has asked you to meet her at the referral hospital. She's taken Chotu there."

Wordlessly, he hoists himself off the stool, and I watch as he rushes as fast as he can despite his limp. He moves sideways to avoid people, his blue bandanna bobbing through the crowd until I can't see him anymore.

I turn back and head toward our home. Sania has grabbed my hair in one little fist; her other hand is shoved into her mouth. The gentle tug pulls me back to her.

"Hungry?" I ask.

She nods. I spread out our reed mat chatai and put her on it. There is nothing I can do about Chotu for now, but I can look after little Sania and wait here until Salman gets home. I take an egg from my precious stash and mash it in a bowl for her. Her face lights up when she sees it before she proceeds to wolf it down. I wonder if my mother has fed her at all today.

I wet a rag and wipe her face, hands, and feet. She is dirty, the poor thing. Mai hasn't had a lot of time for her of late, and I should have paid more attention. My chest aches, as if a knife is sticking into my heart. But when I look down, there is no red blood flowing down my black kameez.

When Salman walks through the door, I hurriedly tell him what has happened.

Without hesitation, he dumps his schoolbag on the floor and runs out the door.

"I'm going to the hospital," he says.

"I'll come too!" I scream after him.

"No, you stay here with Sania," he says, turning back. He is insistent. "We can't leave the house empty."

"Why not?"

But he's gone with no answer.

It's nearly midnight and no one has come home. Sania is asleep. I can't leave her and go to the hospital, and I can't take her out in the cold. I haven't eaten, and I can't sleep. The winter wind has picked up. The incessant Bollywood music gnaws at my eardrums. The oil of the fried food stinks. Every sound and smell feels oppressive—jangling and discordant.

My chest constricts and I pray to all the gods and goddesses, the sun, moon, and stars for my little sister. "Please make Chotu okay," I repeat again and again in the dark. I haven't bothered to light a candle.

When Salman finally walks back through the door, I decide to put some rice on for him. Mai must have gotten it from our uncle next door. I know I shouldn't, that there might not be more tomorrow, but it's here tonight and he is hungry. I pull out the boiled eggs.

"Where did you get those?" asks Salman.

"Sunil Sir gave them to me," I lie. I don't want to tell him about Rini Di or kung fu. Not now. "One for each of us. We'll save the others for Mai and Baba."

Finally, I overcome my foreboding and ask the question I'm afraid to know the answer to. "What's happening there?"

"Chotu is in a bed now. The doctors took a long time to come to her."

I know from the despondency in his voice that things are not good. "What are they saying?"

He shakes his head. "Her fever is very high and not coming down. They won't let anyone be by her side except Mai now."

My eyes burn. I change Sania and we try to sleep, lost in our own thoughts. I'm so tired that despite myself, I drift off, one arm wrapped around my sister's tiny body. When I wake up in the morning, my father is back in his corner of the hut, but Mai is nowhere to be found. And just like Mai always says, as soon as I move a muscle, Sania begins to cry.

Baba says nothing. He lights a beedi and sits on his haunches, staring into the distance. I'm too afraid to utter a word.

I take Sania out for our morning wash.

When we return, Baba is in the exact same position that I left him, but my mother is home. I relax my tight shoulders and exhale, trying to calm down. Chotu is not on her lap. She must be at the hospital. Maybe Salman has gone to sit with her.

The air is pale gray and chilly. Mai sits in a corner.

As soon as the fresh tears begin to stream down her face, I know. Chotu is dead.

I sit at her feet and Sania crawls out of my arms and into hers. Mai holds her, rocking back and forth. The sobs start slow and then become uncontrollable.

I watch helplessly.

Tinny music from a microphone drifts into our hut; some boys kick a can around; someone, somewhere, is frying pakoras. We are suddenly surrounded by the everyday morning sounds and smells of people waking up, opening their shops, getting ready for the day, leaving for work. Yet the morning seems unreal.

How could the rain take someone as small as Chotu? Again, like clockwork, I am struck with the reality that our family is destined for all the ill luck in the world. She was the most spirited of us all and her life had not even begun.

My mother continues to sob and all I can do is clasp her hand.

Despite myself, my stomach growls with hunger. Mai hears that and snaps to attention.

"Come, let's go get the water," she says.

She wipes her tears with the corner of her sari, gives me a bucket, and gets one herself. We leave for the water pump at the station. I pump the water as Mai puts the bucket beneath the iron spout. We do our chores mechanically without saying a word to each other.

As we walk back with the water, my hopes dissolve. I can't let what happened to Chotu happen to Sania. I can't waste my time with frivolities. Kung fu cannot stop the roof leaking. I have to pull my weight to help my family now. If I have to go into the line so that my family can have a tin roof, so be it.

School is not just a luxury for girls like me. It is an avoidable luxury, filling our heads with impractical dreams.

Chotu is buried.

Her eyes are closed and I wish more than anything that they were open. I would have liked to look at each other one more time. Mai has dressed her in a new pink frock with white bows. She looks like a doll and smells of soap and water.

I wish more than anything to hear something from her, even a cough.

Baba doesn't say a word, just looks at me with pity as he leaves for the funeral with the other men.

I hear Salman's muffled sobs as he joins them.

Later, after the men come home from the funeral, I walk in on

Chacha's shouts. My mother sits on the other side of them. He says she has brought nothing but bad luck to the family. That fate has not looked kindly at us since she decided to send me, a Nat daughter, to school.

She has challenged destiny.

"Nat girls are meant to be prostituted. That is what the gods want," he yells. "Their wrath has descended on our family because of your pride."

He adds that that is why my father has a lame leg, why we lost our home, why Chotu is dead. My mother sits there, taking it all in, and my father does nothing to defend her. All the while, I feel my uncle's gaze flitting between Salman and me. I can see it in his eyes: Who do they think they are to be coasting along, not doing what everyone does in our Nat community?

One by one, as news spreads, women from the neighboring huts come by, shedding their tears for Chotu. Many whisper that had I done what my father wanted, Chotu might still be alive. Our hut would have had four walls and a proper tin roof. The rain would not have torn it down. Chotu wouldn't have gotten so wet. She wouldn't have caught a cold. She wouldn't be dead.

Others blame Mai. Chotu was taken away to teach her a lesson. Mai did not withdraw me from school, even after my puberty. I should have been married to a banana tree, had my Bisi Bele wedding rite, and been given to a man by now, they say.

"It is bad luck to have an unmarried girl in the house, especially after her puberty," one woman says. All the others nod in unison. "The gods took the other daughter because she tried to save the elder one," another woman adds. They don't bother to lower their voices. I can hear every word.

Something inside me snaps as I hand out glasses of tea to the visitors, as I try to repel their superstitious chatter. Chotu would have lived if she had been given proper medicine for her cold instead of the bit of banana that the bhagat gave her.

I watch my mother cowed and silent as she sits in mourning on a reed mat. No one seems to stand a chance against this so-called destiny. My sorrow turns to anger. I don't understand why death from prostitution is better than death from a cold. Chotu might not have died this week from the rain, but both she and I would be dead by the time we reached our twenties anyway. Once the "business" took my life, Chotu would have replaced me, and then it would be Sania, and so it would go. I've seen it before.

Is that any better? Can they not see what Mira Di is going through? How long do they expect her to survive the beatings and torture?

I picture myself on a bed in the back room, waiting for a customer. I imagine Mai sitting on a bench outside our hut taking their money. But the face of the girl on the bed is not mine. The face of the woman on the bench is not Mai. We have become something different entirely. We no longer belong to this world.

I close my eyes. I see the darkness, and then I see a yellow light behind my closed eyelids. The light turns purple and orange. I bend my legs and rest my chin on my knees. For a moment, I am not in the hut. I tune out all the blame. I wrap my arms around my knees and think.

I hear Rini Di's words. *No one has any right to a woman's body . . . No one owns her. She has the right to a life without fear.*

I peer through my eyelashes at the women chattering around me, at Chachi's beaten-down face and hard, cruel demeanor, at Mira Di's empty, glazed eyes, at my mother. Mai does not look like Chachi. She looks tired, she looks sad, but there is a spark in her eyes. I'm sure I have the same spark. Our lives are not run by superstition and acceptance.

Sania plays with her rag doll, her body thinner than it used to be. Her threadbare smock can hardly keep her warm, giving her a permanent sniffle in winter.

"Chotu, Chotu," she says, running toward me, looking for her playmate. She has only just started speaking.

I engulf her in my arms to keep the emptiness away. I want to keep her warm. I wipe her snot. I can't tell her that Chotu has gone to sleep forever. But I can protect her.

Our tiny home is empty at last. On a normal day, you wouldn't think it would be able to hold any more people than just us. It's always been crowded with six, hardly less so with five. But yesterday, I saw just how many people can fit into a space the size of a floor mat. And the people who didn't fit in spilled out onto the pathways and into our neighbors' homes. For one day, Girls Bazaar held us in its arms. For once, we don't have to worry about food: We have rations donated from the mosque to last us the week.

Salman has skipped school as our household mourns. I brew a cup of tea and we sit, leaning against the door of our hut. I rest my chin on my bent knee, my favorite posture.

He stretches out his legs in front of him and I study the creases on his white pajamas, all the way up to his face. Traces of his afternoon nap are still on his cheeks, his eyes still a little puffy, his forehead a little marked from the straw of the mat.

Finally, I decide to tell him about the kung fu, about Rini Di. I share my fears. I share my guilt. He's the only one who will fully understand.

He tugs his ears and I know I have his full attention.

"I want some kind of sign that God won't punish our family. I want him to send me a message," I say as if Salman has the power to grant me this wish.

Some dead leaves blow our way as a truck trundles along the highway.

"Which God?" asks Salman with a small, sad smile. His dimple has completely disappeared.

He picks up a twig that has blown toward us along with the leaves and draws a circle in the dust. He adds in eyes and then a mouth turning down. I wait. He wipes away the turned-down mouth with the twig and replaces it with a mouth turning up, smiling.

"It's up to us, Heera. You have to create your own future," he says, waving the twig at his drawing. "God is everywhere. In this twig, in the dirt, in you and me. You can make a smile; you can make a grimace; and you can erase it too."

I nod twice.

"God can be a goddess, a tree, or a stone too," Salman continues. And I know he's right. We Nat tribes worship trees and stones, the forest goddess up in the mountains. We follow rituals from both

Muslim and Hindu religions as well as our own. "You can create your own faith and rituals to be the markers of your life. Nothing to do with destiny."

I listen, wide-eyed, taking it all in. A line of ants crawl toward a jar of sugar. Is it their destiny to make a line and crawl to food? Or do they decide that sugar is what they want and go for it?

Salman picks up Sania, who has crawled over to us. He throws her in the air, and she chortles. "Why don't you ask Mira Di for help? She can talk to Rini Di," he suggests gently.

He washes our glasses with a little water from the bucket, slings Sania on his lap, and picks up his schoolbag. "I'm going to go to the highway and study a little. The streetlights are on and the orange light of the new neon lamps is much easier on the eye."

I give him two of the eggs that are still left—one for Sania and the other for him—and wave goodbye. I light a candle. Our hut is full of light and shadows. A moth flies near the wick.

I take out the Bruce Lee book from my schoolbag, looking again and again at the photos of him kicking, meditating, playing with children. There is one photo that I look at at least a hundred times. Bruce Lee is flying in the air, arms apart, one leg parallel to the ground and the other kicking out at a man in a similar position. The fight looks like art, like the men are dancers.

I practice a bit. My body looks longer in the shadows. Some of the shadows change shape as the flame flickers or I move. It does look like a dance. My arms look like a bird's wings, as if I'm flying.

CHAPTER FIVE

After days of mourning, Mai returns to break stones on the highway. She says we can't afford another day of no wages. We have loans to pay and food to buy. I'm ordered to stay at the hut with Sania, who is gurgling and happy, yet I can't help but feel entirely alone. I have one eye trained to look out toward my uncle's back room, one ear attuned to the noises.

Finally, Mira Di comes by between clients. For once she isn't drunk.

She helps me make cow dung cakes to fuel our stove for the night. We pat them to dry in the sun and the words begin to flow out of me.

I tell her everything that has happened, about Manish and the school principal. About Rini Di and kung fu. It seems like a lifetime ago.

She shakes her head in anger. *Plop* goes the cow dung patty as she throws it on the ground ferociously. I laugh and realize how long it's been since I've felt that particular urge.

"That's not Manish, Mira Di," I say, still smiling.

She turns to me with a conspiratorial smile. "I know, Heera, but I just hate how they treat us. We are human. Our blood is the same color. We have the same two eyes, two ears, one nose, two legs and hands." She does a little jig with her arms and legs to demonstrate. Our laughter helps to transform the feeling in the air.

Mira Di ties her dupatta scarf behind her as she pulls out our little bamboo stool and comes to sit near me. "Heera, now more than ever, you need to go to school," she says with a shake of her head.

I chew on my bottom lip, waiting for her to suggest something.

"Tomorrow after your mai and baba are gone, go to the girls' hostel and meet Rini Di. She sits there every afternoon. I will send her a message today. She will help get you back into school, I promise."

"What if something goes wrong, like it always does?" I ask.

She gives my shoulders a shake. "Do you want to end up like me? Don't you know my father is telling yours right now that this is the year to take you to the fair?"

Her arms drop to her sides. She knows she has said too much.

I feel my hands go cold. "This year? So, it's true. Even after, after—"

"What? You think your sister dying will save you? It only makes matters worse!"

We are both sitting on the ground now, desolation hanging heavily between us.

I think of what the women said when they came to pay their respects after the funeral. They are older than me. Perhaps they know something I don't. I look out at the lane. An old man is sitting outside Jamila Bua's café, watching the latest news on the TV screen that she's put up for her customers. I wonder how he can hear anything over the noise.

"What if everyone in Girls Bazaar, Chacha, and Baba are right? Did Chotu die because of me? What if I did bring bad luck to the family?" I voice my doubts aloud.

This grabs her attention. "Since when did you begin to believe in this superstitious nonsense?"

I don't meet her eye, focusing instead on Jamila Bua as she fries the onion fritters for the lunchtime rush. A black crow drives a sparrow away from the garbage. It's a stark reminder that the mightiest will survive. That destiny decides who will be mighty.

"It's the way of the world, Mira Di. If destiny hasn't decided where I was born, who has? It's all a birth lottery," I say bitterly, walking up and down inside the small space of our shack.

Mira Di comes and hugs me. She strokes my head. "I know you feel frustrated, but do you have a choice? What else can you do?"

I steer the conversation away from destiny. In my heart, I know that I don't believe the superstitions. All the women in our lane believe in the eternal, inescapable fate of our nomadic Nat tribe because they can't imagine anything beyond it. There was no defiant mother or cousin or sister to fight for them.

I decide to spell out my other fear. "What if I don't understand anything?"

There. I've said it. I don't want to be the stupidest kid in the class anymore, especially knowing what the boys will do to me.

She looks at me with no expression on her face. Then her brow furrows into a small fold. "As far as I remember you did fine in school. At least, when you were a kid. You used to get the highest scores for reading aloud in both Hindi and English. You used to be so fond of books. I could not tear you away from the school library." She smiles at the memory.

I smile back. I used to love the dusty library, the smell of books and the stories I read in the privacy of the desk between the shelves by the window. Tagore, Saratchandra, Mahadevi Verma . . . and the adventure stories by the English writers Enid Blyton and Laura Lee Hope. Words have always come easily to me.

Then came the hunger, the bullying, the chores at home, my first menstruation. Everything slipped away.

"That was because you and Salman would help me when I got stuck," I mumble, my head down.

"Then ask Salman to help you," she suggests.

"He's always so busy with his studies," I mutter. "Can't you help me?"

"Do you think I remember anything after the hell I've lived through these past few years?" There is an aggressive edge to her voice. I see a small, worn spark of hope fight the fear in her eyes. She wants to convince me to go to school, against all the odds I must face. Under her clumsy makeup is a desperate appeal.

I look at her and remember her full-throated and happy laugh as a girl. I resolve to rekindle the laughter, light, and hope in her eyes. I will overcome my fears for her. I will fight for my future, for the dreams that she could never make come true for herself.

Outside, the sky is gray, the sun sending out weak rays through the mist. Far off, a train whistle blows. I give Mira Di's hand a squeeze. I promise I will go meet Rini Di. I want to, anyway.

Mira Di finally smiles again. She gets up to go. She can't stay too long, in case Chacha or Shaukat start looking for her as soon as a new client appears.

"I will send word to Rini Di that you will go to her tomorrow," she says as she ties her scarf around her head. Her body language changes. She stiffens, drawing in her shoulders as she walks away. Selfishly, perhaps, I realize that I'm not just doing this for her. I want to be a person. I want to kick and fly. I want to win. I want to have the courage like Rini Di to demand a life without fear.

The following afternoon, after I finish all the household chores, I sling Sania onto my hip and step out of the hut. No one asks where we're going. No one is there. I tiptoe down the lane to avoid Baba in case he's at the gambling joint or the liquor stall, walking as fast as I can just to make sure no one stops me. The winter mist from the fields has not lifted today. It wraps its foggy blanket around us, helping us hide in its shadows.

Earlier this morning, everyone went about their tasks reflexively, caught up in their own grief. They looked like pale shadows, wispy spirits from a Himalayan forest, as they went about their business. Mai has not talked to me about school, or anything else for that matter, since Chotu died. She cries when she thinks no one is looking. To be honest, I want to cry too. Our world has become smaller without her. I can still feel the warmth of her breath when the five of us sleep next to one another at night, as if her little body is still curled up into mine. Perhaps in the spring, yellow mustard flowers will grow from the seeds I sprinkled around her grave.

I cross in front of the tailor shop that is just at the turn of the road near our school. Mira Di often used to go there to learn stitching and sewing. Uncle Darzi used to say she had a gift. He said her tiny stitches were miraculous, not visible to the naked eye. He was going to teach her how to cut blouses, but that was all before she was pulled out of school.

I can see him behind the sewing machine, stacks of fabrics near him, peering into the needle. He looks up to wave. I wave back. I can see he has grown older.

My palms sweat the closer I get to school. The compound is silent. Thankfully, I'm too late to meet the lunch crowd in the playground. I walk slowly toward the hostel to the right of the school building. Bees buzz around the red flowers of the semal cotton tree at the entrance.

"Hede himilye . . . ramto—let me linger near the semal tree that I love because . . ."

I can hear the words of a song that Salman and I often sing. Each line is a different excuse to stay longer in the shade of the beautiful flowery tree. I want to linger to gather the fallen flower buds. Mai could peel, chop, and cook them to make a vegetable curry. Or Mira Di could make a tisane for her constant migraines. But today I don't have a minute to waste.

I hum the tune to Sania, my heart beating with anticipation. The fear is gone, if only briefly. I will meet Rini Di. We will talk about my future. I will enroll in her kung fu class and reenlist in school.

The tree casts its shadow over the green door and low wall that surround the hostel. As I approach, the guard seems to recognize that I'm merely a fourteen-year-old girl and lifts his chin in a gesture to go inside. I climb up the three steps to the wraparound porch and try to decide which way to go. I wish I could bottle this feeling of freedom and promise. I would sprinkle it across the sky.

"Yes, may I help you?" A short and plump lady, sitting behind a blue wooden desk in a yellow sari, greets me. A small black table fan whirs on her desk, away from her face to shoo away the flies, I suppose. I can't help but look behind her to the courtyard, where some girls are hanging out clothes on a line to dry.

"Namaste. I am here to see Rini Di," I say with a smile on my lips, my stomach now twisted in knots.

She nods, as if it's not uncommon for girls to show up and ask for Rini Di, and points down a corridor to her left. "Look for a sign that says 'Library' on the fourth door. She's usually there."

I walk down the red-cemented corridor, begging Sania to stay quiet and obedient for just a bit longer. The door is open. Inside, cushions and colorful dhurrie rugs decorate the floor while shelves filled with books of all sizes coat the walls. Rini Di sits behind a machine on her desk, the mango tree swaying through the window behind her.

"Namaste, Rini Di. I'm Heera," I say timidly. My heart races and I realize this is the first time I've ever spoken directly to her.

Rini Di stops working and gets up. She is dressed in a cotton salwar kameez, like me. It's blue and white, while mine is the inevitable black. "Hello, Heera," she says with a smile. "I was expecting you. I got a message from your didi, Mira." She gestures toward the chair in front of her. A little courage seeps back inside my veins.

I take a seat. A tray of cookies is already set right in front of me.

She stretches forward and gestures toward the tray. "Take some."

I wait politely, though I'm hungry. The school bell rings. I hold in the little flutter of anticipation in my chest. Sania has already grabbed a cookie in her sticky fist and is happily inhaling it.

Rini Di turns her head toward her, her face lighting up with laughter. Her eyes twinkle through her glasses.

"Tea or milk? A cup of milk for your little sister?"

"Tea," I say, feeling like a grown-up.

Behind the books and the files there is a photo of a tall woman holding her fist in the air with the words spelled out in English: *Courage Is Contagious*. I wonder what "con-tag-ious" means.

"Eat," Rini Di says. I grab a cookie because I haven't had breakfast, as usual. I still don't know where to begin. For a moment we sit there in silence as Sania and I devour the treat.

"So, how can I help you?" Rini Di asks as she puts her cup down.

The sugar from the tea and cookie has reached my stomach, providing the only sustenance I've had all day.

I think of the fights, the tears, the hunger, the shadow of the fair hanging over me. Suddenly, my fearlessness melts away and I question why I'm about to have this conversation when next week I might be auctioned to the highest bidder.

I look at her kind face and curious brown eyes peering through her wire-rimmed glasses.

"What's wrong?" Rini Di asks.

I try to smile and realize that I'm actually crying. The night of the rain, when Chotu caught fever, flashes through my eyes in vivid detail. My throat feels as if it might close up.

"Tell me why you are crying, Heera," she says gently.

It takes me a moment to gather the words. "My little sister just died. My father is planning to sell me to Ravi Lala, who will auction me at the fair, just like my uncle sold Mira Di, so that we can put in a roof," I begin with a sob.

She nods understandingly. "I am so sorry about your sister. How old was she?" She covers my hand with hers.

"Only five," I respond with a sniff.

"Far too young to die." She shakes her head in sorrow and asks, "How old are you?"

"Fourteen going on fifteen," I reply softly, wondering why it matters anyway. The day is getting darker. I need to get home before Mai returns or Baba begins to look for me. There is no time to waste. "I want to learn kung fu from you. I know I don't have to be sold. But then we won't have a roof. And Sania might catch a cold the next time it rains. It will be all my fault," I say desperately.

"You can't blame yourself for your sister's death. She should have gotten proper medicine and food. Nothing to do with you. Your baba is not selling you because she died." Rini Di's face is serious. Her eyes search mine. "Girls are being sold in Girls Bazaar all the time. Your aunt was sold. Mira Di was sold. All this happened long before your sister died. These things are not in your control. You are just fourteen. Do you understand?"

"Yeah. I suppose so," I say, my voice cracking.

Rini Di writes something in her notebook.

I grip the end of the table with my hands as I lean forward and continue. "I saw you teach the hostel girls to fight. To kick and punch.

I want to fight too and win prize money to look after my family. My mother's brothers are pehelwans. It's in my blood." I look at her questioningly.

She responds with an approving nod. "Go on," she says.

"My parents, my brother, and even my pehelwan mamas say girls can't fight. But I saw you teach girls to fight," I add in a rush.

"I will teach you kung fu, of course, but you have to also find your inner strength. Self-esteem is essential to any battle. You have to know you are worth fighting for."

I turn this thought over in my head a few times.

I glance at her with clear, steady eyes. I think of Manish, the boys, the principal, Ravi Lala, the mourners at Chotu's funeral, the customers, even police officers like Suraj Sharma who presume people like me are incapable of anything but prostitution. But somewhere deep down I know I am worth fighting for.

"That's why I am here," I finally blurt out.

A smile creeps back onto Rini D's face. She reaches out for a fist bump. I raise my fist too and then pause.

"There's something I need to tell you first," I say.

She looks puzzled.

"The principal has told me not to come back to school. I broke a boy's tooth because he stole an egg from me. We have nothing to eat at home and I was just taking the egg for my mother. But if I don't come to school, I can't eat the midday meal. And if I can't eat the midday meal, I can't even stand straight, let alone learn kung fu."

I slowly stop crying. She hands me a tissue. At last, I have told her everything.

I then ask the most important question: "The school lunch is all I have. Please, Rini Di, can you talk to the principal?"

Rini Di empties her cup and sets it down decisively on the table. She comes over and pats my back. Then she proceeds to hand me an orange and a promise. "Sunil Sir and I will talk to the principal today."

"He'll let me back in school?" I take a breath.

"Yes. I believe he will. But you must agree to come regularly. Even if it's harder with everything at home." She glances at me to make sure I'm listening.

I nod. But I have a few more things on my mind.

"Everyone knows I will be prostituted. Manish told the whole school," I mumble, my humiliation an obvious thing in my throat.

"Manish, the police officer's son?" Her voice is angry now.

"Yes," I say, barely getting the word out. I balance Sania, who has happily finished off the cookies on the tray and is now restless.

Rini Di sighs. "Don't worry about Manish. Sunil Sir will talk to him." Then her tone changes. "No one decides your fate but you. In the meantime, you must make other friends. Ones who will stand by you."

I listen, all ears.

Her face is set in firm, serious lines. "Manish picks on you because he knows he can get away with it. You have to learn to stand up to him, but in a different way." She speaks slowly now, choosing each word carefully. "The school is your protection. As is kung fu. If Sunil Sir and I can convince the principal to keep you in school, will you promise to study hard?"

I nod vehemently.

"What if I told you that there is a kung fu competition coming up? And I can train you to fight."

I'm not sure I have heard her right. "Really?"

Rini Di smiles, reaching under her desk to pull out a black cotton bag. She hands it to me. "Open it. It's for you."

I dive in, and despite myself, I feel a thrill of excitement. Inside is a white uniform—a loose jacket and pajamas. Like the one Bruce Lee wears in the book. And at last things are beginning to feel *real*. There is no right word to describe it.

Rini Di watches me as I turn the uniform over in my hands. She is trying to look stern, but the hint of a smile forces its way through. "You know why this uniform is white?" she asks.

I shake my head, eager to know. I want to learn everything I can about kung fu.

Her voice is quiet, and hints at promises. "Because white represents the values of purity, avoidance of ego, and simplicity. It gives no outward indication of social class, so all students begin as equals."

My heart beats with excitement, and then reality strikes. "But how will I be able to do this, Rini Di? My father . . . Ravi Lala."

"Your father wants money, doesn't he? I think I might find a way to convince him to let you come to school," She stands up abruptly. "Come on then. You bring your sister home. I will speak to the principal today and then come speak to your parents as soon as I have things figured out."

She hands me some bananas and apples that she has on her table to take home with me.

Then I shake hands with someone for the first time in my life.

CHAPTER SIX

When the bone-chilling northwesterly wind sweeps through our town and a damp mist hangs over the arhar fields, when we feel the cold in every pore and couldn't imagine a more difficult place in the world to live, that is when the Mela fair, called the Kali Mela, dedicated to the dusky, dark ferocious goddess, camps right next to our Girls Bazaar.

Farmers begin to gather from near and far to sell their produce—milk, cheese, ghee, cattle, vegetables, grain, seeds, fertilizers, and manure. Mira Di says that, for so many of them, it's the only time that they'll leave their isolated hamlets and remote landholdings and have money to squander. Merchants from all over the country bring their choicest wares to trade with the farmers. The streets are becoming jam-packed with stalls selling jewelry, toys, clothes, medicines, souvenirs. Everything you could imagine—from needles to tractors.

And then, jostling in the narrow aisles between the farmers and merchants, are the performers—acrobats, magicians, jugglers, games, gambling, cinemas, and supposedly nautanki folk dancers.

Mira Di says that in the past, famous nautanki dancers were invited to perform for kings and nawaabs along with live singers and musicians. They were performers practiced in the arts and graces of dancing. But we girls from the lane know that the nautanki has been replaced with a cheap striptease dance called an "item number" for which no practice is needed and no grace is required.

As the bright lights go up, the girls in our lane shiver. They shiver from the cold in their skimpy bras and panties. They shiver from the fear of the dance party owners, from the overwhelming volume of sex buyers who arrive with the fair, of having to wear no clothes on cold, wet nights.

I have lost count of the number of times I have slunk in to watch. It's far too easy to lift the tarpaulin of the dance tents and stay in the shadows like Rosy and I used to do. When I was younger, I could barely understand what I was seeing. Even now, I'm not sure that I do—girls in bras and panties gyrating to music on the makeshift stage, their eyes looking toward an unknown future.

The younger ones stuff their bras with rags and plastic balls to make their breasts look bigger. I remember crouching in the shadows as I watched them, intensely aware of how uncomfortable it made me feel, yet curious. Some of them danced well. Some of them barely moved. The audience full of men would say things I didn't understand then, and now wish I didn't.

As the women—girls—stood there, trying to attract attention, a boy would come out from time to time from the wings to throw water on them. I've since learned that the little sprinkling is to make their clothes stickier, sexier. No one cares that it is the coldest day of winter.

And then, one day, Mira Di became one of those girls.

After years of lifting the tarpaulin of the dance tent, it was Mira Di onstage, dressed in the tightest red dress I had ever seen. She stood still, watching the other girls before a particularly loud whistle came from the crowd. A man with bulging eyes and big paunch pushed her from the back. She stumbled forward suddenly, trying to sway her hips.

I'd seen Mira Di dance plenty of times, but it was never like this. She was a lively dancer, light on her feet. She'd learned every folk dance taught in our school. I remember watching her at a school dance, twirling enthusiastically, her skirt ballooning around her in a dance called ghoomar from Rajasthan. I'd seen her step briskly forward and backward in the fast-paced Bihu from Assam. She could outpace the boys, stomping away at the Punjabi Bhangra, her arms in the air, her legs kicking up.

But this time, Mira Di danced slowly and suggestively, her black hair moving around her hips. The boy pouring buckets of water on her was my cousin Shaukat. Her face stayed frozen, fixed with a smile, her eyes in a trance. Maybe she would have seemed okay to anyone else. But I knew Mira Di better than anyone.

At the time, I didn't know what was really happening. I hadn't yet learned what actually takes place when the Mela comes. That the owners of the dance parties buy girls from their fathers or guardians, pay for a marriage to a banana tree in a Bisi Bele ceremony, and auction the girl's virginity to the highest bidder. That after the first night, the dance parties parade the girls onstage to perform their item numbers, numbers tied to their arms. That the men in the audience choose the girl they like, pay the dance party owner, and take her to a makeshift room behind the stage. Then, when the Mela leaves town, the girls go with the dance party that owns them. In exchange, older girls from the dance parties stay behind in the mud huts of Girls Bazaar. And so it continues, year after year.

I still remember Mira Di's Bisi Bele—the delicious food, music, and dancing. Mira Di was smeared with turmeric and oil, then bathed and dressed in a red sari. The clan priest came and performed the ceremony, piercing her nose and adorning her with a gold ring, or nath. He chanted some mantras as he garlanded a banana tree with marigold flowers, blessing both her and the tree. And that was that—she was officially married to the tree.

After her wedding, my chacha handed her over to the highest bidder. The winner took her to one of the makeshift rooms behind the stage, where he took off her nose ring and stole her innocence. Nath utarna, the removal of the nose ring.

I didn't know it then, but later Mira Di told me that the owners of the dance party paid for everything—the meat and the alcohol, the red sari and gold nose ring. It is an investment that they recoup instantly after the ceremony. A virgin fetches a higher price from clients.

Mira Di was beautiful, is beautiful. A dance company wasted no time buying her. We didn't see her for three years after the dance party left with the Mela.

Something in my aunt broke when my chacha came back with a sari, a sackful of rice, a new older girl in the back room, and no Mira Di. When she asked where Mira Di was, Chacha hit her.

Without Mira Di, everything about Girls Bazaar lost its joy and color.

Once, when she came with the fair, Mira Di sent a tiny mirror for me, a new sari for her mother, a walking stick for my father, and money for our textbooks. We did not meet.

But three years later, she came back. I remember just how thin she was. I remember the marks all over her body. She was so ill that her parents decided to let her stay. But Chacha put her to work at home in that back room. She was only seventeen.

At first, she didn't want to see me. But I went to see her anyway, offering her all that I had. I took out a raw green mango and placed it on the bed, the kind that she used to love nibbling on, and for a moment I recognized the girl I once knew.

Over the next few months, Mira Di began to tell me things. How the dance party took her from town to town. How they taught her to sing and dance. How they started sending men to her room, clients.

"I didn't like it and used to plead with the men to leave me alone. I said I only wanted to sing and dance. I used to try and run away. But then I stopped fighting it. And that became my main job. We were sold repeatedly, from one dance party to another, one night after another. We were worse off than the cattle."

I had resolved then and there, as I heard her words, never to let Baba do this to me. I didn't know how, but I had decided I would run away rather than be sold to a dance party.

Now, as I hear the merchants setting up their stalls, as I wait for Rini Di and dream of school and kung fu, I tell myself I don't have to run. I can fight.

There is an hour after Mai returns home when it's just the two of us—a rarity that I decide not to take for granted. For two days, my eyes have been trained on the door of our hut, waiting for Rini Di to walk through the threshold and change my fate. But for now, I allow myself to relax and enjoy Mai all to myself.

"Should we lie down for a bit?" Mai asks through a smile.

She is tired, and I bring her a glass of water. I put my arm around her and she pulls me in close. I can't remember the last time Mai has lain down in the daytime like this.

At last, when I pull away, sitting up so I can get dinner started, I see she is crying. Of course, her tears are for Chotu, because from now on all of Mai's tears will be at least partly for Chotu. But as we listen to the hammering outside, to the preparations for the Mela that will begin in only a few days, I know there is more. I recall a time when the fair used to fill me with excitement. Now it just fills me with panic and revulsion.

"When will we know if Rini Di was able to speak to the principal?" Mai asks when her tears begin to slow.

The truth is that I don't know. How could I bear disappointing her if Rini Di doesn't pull through?

The darkest parts of my mind force me to imagine my own Bisi Bele. I picture the clan priest taking a needle to my nose, giving me a nath, but stop myself from going any further. We both know that Ravi Lala is on the prowl. That Baba wants to do my Bisi Bele during the Mela to get the best price. The longer I stay at home, the more likely it is that they'll notice me.

I look at her woefully. "Maybe I could break stones with you? Just long enough to save money for our hut. Then Baba wouldn't feel the urgency to sell me," I suggest, avoiding her question.

She looks at me as though I have lost my mind. "Baba wouldn't hear of it. And that would take a lifetime."

My eyes gravitate to the door to the hut once again.

"Why does it have to be this way?" I say, almost in a whisper. "Why does it have to be the highway, the dance party, or Ravi Lala?"

Mai gives my hand a squeeze. "We are nomads who no longer have any place to go. They banned us from moving from one place to another. They jailed us if we traveled. They cut our forests down."

I stare into Mai's eyes as she looks to somewhere beyond our hut walls.

"We used to come to the plains to sell our medicines, perform acrobatics, put up wrestling shows, sing and dance in villages along the way. The Angrez forced us to stop everything. Medicine, rope bridges, iron utensils." She counts them on her fingers. "Their own factories in England were making the same things. They wanted to sell those."

"So what did we do?" I ask, already knowing the answer.

"We had no land. Our skills were outlawed. We ended up squatting on other people's land and doing odd jobs. The landowners took away our women in return. That is how it started. Our lives hang on a very fragile thread." She removes a strand of hair that's fallen over my eyes.

"But English laws don't matter now. India is no longer ruled by the British. Why can't we do something else?"

"People will always believe we are thieves and prostitutes. We can never escape the stigma."

"So, this is what they mean when they say 'fate'?"

Mai's breath becomes heavy. "I don't want to scare you, but I need you to be aware of the danger you're in."

I feel a chill go down my spine. But before I can respond, the door to the hut opens. To my disappointment, it's not Rini Di.

Mira Di stands in the doorway, looking beautiful in her red sari and red lips stained by the betel paan leaf she is chewing. She offers Mai an apologetic smile and signals to me to come over to her. I do as I'm asked.

"Can you do something for me?" Mira Di whispers. She slips me some money, and I know she is asking me to fetch alcohol for a client. "Keep the change," she adds.

There is a fresh cigarette burn on her arm, just beginning to blister.

Without looking back at Mai, I run to the Bhatti brewery down the street where they mix up moonshine. Perhaps if I keep moving, the fear and anxiety will go away. I buy a bottle and then head to Jamila's tin shack café, where I buy four samosas. I know better than to go home with any cash that my father can take from me.

The bottle isn't sealed and I take a few sips of the brew. It tastes nasty but I know it will warm me up soon. It's a full moon tonight. The highway is empty. I go there. I remember something from Bruce Lee's book about a finger pointing to the moon.

Don't concentrate on the finger or you will miss all that heavenly glory.

CHAPTER SEVEN

The next morning, my mother does something I never thought possible. She marches over to Ravi Lala's house and asks for a loan, assuring him it will only take her a few months to earn enough to pay him back. Ravi Lala hands over the money to Mai, no questions asked.

But Mai does not come home with cash, only the news that bricks, straw, rope, bamboo, sand, cement, and nails will be arriving soon and that we better get ready to get to work.

Baba listens, open-mouthed. I can't tell whether he's furious or impressed.

Salman and I immediately fight about who will do what. We both want to tie the frame tighter. No one wants to mess with the mud.

"You will both do everything," says Mai. "You too," she says to my father.

Mira Di comes over when the news makes its way across the street. "He just handed you the money?" she asks Mai.

"Yes," Mai says, beaming with pride.

"You know why, right?"

My mother is instantly defensive. "It doesn't matter why."

Mira Di shakes her head. "You are fooling yourself."

"Don't you dare talk to me like that!" Mai snaps. I've never seen her speak like this to Mira Di before.

"He keeps count of the number of girls in our area," Mira Di continues. "And now he has his eye on Heera. He never lets go. Now you're indebted to him."

There is truth in what Mira Di says, but Mai has a counterargument. "He wants money, right? I can repay his loan in a few months."

Mira Di shakes her head. "That's not profit. Even if you break millions of stones on the highway and give him his money back, that is already his own money; you cannot add to his wealth. Heera is pure profit to him."

Mai's face turns grim. "Do you really not see why I did it? The fair is here. But now Baba cannot say that Heera must be sold to put a roof on our hut. I can save her for a year. If your Rini Di will get her into school, that is."

At last, Mira Di is quiet.

Some risks are worth it. Mai has done what is in her control to save us. She has done it for Sania, for Salman, and for me. It's her way of fighting to protect me from the Mela. But I also know that

Mira Di is right—Mai is playing with fire in taking money from Ravi Lala.

For now, the knowledge that my mother has fought for me is more than enough. It's everything.

Over the next two days, we all work together to make the hut. We put our new bamboo poles in the four corners and the center of our shack. We gather the straw into bundles and twist the tops to hold them together. We weave cross strips into them and fasten them to our sturdy bamboo frame with jute ropes. We pile on the bricks to make the walls as my father adds the cement he's mixed. We all help layer the wall with mud and dung.

From the moment our walls go up, there is a sense of safety that I never understood how much I needed. The nights are not as cold. The days are not as hot. The ground is dry and easy to clean. Mai uses some of the loan money to buy a lantern so that Salman can finally study at home.

The walls are smooth, cool, and brown. I run my fingers down them again and again, but Mai wants to do something to make them even more special. She mixes up a batch of white rice powder with turmeric and we paint on the walls, just like she used to do with her family as a child.

Sania can't contain her excitement. As we work together to create a border around the door, and designs on the walls within, Mai starts to hum. She runs to stop Sania from turning our scenery into one giant blob of handprints, grabbing her by the middle and tossing her high up in the air. In this moment, my heart feels as though it might burst. I never imagined I could be this happy again.

The next day, after days of working on our hut in addition to breaking stones on the highway, Mai can barely stand. She lies flat on her stomach on the mat as I walk on her back, careful not to put too much of my weight on her. But she says my small hands aren't strong enough to take care of the throbbing ache in her spine.

It's almost dark when I begin to help my mother cook while trying to keep Sania away from anything hot or sharp. Mai has been spending the money she makes before it's taken away, hiding what's left of the loan money from Baba. So today we have a little rice, a little daal, and a few veggies for dinner. As I chop the meager onion and tomato for the daal and give Sania the scraps to play with, we hear a knock at the door.

At last, we receive our eagerly awaited visitors.

I open the door to find Sunil Sir standing beside the person I've been longing to see. Rini Di offers me a kind smile.

"Namaste, di. Namaste, sir." I fold my hands in greeting.

"Hello, Heera. May we come in?" Sunil Sir asks.

"Of course!" says Mai, immediately getting up.

I lead them into our hut, which finally has walls and an opening for a door. It is neat and clean. A candle burns brightly in the small alcove in the wall. Mai's wall paintings look beautiful in the flickering light. Rini Di hands a bag to Mai, who takes it wordlessly. I can already see that it is filled with grains and fruit. Enough to keep us fed for a week.

Courteous, as always, Mai pulls out a small plastic chair for Sunil Sir and gives her bamboo stool to Rini Di. It is our only one. Rini Di quickly takes a seat beside Sania on the floor and Sunil Sir takes the stool.

"Please, take the chair," Rini Di insists.

But Mai has never taken the chair. Ever.

She joins Rini Di on the floor.

For a moment, it feels too good, too safe to be true. A room full of people who want what's best for me.

"I have spoken to the principal. He wants Heera back," Rini Di begins to say just as Baba walks through the door. She turns to me then as Baba looks to Mai for answers. "Heera, we'd like to have a word with your parents, if that is okay."

I'm supposed to leave them alone, but I stand behind the plastic sheet that is our door, where I know I'll be able to hear them without being seen.

"We heard what happened to Chotu and wanted to come earlier, but we knew you'd be busy with your family," Rini Di says.

I hear my father grunt.

Rini Di asks after Sania and Salman. She and Sunil Sir both have plenty of questions about how Salman is doing in school. They are impressed, as everyone always is by Salman.

"And Heera—" I hear Rini Di say.

"She is still needed at home," Baba says.

There is a silence within as I hold my breath.

"She is home all alone through the day?" asks Rini Di.

"When I am at work, she looks after Sania," Mai says.

Their voices are so low now that I can hardly hear.

Then Rini Di speaks up. "Of course, she also needs time to grieve, but being in school might help her move past this tragedy."

"How would studying help?" My father now.

"Being among her friends and teachers might be a healthy distraction," Sunil Sir offers. "It will help her get back into a routine."

"Who do you think you are, coming here and telling me what is good for my family!" growls Baba.

"That—" Rini Di begins to respond but is cut off.

"What we need is money. So we can eat twice a day and stay warm."

The blood in my head is pounding so hard that I can't hear what is said next, and before I know it, Rini Di and Sunil Sir are outside and have discovered me eavesdropping.

Rini Di looks at me with an expression I have not seen before: shared conspiracy. She winks. "Remember, I never give up. He wants money? I will find a way."

She winks again as she and Sunil Sir wave goodbye.

Peace doesn't last long in Girls Bazaar and the very next day, the spell is broken.

We hear the sound of sirens. Outside, there are two police cars in front of Chacha's hut. Eight or ten police officers are standing there, batons in hand. I watch Shaukat as he's dragged into the van. A crowd begins to form, watching in silence as Chacha wails and Mira Di cries into her arm.

"It's all your fault," Chacha shouts at Mira Di. "Shaukat would never have said no to that client if you had not shown him the cigarette burns on your arms."

For once Mai speaks up. "What could she do? Let that man burn her again? If she can't tell her brother, who will she turn to?"

It seems that Baba has finally had enough of Mai's newly found confidence and candor. "You stay out of this," he yells at her. "Do you know that the customer was the police officer's brother-in-law? You cannot insult a man of his stature."

Without acknowledging Baba's retort, Mai goes to comfort Mira Di. She puts her arms around her, pulling her into the hut and away from the prying eyes of the Girls Bazaar crowd of onlookers.

At last, Baba and Chacha leave for the police station in a rickshaw.

Inside our hut, Mira Di holds my hand tight. Jamila Bua knocks on our door soon after with some tea leaves and sugar. She's been there for Mira Di many times before. One night, Mira Di came to her hut with bloodied lips and a bruised eye. Her cheeks were marked with a hand-print. Her blouse was ripped. Jamila Bua had quickly soaked some soft rags in the leaves of the marigold plant, wiped the wounds clean, and treated Mira Di's eyes, lips, and cheek with an ointment she had made from neem and turmeric paste.

I brew a pot as Sania silently plays and Mai makes Mira Di comfortable on the straw mat. Mira Di wipes a tear with the end of her sari and shows us her arm. I hope that she can feel momentarily safe among us women. Her skin is full of small dark scorched circles.

"There is this customer who likes to smoke beedis and puts them out on me," Mira Di says. "When I cry in pain, he laughs. Finally, I told Shaukat that I don't want him near me." She pauses, crying softly. "For once, Shaukat stood by me. He turned the man down when he tried to buy me. But he continued to wave money at Shaukat in front of everyone." To my surprise, Mira Di begins to laugh. "Shaukat actually boxed him. The man went right down. He just did not expect small and tiny Shaukat to hit him."

Jamila Bua starts to giggle as well. "Everyone near the tea stall saw the whole thing." She becomes serious then. "But the man walked off cursing Shaukat, promising revenge. God knows what he went and told his cop brother-in-law. That creepy Suraj Sharma."

We sit around in our familiar surroundings, frightened and dry-eyed, wondering if the police will punish Chacha and Baba too. They cannot read or write. They certainly cannot afford a lawyer. Shaukat is a sickly boy and won't be able to bear the atmosphere of a police lockup for long. His dilapidated body can only take so much.

It's the afternoon when Baba and Chacha return. We breathe a sigh of relief as we see them walk back. But our hearts sink when we hear Shaukat's news: They need money to get my cousin out of prison. Suraj Sharma, Manish's father, has booked Shaukat for human trafficking.

"He's asking for a big bribe to drop the charges," Baba says. "It's a lot of money, more money than we have."

We all know what that means. They will have to turn to Ravi Lala for another loan.

Shaukat will be home by the evening, but at a price.

That night, the back room is closed for business and Mira Di calls me to join her.

She pats a spot beside her on her bright pink bedspread. The tiny room is only a little bigger than the wooden bed itself.

I sit on the edge of the bed, my feet dangling. I can tell from her smell that she is drunk. The room is dark aside from some outside light that filters in from the railway station through the small window with iron bars.

I'm the only one who sees this side of Mira Di—shaky and vulnerable, weepy and completely drunk. To the world outside, she is someone else entirely. She takes long steps when she walks the streets, her body uncoiled, her long hair hanging to her hips, red lipstick contrasting with the black mascara and sky-blue bindi on her face. She walks with confidence, talks very little, and always has a smile fixed on her face. Nothing like the disheveled, frightened woman I see in front of me who is holding her body in with her arms wrapped around her knees.

"Shaukat and my father had to promise that I wouldn't turn that client away ever again," slurs Mira Di. Her feet are on the bed; her knees are bent; her hands cover her eyes as if she is blocking a glare.

"What do you mean? The police made them say this?" I'm taken aback, though I shouldn't be surprised.

"Who else? The police are the worst of all! Especially Suraj Sharma! I'm sure he does business with Ravi Lala."

I stop dangling my legs and sit up at the thought of Manish's respectable policeman father in business with Ravi Lala.

"Don't act so surprised." She twirls one of her bangles as she speaks, her voice low and urgent. "Ravi Lala knows how many girls the fair needs every January. He keeps track of our homes to see who can be made available to the dance party. The police and all the local politicians are in his pocket. He sends girls to them too. If a girl runs away, the police will only bring her back to him." Her tone is desperate.

Outside, the sounds of the Girls Bazaar blare—men quarreling over their bets in the gambling joint, the "clients" haggling over the price of girls, Bollywood songs playing over the chorus of children crying from hunger.

"It's important that you know this, Heera. Rini Di says Suraj Sharma and Ravi Lala are part of a trafficking ring that smuggles girls from India, Nepal, China, and Korea to the US." She pauses, looking at me intently. Her forehead is covered in sweat and I realize that she's sharing secrets she is not even supposed to know. She inhales deeply. "Rini Di wanted Shaukat and me to hide cameras on our bodies and record Ravi Lala's and Suraj Sharma's comings and goings. She said if we get enough evidence, we could put them all behind bars and all of us in Girls Bazaar would be free from their clutches."

I breathe out softly. I don't want her to stop.

"But I said no. These people are vicious and vindictive. I'm not very smart, perhaps, but I'm smart enough to know not to make matters worse for myself."

"I don't understand," I exclaim. "Why didn't you take Rini Di's help? You could have brought Ravi Lala down!"

"Heera, Heera, Heera," Mira Di says, shaking her head, a sad smile on her face.

"If anything were to go wrong, no one can protect us. Not even Rini Di. Ravi Lala owns everyone. And on top of that, my client would have come at me for revenge. He'd find a way to take it out on me. He's from an upper-caste gang with links to politicians in Patna and Delhi. They own some of the routes and the dance parties in the fairs too. See what happened when Shaukat stood up to one of their people?"

I say nothing as I try to take it all in. I want to tell her that the only hope of us surviving at all is to take these people on. That Rini Di is our only chance. But then I decide I have to be careful. She will stop telling me anything if I challenge her. So, I just nod and say, "Yes."

"You know, Heera, they treat us like fools. They send us off with no knowledge of what will befall us. I don't want you to make the same mistakes as me," she says, turning her head away.

"What mistakes?" I ask.

"Don't trust anyone, Heera. Not even your mother. Your mother thinks she can handle Ravi Lala when he comes for you, but she's wrong."

I open my mouth to protest, but she puts up her hand. "Your mother doesn't mean to hurt you. She's on your side. Not like mine. But by taking money from Ravi Lala, she's set a timer on your freedom."

The lumpy mattress begins to feel unbearable. I stand up at these words and start to pace the room. "So, what do you think I should do?"

"I wish I knew," says Mira Di sadly, her brightly painted lips quivering. "I know I said you should stay in school, but I was in school, wasn't I? Such a lot of good that did me."

Her body is trembling, and I realize that mine is too.

"Mira Di, I don't know how much longer I can wait for Rini Di to come again. Please, is there anything you can do?" I beg.

She nods. "I will send her a message."

CHAPTER EIGHT

The fair is open for business, and the sounds and smells fill every corner of our little home. It's only midday but I feel as though my eardrums will burst. The hammering and nailing of the tents and stalls has disappeared as they put the final touches on their displays in the din. Now multiple speakers announce fair rules, events, competitions, missing children. More speakers compete with one another to play Bollywood songs as loud as possible.

There is nothing subtle about the gaudy posters of girls in bras and panties on the numerous nautanki stalls with names like Paradise, Dreamy Nights, and Love in London. Or the owners of the dance companies who have begun to walk up and down the street, soliciting customers. I stay inside, determined to be as invisible as possible until I hear word from Rini Di.

My senses are overcome by the aromas of frying food—the golden jalebis, crisp from the pan. I imagine the confectionary cook tossing the syrup-soaked rings onto an old newspaper to drain out the oil.

Mai has decided we will eat less in order to pay Ravi Lala as quickly as possible. She has begun hiding her earnings from Baba to repay the loan before he can get his hands on me. She keeps the money with Jamila Bua and tells Baba that the contractor hasn't been paid yet.

I recall Rini Di's words to my father. *She is home all alone through the day?*

I'm not entirely alone, though. Sania is here with me.

A knock at the door distracts me from my hunger and I'm relieved to see the kind face of Jamila Bua, her eyes beaming with excitement.

"Rini Di wants to meet you at the café near the referral hospital," she whispers, out of breath. "She has something important to discuss, and she'd like to know how you feel before she tries to speak to your baba again."

"How can I leave, Jamila Bua?" I respond uneasily. "Baba has been coming back to check on me. He's watching me like a hawk now that the fair has arrived."

"Your mai and I have worked that out. She's told your baba that you will be taking Sania to the referral hospital to get checked up. Nothing unusual in that."

Before I can think twice about it, I scoop up Sania and do as Jamila Bua says.

I walk through the throng of customers and vendors, trying to take it all in while hoping to stay invisible. There are men in pants, dhotis, lungis, and pajamas with sweaters over jackets, kurtas, and shirts made from every possible fabric. Women in saris and salwar kameezes, children in clothes of different hues, cattle with their horns painted, performers in their costumes. Someone has set up a small zoo with animals from the forests of Nepal.

I bury my head as I walk forward, trying to go through unnoticed.

Just past the referral hospital, Sania and I enter the tea stall. A bamboo fence surrounds the little patch of land with its little red plastic stools and tables set under two mango trees.

Rini Di walks in with purpose, flinging her bag on the closest table. She sits down and asks Sania and me to take a seat next to her. We are just beginning to order tea and bread pakoras when, to my surprise, Mai walks through the door and sits at our table.

"I wanted to see you today because I think there is a way to convince your father. But I have to be sure that you both agree," says Rini Di.

We eagerly hang on her words.

"You know I have talked to the principal, and he has agreed to let Heera back in school," starts Rini Di.

Mai clutches my hand beneath the table.

"I have a few conditions, though." Rini Di looks at Mai with a question in her eyes. "I want your commitment that she will attend regularly. I know food is important, but school is much more than that. She must study hard. I will make sure some other girls in my hostel help her. She can stay after school or come early to do her homework with them."

Mai nods vigorously. "Of course."

Suddenly, I feel the need to clarify something. "What about Sania? Where will she stay when you're breaking stones for the road construction?"

"I can leave her with your chachi on some days. On others, she is still small enough that I can carry her in my sari while I work," Mai says with certainty.

"You will both get hurt, Mai."

"She is hardly bigger than when I did it before. And the weather is better now." Mai turns back to Rini Di. "She'll go. Don't worry."

It's harder for her to answer my next question. "What about Baba?"

Before Mai can answer, Rini Di responds. "I've figured out a way to get your family the money you deserve. If you agree, I will come to your hut and explain to all of you together. The government has put aside a lot of money to make sure that girls from poor and marginalized castes get food and education. There is also a budget for housing and health care."

"That will take time," says Mai. "We have been trying to get dry ration under the government policy for low-cost food for years. The authorities just send us away. They say we are prostitutes. They don't event put us on the list, let alone give us ration."

"The organization that I support, the one that runs the girl's hostel, has an outreach program to make sure families like yours get this allocation," Rini Di continues.

Mai shakes her head in disbelief.

"I promise you that it is not impossible," Rini Di says. "It just requires a lot of persistence and tenacity. We'll have to fill out forms, show up at government offices, speak to higher-ups, even to the media if we have to. Sometimes we'll even file police complaints, appeal to the court. It may happen in weeks, months, or maybe years. But we don't give up."

She looks at my mother to see if she has understood, and continues. "You are not alone. And it is much easier when you are not alone. Women like you can form groups. You already have some friends. And together, we will see to it that it happens," says Rini Di reassuringly.

Mai's hand begins to tremble.

Rini Di reaches for her. "That is why, if we invest so much time and resources, you have to promise not to give up."

"I understand," Mai says with resolve. Then adds in a shaky voice: "Can you convince my husband too?"

Rini Di nods and makes one last point.

"One more condition. You know Heera is bullied at school? We have to teach her to fight without spitting or breaking teeth."

Mai shakes her head. "She is a girl. She should not fight—"

"I want to learn kung fu, Mai," I interrupt. "It's self-defense. If someone beats me, I can block them. I've seen girls practice it in in our hostel compound."

Rini Di smiles. "Have you been reading the Bruce Lee book?" she asks.

I nod shyly.

Rini Di continues. "At the hostel, we teach the fighting art called kung fu. It's a kind of kushti," Rini Di explains to a bewildered Mai. "Manish picks on her because he knows he can get away with it. She has to learn to stand up to him, but in many different ways."

I can see from Mai's expression that she wants me in school but doesn't care about kung fu.

"Mai, you remember how I used to wrestle. It's in my blood. The classes are within the school compound," I implore.

Mai sighs, relenting. "If it means she can stay in school, and that she is safe, then so be it."

That evening, it is just Mai, Baba, and me at home when Rini Di walks into the little space outside our hut where Mai is cooking.

Baba grabs me by the arm. "Why is that woman here again?"

"She is trying to help us, Baba. Just listen."

"Why would she want to help us?" Baba shoots back, adjusting his bandanna. "Has *anyone* ever helped us?"

Rini Di waves us over as she sits on the cane stool near Mai, samosas and jalebis in hand.

Baba's face softens at the sight of the food.

I quickly get the red plastic chair for my father. Mai gives him the jalebi and samosa on a plate as he sits down.

"I would like Heera to come back to school," Rini Di says as we eat. "The government is giving nearly a thousand rupees a month for girls from backward castes to go to school to cover their expenses. You will get that. It will contribute to the household."

I smile inwardly. Rini Di has found the perfect bait.

Baba eyes her suspiciously. "We never got it when she went to school before."

"This year I will make sure she gets it. You have my word. And we can help you get food ration cards."

Baba and Mai look at each other. "How can we be sure?" asks Baba.

"It is what I do. The organization that runs our hostel works to ensure that people from poor communities get what the government owes them."

But Baba shakes his head. "There are other things to think about too. Both my wife and my brother have taken loans from Ravi Lala. Our hut is on my brother's land. Ravi Lala can decide to collect his debt whenever he wants, and if my brother has to evict us, he will."

The reality of his words knocks the wind out of me.

Finally, Mai cuts in. "I am earning from my work," she says desperately. "I'll repay him."

I can see the frustration building beneath Baba's skin. "You will have to crush a million stones before you have that much money!"

Rini Di interjects. "I will make sure that you are taken care of for a year. You will not need Heera to earn. The school owes you money for the years they didn't cover her expenses. I should be able to get that for you. And the thousand rupees will start coming now. One year. That's all you need to agree to for now."

"I don't have a year," Baba says, twirling his mustache. "Ravi Lala is willing to take Heera in place of the repayment *now*."

It feels as if all of us hold our breath at once.

"Baba, what are you trying to say?" I ask, my voice quivering.

Baba rises from his chair and wipes the crumbs of the samosa from his lips. "Ravi Lala says it's time. Next week, he'll forgive our loan and pay for the Bisi Bele."

"What about Rini Di's offer?" Mai begs.

Baba stares down at me, ignoring the tears in Mai's eyes. "These fancy people have never helped people like us. She is only filling your heads with garbage. This is the way of our people, Heera. This is your destiny, your duty. You are a Nat daughter."

I can't bear to look at Mai or Rini Di.

My heart stops beating. My stomach feels empty. I squeeze my eyes shut.

The ground seems to have more gravity than before.

It wants to pull me down.

CHAPTER NINE

"I was afraid this might happen, but you must promise me you will stay calm." Rini Di looks into my eyes behind her wire-rimmed glasses. "The Bisi Bele will take a few days to plan. I will come before that. Even if the fair is here, Ravi Lala and your baba are both superstitious. They will not sell you without going through the rites and meeting with an astrologer. Give me a day or two, and I will come for you," she promises.

The sun has barely risen, but I could not sleep. I couldn't bear to stay home. I had to run.

In the cold morning mist, I ran away from the bright blues, pinks, yellows, and reds of the tents and the stalls, the dancing lights and the big wheel whirring through the air from our lane, past the railway station and over the tracks, through the fields and beyond the vegetable market and the district court. All to skirt Girls Bazaar. To walk up the three steps to the hostel and hear Rini Di say, once again, that she never gives up.

"What happens if it happens sooner than that?" I ask with a trembling voice.

"Then we can bring you here, to this hostel," Rini Di says.

Outside, some of the girls wash their clothes under the hand pump in the hostel courtyard. Down the corridor, I can hear other girls watching something on TV.

"What do you mean? I thought this was a place for orphans."

"Many of them are. But this is also a hostel for children who have all sorts of problems. Some of them are from homes such as yours, and they're here so they won't be sold into the sex trade."

At last, my hands stop shaking. I look up. "Really?" I ask hesitantly.

"Yes, but to do it against your parents' wishes would mean involving the police and a court case. I don't want to do that, and I'm sure you don't want that either," Rini Di explains as she gently pushes a plate of cookies toward me.

I take a big bite. And then another.

"No! I don't!" I say, speaking as I wolf down the cookies.

"Right. So, it's best for everyone that we find a way to stop this without disrupting your family. That's why I need time."

I can picture Ravi Lala's dirty hands. Every finger has a ring with a large stone that the astrologer has advised him to wear.

I am not sure we have time. But I see Rini Di's point. Baba cannot move forward without talking to an astrologer. Nor will Ravi Lala.

That night, before bed, I tell Salman that I would like to chop down every banana tree in the lane. "No banana tree, no bridegroom, no marriage, right?" I ask Salman, with a lift of my chin and a grin on my face.

After I'm married to the banana tree, I will be a wife, but not to any man. I can be sent off with a dance party with no one feeling guilty. The rituals will be followed, the gods and goddesses appeased.

Salman laughs anxiously and I go to sleep thinking of chopped banana trees, trying with all my might to ignore what I heard from Baba earlier. That the astrologer wants us to visit him tomorrow to fix a date for the Bisi Bele.

Salman has already left for school by the time I awake to the sounds of the morning. Jamila Bua has lit her fire. Sania is clean and fed. Shutters open. Bicycle bells and bus horns declare that the day has begun, as if it is any other day and not the last day of my freedom.

Today is the day of the astrologer's visit. He wants us to meet him at 5:30 p.m., when Mai comes back from the highway. Even Baba realizes that we cannot afford for Mai to take a day off.

I'm not sure what I'll do if Rini Di doesn't arrange things in time. If I'll run. If I'll submit to my fate like Mira Di.

I never give up.

I sweep the house, fill our bucket with water from Chachi's hand pump, and go for a wash with Sania at the railway platform.

Mai is about to leave when I hear Baba seethe. "How dare she set foot in here again."

Rini Di walks down the street, her head held high.

Luckily his morning cup of tea is still brewing, so Baba does not leave.

"You have some nerve coming back here after my decision has been made," Baba says.

But Mai is smart. She knows that the last thing that anyone, including Baba, wants is a scene, or the sharp ears of Chacha and Shaukat. The Girls Bazaar drumbeat would reach Ravi Lala in minutes. "Please, let's have this conversation inside," she says softly.

Behind our door, Mai offers Rini Di a glass of piping-hot tea. Baba scoffs when she insists that Mai bring a glass for herself too.

I am allowed to sit with them, sipping tea on the straw mat, our backs against the mud wall as if we have all the time in the world. Sania chortles as Rini Di gives her a cookie. Mai's sari is tucked into her waist, her hair tied up in a bun. Every moment here takes her away from her work on the highway, but she doesn't rush the process.

"I have good news," Rini says with a broad smile on her face, as if yesterday's conversation never happened. "I spoke with the headmaster, and he has agreed to give the stipend due to Heera from the last year. It will cover your loan."

My mother looks at me. The joy on her face is an unexpected punch in the stomach. I realize then how long it's been since I've seen her smile like this—her eyes lit up, her lips curled so that I can see the laugh lines near her eyes crinkle the way they used to when she played cops and robbers with us four children.

"She is also due arrears for the years that have passed; in total it is around twenty-five thousand rupees," Rini Di announces. I've never even heard of such a large sum of money in my life.

My father shifts. I know this is a number beyond his wildest dreams. He puts his teacup down and turns to face us women, finally. For once, I can see an expression that is not anger but curiosity.

The blare of a train's whistle fills our hut. Rini Di waits patiently as it passes. "I wish I could tell you that the money is coming to you soon, but unfortunately, the headmaster can't pay just yet. I will take up the matter with the educational department. But in the meantime, I have brought the money to repay the loan for now."

"Why?" asks my father suspiciously. But his body language changes as he strikes a match and lights his beedi.

"Because it's a small price to pay to get Heera in school. I have gotten to know her, and she is talented. This is the least I can do," Rini Di says.

Mai wipes a tear from her face with the corner of her sari. She pulls me close to her.

"When would we have to pay you back?" Baba asks in a softer tone than any I have heard him use with Rini Di before. "And how long will that take?"

"We will see," says Rini Di gently. "When I get the school to pay your arrears, we can settle it then. But I'm not Ravi Lala. I will not expect you to sell your daughter to settle your debt."

Baba says nothing. He takes another sip of his tea and inhales a long whiff from his beedi.

"We agree," Mai says impatiently. "Right?"

Rini Di has already pulled out an envelope of money from her backpack.

My father looks at her. For a moment, my heart is in my throat. "You are the one who took the loan from Ravi Lala in the first place," he says to Mai at last. "It will be you who pays it back and tells him that Heera won't be joining the dance party this year."

I have hardly moved a muscle during this entire exchange at the risk of altering the outcome, but as I stare at Baba from the corner of my eye, I realize at last just how scared he really is.

"I will wait here until she returns," Rini Di says, her eyes fixed on my father's. "I would love to play with Sania and chat with Heera about some school things. I have the time."

Baba gives a tiny nod, as close to a thank-you as I have ever seen from my father. Slowly, Mai reaches for the envelope from Rini Di's outstretched hand. "Shukriya," she says shyly.

Then Mai storms out of the hut, her chin jutting out, her pace hurried.

Rini Di pulls out a packet of chips and two books for me—a picture book with a story and a brand-new exercise book to write in. She begins to read from the book as we munch on the chips, ignoring Baba as he paces. He finishes one beedi and lights another.

The winter sun comes in through the window and our open door. With Rini Di here, the world outside feels friendlier. A woman laughs. The whistle of another train, the splashing of water being pumped, the shouts of vendors selling fresh bananas is only noise.

Each minute feels like an hour as Baba circles us with his pacing, orbiting around us as we play with little Sania for distraction.

There was another time, years ago, that I remember Mai being this excited.

We had been lying on our mat one evening, shortly after we moved to Girls Bazaar.

"I think I could start a betel paan leaf shop in the front of our hut one day," Mai whispered in my ear. "Everyone in our lane chews paan. My special mix of nuts, seeds, and tobacco is famous. I have a special way of smearing the lime paste across the leaf and mixing in the ingredients before I fold it into a triangle. I could teach you."

It was the first time Mai ever told me what she wanted to do.

"We could set up a neat wooden stall with a platform for small jars of lime, katha, fennel seeds, sweets, and nuts," she went on. "Some tobacco. I could keep the betel paan leaves fresh soaking in a mug of water. All lined up nicely. No back room like Chacha."

We smiled at each other, imagining the paan shop. I told her I wanted to choose the colors of the wooden platform. I'd pick a brilliant peacock blue.

I picture her now, sitting cross-legged on a cotton rug, dressed in a crisp, new starched sari. The jars of colorful ingredients laid out in front of her. A long line of customers as she folds paan after paan.

Just then, the door to our hut flings open. "It's done," Mai announces. Her bun has come fallen out of its knot. But she looks more energetic and in control than I've ever seen her. More even than when she took the loan and built our hut.

"I told him straight," she recounts in a loud whisper, as if Ravi Lala is in the room. "My Heera is too young to be sent away. She will be staying in school yet."

Baba stands by the door as if someone might burst through it. "And?" asks my father. "What did he say?"

"What could he say? He doesn't own us, after all, not now that the money is paid back." For once, I hear my mother speak to my father with some authority. She looks at him directly from the floor as he stands near the entrance. She does not look down or avert her eyes. She does not leave her sentence half-finished.

"And all the plans for Bisi Bele?" Baba asks, taking another drag from his beedi.

"Canceled," my mother says through a big grin.

"And he was happy with that?" Baba is still skeptical.

"Happy or not, what's it to me? What business is it of his if Heera goes to work or not?" challenges my mother with a shake of her head.

This time I think Baba is right to be skeptical. Ravi Lala runs Girls Bazaar. He won't give up easily. Such people never do.

As if she can read my mind, Rini Di gets up to leave. "I'll see you in school on Monday," she says to me, giving me a big, reassuring hug. "Remember, we are all here if you need us. It's the weekend, so Salman will be home. Don't go anywhere without him. And remember to bring your uniform." She winks.

I bury my doubts beneath my excitement. There will be no astrologer visit today. No marriage to a tree.

For now, I am free.

I think of Bruce Lee.

There would be no bright stars without dim stars and without the surrounding darkness no stars at all.

PART II

Be like water.

~Bruce Lee

CHAPTER TEN

I had somehow imagined this moment to be so much more difficult than it is. Like crossing a river full of crocodiles. The boys would encircle me. The principal would block the gate. I would have nowhere to run.

In reality, nothing happens.

The school is the same as it's always been. It's the same building, lined with the same verandas, behind which are all the same classrooms. The same everyday sounds: children chattering, footsteps running, someone laughing. A cycle bell rings. A door slams. It's the same comforting, underlying tone of my school humming with morning activity as if I never left.

But today is different. Today, I've gotten a second chance. The pink paint on the walls looks brighter. Why did I ever think it had become gray? A squirrel runs ahead of me into the open gate toward the court-yard. And Sadaf walks beside me, her curly brown hair pulled back into a ponytail.

Her parents don't even allow her to come into the red-light area. And yet she decided to walk me to school. I could hardly believe it when Jamila Bua told me the plan. But at 8:00 a.m., there she was in front of the referral hospital, waiting near the café by the red plastic chairs.

As we get closer to the doors, I notice Sadaf's customary blue jeans and a freshly washed T-shirt, sparkling white. As usual, I'm wearing my patched black salwar kameez, one of three sets that I keep alternat-ing. But no one seems to notice. I see the usual sights—kids going about their business, playing in the grounds, heading toward class. No one seems at all interested that I'm back. Perhaps it's a good thing.

School means food, I remind myself. School means food and kung fu.

Sadaf takes my hand. "It'll be fine."

Whatever lies inside these walls is far less frightening than the fair.

"You going to kung fu after school?" Sadaf asks.

I nod, trying not to act too excited. It's the main thing getting me through the day.

"Rini Di says she'll be picking someone for the next competition soon."

I look at her to make sure she's not joking. I don't even know what it would take to compete. But I know that I want more than anything to be chosen.

Still, I hear Manish's voice dance in my head. "Heera laid an egg,

Heera laid an egg . . ." I can hear his friends. "We know what you'll do when you grow up." Their words tap against the walls of my brain. "We know, we know, we know, we know, we know . . ."

My steps falter.

"Let's sit together," Sadaf suggests as we walk to class.

Before I can stop her, Sadaf automatically walks to the front of the room, where Razia is sitting on the first bench. This is new for me. I've only ever sat in the back. And there are hurdles to get from here to there—I would have to cross the chief crocodile Manish, sitting in the middle row, surrounded by his cronies. Their whispers and stares prick at my skin. Memories surface and feelings that I have ignored rise to the top. My hands begin to shake.

Sadaf turns around as I slow down. "Heera, come on." She pats the seat beside her.

My confidence returns just long enough to avoid their eyes and find my seat. Maybe it's just a glitch, but if I'm not mistaken, the boys seem puzzled. I've never had friends. Not after Rosy left. And now I'm invited to sit with two of the smartest girls in our class. The truth is that I never wanted to make new friends after Rosy left for Nepal. Nor did anyone want to make friends with me. Finding a new friend would mean replacing Rosy. It would mean that she was really gone.

I remember what Jamila Bua once said: *We can always do with more friends.*

Today, I am grateful. But I can't help but wonder how long Sadaf plans to stick around.

I spend every moment for the remainder of the day waiting for something bad to happen. But as each moment passes, I somehow remain unscathed.

In science class, Sadaf pulls out her books and shows me the lesson we're studying today. It's the cosmos. Luckily, Salman has already explained some of the basic concepts. For once in my life, I actually know what's going on. The teacher explains our solar system, drawing a diagram on the board. I copy it, taking notes, but also trying to listen. I realize that at the front of the room it's easier to hear—there's less noise around me, less chatter, less distraction. When he asks what galaxy our planet is in, I don't raise my hand. But I know the answer. The Milky Way. I make it to the end of the lesson without losing track.

The bell rings. Sunil Sir enters the classroom and behaves as though me sitting in the front row is an everyday affair. He launches into a new topic: negative numbers. We did this last year too, I remember. My brain seems to function again. A little food and a little friendship go a long way.

At lunch a dollop of rice falls onto my plate. I mix it with the fried potato fritters and sautéed spinach, savoring the first bite. My instincts urge me to eat as fast as possible, but I tell myself I have to slow down. Especially after Sadaf and Razia place their mats next to mine.

This too is a first. Nobody has ever wanted to sit next to me at lunch since Rosy left.

Even the kids who were forced to sit closest to me made sure to maintain distance, their steel plates angled away from mine. The lunch ladies would drop the rotis and daal onto my plate from way above so that their hands didn't touch my hand when they served the food. They didn't want to come into physical contact with someone of my caste. But today I'm eating in between two of the top students in the class.

Finally, I cannot take the uncertainty. I have to know.

"Why have you decided to be my friend?" I ask, keeping my eyes on my plate.

"We don't like bullies," Razia says with a toss of her head, as if the answer is that simple.

Sadaf nods in agreement. "When Rini Di told us that you might drop out of school because of Manish, we made up our minds to find a way to help you," says Sadaf. "I asked her if I could walk with you to school on your first day back."

I smile, hoping my face is capable of conveying the gratitude I feel.

Suddenly, the aroma of the potato curry with red chilies and tomatoes fills my senses. Sadaf and Razia chat like long-lost friends. I don't talk much, but I listen. The food at school has never tasted better. But I'm also acutely aware of Manish sitting at the far end of the room. The boys around him throw the occasional look in my direction and laugh. My face begins to grow hot, but I pretend to ignore them.

After lunch, I wash my hands and head back to the classroom for English when Manish and Rahul, his acolyte, walk toward me and smirk. At last, my time has come. I knew it had to happen sometime, though I had begun to think it wouldn't be today. I keep my head down, hoping I can somehow learn how to disappear into the wall. They pass, and for a moment I think I'm in the clear. But then Manish stops and turns back to me.

"Watch out!" he whispers, opening his cupped hands. A small animal scurries out. A mouse, maybe even a small rat.

I think of what Rini Di said. That I need to learn to defend myself in other ways.

I break into a jog away from him, his laugh fading behind me.

I feel the spices from my lunch in my throat as I fight the urge to cry. When I make it to the desk, I'm quiet. Sadaf and Razia discuss something that I don't even pretend to follow. I stare ahead at the blackboard. Just like old times.

To get through an entire day of school without trouble was more than I had expected. Now the bubble has burst. I feel exposed. Alone once again with not even an egg in my hand.

Suddenly, my ears pick up some music, slowly forming into a song from the chorus rehearsal in the other classroom. The notes begin to cut through the tension. I close my eyes, trying to listen to the words. It's about the soul flying in the air with the wind, over the clouds, free as a bird . . .

The start of class jolts me back to attention. Our English teacher asks someone to read a poem about a flower called a daffodil. There is a picture of a cluster of them in our book growing down the side of a mountain in a country called England. They are yellow—just like our sunflowers and mustard blooms. I wish they had a poem on the yellow mustard fields in our syllabus. A poem about India. But I understand what the poet is trying to say. It's the same way my heart has often danced when I see the miles of knee-high yellow mustard flowers.

We may be from different countries, but our feelings are the same.

The way that Bruce Lee is from America, but is also Chinese.

The way kung fu began in China, but had Indian teachers and is popular in America. And here in a corner of Bihar, where us girls are ready to learn to defend ourselves.

The bell rings. This time I forget about Manish waiting to make his next move. Razia, Sadaf, and I pick up our bags and race to the changing rooms. It takes only seconds to put on the robe and the trousers. There's a long mirror on the door where I'm able to look at myself—I'm taller, more powerful in the clean white uniform.

Girls like me can't afford to be mediocre. We barely get one chance, let alone a second one. Sadaf smiles when she sees me looking at myself.

I look at the kwoon, settled between the red and yellow swings and the great mango tree. The tree has more branches and leaves than it can hold, even though it's winter. I've often sat under it, away from prying eyes, listening to the whisper of its leaves. Today, the branches sway toward the kwoon like human arms gesturing to show me the way, inviting me in. Today, I'm here as a practitioner. I will no longer be an onlooker. It's no longer just a long rectangular stretch of pinkish-brown dirt near the swings. It's golden, washed in the afternoon sun. It's where I'll learn speed and endurance. Where I'll learn to become a champion like my uncles.

Two girls from the hostel have taken off their shoes and are dusting the kwoon for leaves and stones. Laughter floats in the air as students line up. Rini Di stands in front of us in her white T-shirt and black track pants.

Sadaf and I take off our shoes and stand in line inside the kwoon.

I catch Rini Di's eye and she smiles at me as if I have just walked in with the sun, her eyes stretching, forming wrinkles at the corners.

"In kung fu a teacher is called a sifu. Just so you know," Sadaf tells me in a whisper. "Just follow what I do."

Rini Di greets us all. "Namaste!"

"Sifu Rini hao," we chorus back as we bow. Everyone greets her with the traditional Shaolin salute, right fist on the left palm. I follow suit.

As we stand in rows, a mix of new and old students, Rini Di tells us that we'll start with a warm-up and then go through the five basic stances. Horse stance, forward stance, cat stance, twist stance, and crane stance.

"When will we practice the high kicks?" asks a boy in the front.

"First you must perfect the stances. Having the right stance centers your gravity and drives your hand and leg motions, giving you power. They're fundamental to the practice of Shaolin kung fu. When an experienced practitioner views a performance, they look at the stances first."

I take a mental note.

The instructions begin. *Left. Right. Press your thighs. Back straight. Shoulders down. Breathe deeply.*

As I relax down into what I think is the horse stance, Rini Di comes and straightens my back. "Don't push your chest inward," Rini Di shows me. "All power in kung fu comes from the ground."

I try to feel the pull of the earth. I embrace gravity, letting it connect with my body. Somehow, it's more natural than I could have ever imagined. Something happens. My body loosens up and lets go. I open up my shoulders, instead of slouching over my breasts in shame. I inhale deeply into my expanded lungs.

I think of when I've felt like fighting in the past. How the tension in my body seemed to swallow me. I wasn't in control then. But now I feel as light as air. The gravity centers me. The earth carries me. The day's anxieties don't exist. The earth has absorbed them. I feel as though I can move my body in any direction.

We move to the forward stance. Rini Di shows us how to shift our weight onto the front leg. We bend the front knee, our back leg straight toward the side like a drawn bow.

By the time we finish the cat stance, the twist, and the crane stance, I am exhausted.

I can feel every muscle ache, every pore breathe. The shame, the guilt, and the fear that have been embedded in every cell of my body seem to have seeped out of me. I have always hated my body—my breasts and hips, the parts of me that gave me away. They marked me out for the fair in Ravi Lala's eyes.

I push my shoulders back and open up my chest without fear. I am calm, though my heartbeat is loud. For the first time, it seems, I notice different parts of my body.

Finally, Rini Di says, "Relax. Remember, kung fu is not just about physical strength. It is about channeling your energy, or chi, to use your strength effectively. The more you practice, the more you train your mind and body to work together, the more you will reach the highest stage of kung fu—a state of complete mindfulness."

"What does that mean?" asks Sadaf.

"It means your mind and body will connect. They will guide you together. You will choose to listen to both unitedly. If a power is stronger than you, you will become flexible and let the stronger power spend its energy out on itself rather than on you."

We nod. I mull over these words.

She leaves us with a final thought. "You cannot be powerful all the time, or you will break. You cannot be flexible all the time, or you will lose direction. Be like water. Flow. Don't crash."

I bow to Sifu Rini, then in all the four directions of the kwoon.

I will flow, not crash.

"Namaste."

CHAPTER ELEVEN

I often wake up at night in a sweat from a nightmare that I've never told Mai or Salman about. I'm skidding down a tunnel and land in a ditch as Ravi Lala chases me, his face like a wolf, the scar on his cheek under his right eye gleaming. And then when I feel I cannot breathe, his face evaporates, my eyelids open, and I'm in the darkness of our hut with four warm bodies breathing evenly around me. I haven't slept a straight eight hours since Chotu died. Even less since Baba announced that Ravi Lala wants me.

Day after day, I catch myself as I walk to and from the school. Day after day I remind myself that I've really gotten away. Or have I?

Sometimes it feels like it's either Salman or me whose life will be ruined.

Over the last two weeks, as I've started going back to school, Baba has turned his attention to the boy to earn money for the family. He wants Salman to join Ravi Lala's gang—to procure other girls, pimp them. Even the thought feels like glass cracking inside my heart. But Mira Di says she doesn't plan on giving up on either of us. That a client of hers who says he wants to marry her and get her out of Girls Bazaar knows someone in the Christian boarding school in Siliguri. She asked him to help get Salman in. To get *him* out of Girls Bazaar. But we've yet to hear back.

I tell myself to focus. Stay present.

The library at the hostel is nearly empty, packed only with a rich silence. I have such few moments of silence in my life that I want it to enter my body through my skin. Its microclimate soothes me to no end after the seething sounds in our lane.

Zehra, my tutor, is staring at me. She's angry, I can tell, after dealing with another one of my bouts of frustration. Her thick lashes close over her dark brown eyes for a second as she tries to calm down.

"Feeling any better?" she asks gently, looking up with an easy smile as she tucks a few stray strands of hair back under her headscarf.

I take a few deep breaths. I'm frustrated that she can't quite understand what I have to overcome. Nobody who has not lived in our lane could possibly understand. Maybe I should ask my mother to tattoo that nobody in our family has ever completed high school on my forehead.

"Fractional exponents are a little challenging at first," she says. "But once you understand the principles, you'll get it in no time." Leaning in across the table, she backs up a bit and takes me through the math and science concepts again, going back to the syllabus from the beginning of the year. I've missed so much and grasped so little.

She has a pile of reference books with pictures so that she can explain more clearly. We inch forward like monsoon snails. They look as if they're standing still, but every few hours you can see how far they've actually moved—slowly and painstakingly. But if we're to finish it all before the exams, we have to move fast. And yet, I have to stop and ask questions, even questions that I felt were too silly to ask in class.

Now more than ever, it matters that I really understand what I am studying.

I've wondered what Zehra's story is. Why does she live in the hostel? Was she rescued from the fair too? Or is she an orphan? She hasn't asked me anything about myself, and I'd like it to stay that way. So, I swallow all my questions and try to concentrate on the work. She's smarter than I could ever hope to be. And she's normally very patient.

The aroma of boiling rice makes its way to my stomach and I'm lost again. I'm not hungry the way I used to be anymore, but my senses haven't forgotten. My stomach still reacts the old way. My mouth still salivates and my attention drifts away from my books and over to food.

The hostel's pantry rooms are stocked with food on shelves all the way up to the ceiling. I hope that Rini Di doesn't mind me eating dinner here for another night in a row.

"How's it going, ladies?" Rini Di asks as she comes by at the end of our session. We're at the long table in the library where Rini Di's office desk sits at the opposite end.

I have begun to like this room, with its long windows and built-in shelves crammed with volumes and volumes of books. I hope that, someday, I will have read all of them. I study the odd objects scattered around, a big brown clock with a pendulum, a large globe, steps to reach the higher shelves. This is the room where I have learned to come up with semi-sensible answers to questions.

"Good," I say. "Zehra is a very good teacher."

Zehra's smile grows wider.

"You hear that?" Rini Di says, nodding in the direction of my comment. Zehra is beaming now and Rini Di pats her on the shoulder. "You're on the right path." She turns back to me. "Zehra here wants to study to be a teacher."

Zehra blushes, her face reflecting the pink of her headscarf.

"Is that why you're helping me?" I ask, turning toward Zehra.

She winces as she thinks, then shakes her head. "Partly. But all the older girls here help the younger ones as needed. We've done it so much we've become quite good at it. I was also tutored by an older girl when I got here."

"That is true," says Rini Di, "but Zehra also has a natural way with teaching, don't you think? If you're done, Zehra, I'd like to borrow Heera for a moment."

I pack my books away and follow Rini Di back to her desk. Nobody can convince me that I'm anything but lucky to have found her, especially not Baba, with his dire warnings.

"How's it going at school?" Rini Di asks as we settle down with the inevitable cookie and cup of tea.

"It's okay, I guess." She asked me the same question last week, but I had been in tears at that time. This week is better. Manish and his friends have finally begun to ignore me for the time being.

"The lessons are getting better?" Rini Di asks, one eyebrow arching in a perfect semicircle.

I picture the classes this week and realize that I don't feel nearly as behind. When the teacher writes something on the board, I actually read it. When they say something, I can hear and understand more than I did before. English still comes easily to me from my early lessons with Mira Di, so I'm even able to enjoy the readings. I have a hard time writing answers in full sentences, but at least I'm catching up. Especially now that I'm shielded, with Sadaf and Razia sitting on both sides of me in class and at mealtimes.

"Yes, a little," I say.

"What about kung fu?"

"That's the best part of the day," I say with a wide grin.

My mind bounces and bolts like the stray puppy that the hostel girls have adopted. I want to tell her about how it feels when I shift my weight from one leg to the other, when I kick in the air, when I roll my palm into a fist, when I stand with my spine straight. How I feel alive and relevant. How I can feel every nerve, bone, muscle, and skin cell sing in harmony as I go through the motions. Like a song. But all I can think to say is, "It's where I feel free."

Rini Di leans back in her chair and loops one arm over the back. Papers are strewn all over her table; her coffee cup is balanced on a pile of books, its blue china sparkling in the light of the overhead lamp. "I've noticed you coming early to practice in the courtyard."

My smile could not possibly be any wider.

She takes off her glasses and massages the bridge of her nose between her thumb and forefinger. I've seen her do this before. It's a habit. "Do you remember it all?"

I nod. I remember, all right. I replay all the stances, all the moves that Rini Di teaches us in my head all through the day and night. I know the Bruce Lee book by heart.

"Easier to remember than math, isn't it?"

"Much."

"For you, maybe. Not for everyone."

I beam as Zehra did before.

Rini Di pulls out a pen from the little elephant stand on her table. She asks me how I've been eating, how things are at home. I tell her it isn't so bad. Mai has been working on the highway again, so we have food most of the time. I decide not to tell her about the pressure Baba is putting on Salman.

Finally, she tucks her pen away, pushes her metal glasses back, and leans forward. "Heera, I wanted to speak with you today because last year we started a new program with two hostels for at-risk girls in New York called Phoenix Group Home and Sunshine House. We have an exchange program with them and the girls there are learning martial arts too. I wondered how you would feel about writing letters to one of them, maybe making a new friend? As long as you feel comfortable writing to them in English."

I can't help but feel disappointed. There was a part of me that hoped she was going to choose me for the upcoming competition, even though I knew deep down that I haven't been training long enough.

I've never written nor received a letter before. Ever. And I've never even seen a person from another country, unless you count Nepal, which I could walk to from here if I wanted. "Exchange letters with a stranger?" I ask awkwardly.

"It can be a lot of fun. We can write and send letters by email on the computer now, so it will help you learn some new skills too."

Something else I've never done. I've barely even laid eyes on a computer in real life, outside Rini Di's office, and I've certainly never *touched* one. For a second, I am terrified. Dust motes weave through the light. A moth circles the bulb. I can hear the girls laying out the dinner, the clank of plates and plonking of vessels. The computer must be expensive. What if I break it; what if I get an electric current from it?

"But I don't know how to use the computer," I say at last.

"That's the point, isn't it? You will learn." Rini Di hands me a piece of paper. "Take a look at her profile. Write your thoughts down on paper and Saturday, you can stop by, type it out, and send it off. Come around lunchtime and eat with the girls too."

There is a blurry black-and-white photo of a face, under which is a name: Connie Wright.

You can't tell much from the picture but apparently, she is fourteen, just like me, and is also in grade nine. She lives at the Phoenix Group Home. Her favorite foods are something called tacos and cheesecake. I have no idea what either of those is. Rini Di suggests that I ask her. All I have ever learned about America is from watching one movie that they showed in the hostel. All the children lived in big houses with swimming pools and had fridges full of food that they could eat anytime. But Rini Di tells me that Connie comes from a home that is kind of like mine; her home wasn't safe for her, and some people tried to hurt Connie too.

Since Bollywood films are nothing like life in Girls Bazaar, I wonder if American lives are nothing like those movies. Perhaps she is a girl just like me.

The next day, I head to class before the bell and take out the piece of paper Rini Di gave me with Connie's profile. I tear a sheet out of my rough book, wrinkle my nose, and begin to write. As always, the English is the easy part; it's the content that I have a hard time with.

> My name is Heera. I am fourteen years old. I live in Forbesganj, Bihar, India.

In my head, I've started this letter so many times, but this is as far as I get. What would I say if she were in front of me? I tilt my head back and close my eyes, trying to imagine her. I can see her face, but I don't know if she is tall or short, fat or thin.

> I study in grade nine. I don't like school much, but it is getting better now that I started kung fu classes. The other fun part is I get to borrow English storybooks from the library. I used to read these books with my best friend, Rosy, and her mother. We used to love the stories about a girl who went on adventures by the sea.
>
> Do you like kung fu? Do you like school?

Rini Di told me to ask personal questions. She said that people like it when we ask about them. I almost asked her to tell that to my family.

We never talk about anything at home. But I think she must be right when it comes to Connie.

> I have one older brother and ~~two sisters~~ one baby sister. What about you? Do you have any siblings? Do they live with you too?

All I want is to be able to write something interesting, but how far do I want to take her down the tunnel of my dark life in the very first letter? I want to tell her about Chotu and how much I miss her. But that can wait for another letter. When we know each other better.

Try as I might, I can't think of another thing to say about myself. So I decide to tell her about Salman instead.

> My older brother wants to be a scientist. He is good at math and has read about an Italian scientist called Galileo who proved that the earth revolved around the sun. My brother wants to study the stars and the cosmos too. I am not sure what I want to specialize in. I know I want to be a teacher, but a teacher of what is hard to say. Maybe kung fu

I don't have the courage to tell her that I can barely write full sentences, not because I don't know the words but because I don't feel I have anything worth writing about. How much of a struggle it's been just to write this handful of lines. Nineteen lines in forty-five minutes. I've crossed so much out that I begin to simply roll up the pages in a ball and throw them away.

I don't know if I can be a teacher of anything. I don't know what my future holds one year from now—will I be sold to Ravi Lala and then the dance parties at the fair like Mira Di, or will I actually be able to escape? All I know is that, thanks to Rini Di, I have a chance.

I hear the shouting. The closer I get to our hut, the louder it gets. Salman stands, silhouetted in the flickering shadows of the candle-light, just inside the threshold.

"Who has filled your head with all this nonsense?" Baba is yelling. "You, your sister, you think things in life come free?"

I wait outside. My heart is hammering. I'm not sure what's going on. The sun has set and I tiptoe into a shadow, pressing myself against the wall of our hut. Baba's back and Salman's face are outlined by the wavering flame of the candle.

"But this is free, Baba. Literally free," says Salman, clearly frustrated. He towers over my father, who slumps to one side thanks to his bad leg.

I can hear a scream from a neighboring hut, or is it the fair? The Bollywood songs blare away with artificial cheerfulness. I watch the drama unfold in my home, trying to determine the latest cause for Baba's anger.

"How can it be free when your family is paying the price for you wasting your time!" Baba snarls.

Salman throws his hands up in exasperation. "Wasting my time? School is the only way to get out of this hellhole. Can't you see that?"

My father wags an angry finger at him. "You think you are so much better than us, don't you? Won't work like all the boys your age around here?"

My heart feels like it will break free from my ribs. I hold on to the wall. For a senseless second, I think I'm going to cry. My adored brother, of all people, is going to be pulled out of school. It can't be. He is going to be a scientist. I've seen the night stars reflect in the blue of his eyes.

"I'll come back and work during the summer holiday like I do now. I'll help." Salman tries to reason with my father. His voice is calm and detached.

I can't see it in the dark, but I know the veins in Baba's neck must be bulging. I see my life beyond this: Salman and his sun, moon, and stars. My kung fu. Mai's betel paan leaf shop. I see all of it consumed by Baba's rage.

"You think that is enough!" Baba yells.

And then Salman snaps. "You think men selling their mothers and sisters is work! That is what you would have me do instead of study?" He's shouting back now. His hand is tugging his ear. His jaw is clenched. I look at the shadows springing on the wall behind him. The shape of my father's face looks dark and menacing. I squeeze my palms into tight fists.

Baba is breathing heavily. He shifts his weight from one leg to another. "What option do we have? It is the work available for our people. First your mother fights to keep Heera in school, though she should be earning for her family, and now you not only want to keep up with this studying foolishness, but you want to move away from home to do it!"

Salman? Leave home? But then I remember. Mira Di's client. He must have found a way to get Salman into the school in Siliguri.

"So, what? Should I stop going to school tomorrow? Should I stand at the corner with all the other boys and bring home men? Who should I send them to? Heera? Or Mai?"

And then I hear a crack. Baba slaps Salman, hard, across the face.

My heart stops. My eyes sting. For a second, I think Salman is going to strike him back. But instead, he takes a deep breath and speaks in a voice so soft it frightens me even more. "If I study hard for the next few years, I will be able to get a job that can get us all out of here. If you can't see that, you are a bigger fool than I thought you were."

I see it all slip away: my future, Salman's future. My mouth dries up. My shoulders slump. Salman turns around and leaves. He walks past me and disappears down the dark lane. I don't know if he sees me, but I have to go inside. I don't want to be Baba's next target if he sees I've been eavesdropping.

That night, Mai and Sania go to bed while I wait for Salman to walk back through the door.

When Baba finally comes home, stinking of alcohol, I keep my eyes shut. He hits the floor and begins to snore. I get up as quietly as I can and tiptoe out. Outside, I sit with my back to the wall of the hut facing the lane, waiting. I don't know what time it is when I finally see Salman coming down the path toward home, but it's late. I stand up.

"Where have you been?" I whisper, in what I imagine is a careful, soothing tone.

"Out." For the first time that I know of, Salman's breath reeks of booze.

A cold wind blows toward us. We walk to a bench on the railway station. I have an egg in my pocket for him. I know he hasn't eaten anything. Sitting side by side beneath the light on the cold platform, I can see his expression clearly.

"You've been drinking?" I say sharply, the egg in my hand.

Salman looks away. A dog comes and sniffs at our feet. I want to tell the dog that we aren't likely to have any treats. But it realizes soon enough and goes away.

"What are you going to do?" I ask, tugging on his elbow to encourage him to face me.

He looks awful. His face sags. His eyes are as big as the pond we swim in. "What is there to do?" He throws me a baleful look.

I want to hug him tight, but I know him well enough to know he'll push me away.

"You could run away," I whisper. A wild idea, but a good one. He's a boy. He can just catch a bus and show up at the school in Siliguri. Baba can hardly do anything once he's gone.

Salman smiles sadly. "I guess I could try."

"Why not? The school will take you in. For free." I feel triumphant at the thought of defeating our fate and Baba at the same time.

He looks at me as though I'm crazy. His hair is smooth and neatly trimmed as always. Then I see the real Salman surface, the older brother. Caring, kind, and responsible. His face is both grim and resolute.

"Say I do. What will become of you after that, Heera?"

I shoot him a panicked glance. "What do you mean?"

"If Baba wants me to give up school and start working, what do you think he'll do if I leave without his permission?"

My brows draw together. I don't want to understand what he is saying. "He will understand it is for the best! Mai will make him see."

His eyes stare inside mine, searching to see if I really don't comprehend. He takes the egg from me and begins peeling it. "And do you think it will work?" he asks in a very reasonable tone. He always asks me questions so that I can arrive at the answers myself.

"Yes, maybe." I nod a few times. I am loath to let go of my idea. It's the best way out, the only solution.

"I don't. I think if Baba can't make me earn to support the family, he will turn to his next child once again. I don't even think it's about the money anymore. He will always need more, not just to feed his addictions, but to feed his ego."

The iron of the bench feels solid and cold under my arm as I turn to grip his palm. I am determined to convince him to leave for Siliguri right away. I shake my head. "No, he has agreed to give me a year. He won't go back on his word."

"Okay, assuming you're right. A year is all you want, Heera? What happens when that year is up? You'll be happy to go to the fair like Mira Di?"

It's the very thought I've done my best to push away. But the truth is, I don't know what I'll do. I focus my attention on the ugly concrete railway station, with its plexiglass banners hanging everywhere, advertising products that I've never touched, inside houses and rooms that look like the movies. I can hear the coughs and murmurs of passengers sleeping around us, waiting for the morning trains.

Salman pats my cheek. "I promised to keep you safe. And I will."

At least his palm smells like him, a faint comforting scent of ink, tea, and coal.

"By giving up on your dreams?" I ask. My voice wobbles.

I turn my head away and look at the bare, scrawny trees on the other side of the platform. Savage, inescapable reality raises its head again, like an uncoiled snake.

Salman is crying silently, without moving a muscle. "What will my dreams matter when my little sister is sold?"

I throw my arms around him. He doesn't deserve this.

"Don't worry, Heera. I won't give up on my dreams; I'll just cut them down to size."

CHAPTER TWELVE

For once in my life, I try to be like Salman and get ahead of the day.

The morning is dark, with only birds calling one another from distant trees. I decide to wake up early so I can go to the school courtyard and practice kung fu. By six o'clock, I have fetched water for Mai, swept the floor outside, finished a meal of a little leftover rice with salt, and put on my black salwar kameez.

The school is vacant, bathed in a misty whiteness. I clean the kwoon of leaves, shimmering with morning dew and the occasional drips from the mango leaves above. I practice the routine we have been working on in class. I bow. Bend at the knee. Take a deep breath. Snap-kick-punch. I practice a series of these moves, trying to keep my back straight like Rini Di tells me.

It's harder than it looks. My balance is good, but I lack strength.

I imagine myself lunging at Ravi Lala, flying through the air till I am almost horizontal, then spinning and kicking him straight in the chest, knocking him backward to the ground. I may not be a master yet, but I will get there. I thrust, swing, flick, and block until the morning rays of the sun are just a blur of red.

At seven forty-five, before anyone else enters the premises, I go to the water pump behind the storage shed and wash myself thoroughly with soap and water. It's freezing, but I don't care. I am alone. I have privacy. There are no railway passengers gawking at me. How quickly all this comes to feel as though I have been doing it for years. This washup is another little secret of mine—I suddenly feel like I have so many. I'm energized, clean, a little farther from the filth of Girls Bazaar.

The pure light of the morning sun filters through the trees.

This, I decide, is my most treasured hour.

Classes seem to drag on even longer than usual, not because they are exceptionally boring but because I have already had a taste of kung fu this morning and all I can think about is practice at the end of the day. But I force myself to focus. After two weeks of lessons with Zehra and three weeks of sitting with Sadaf and Razia, it isn't so hard either. The routine of it all feels, dare I say, comfortable. And today, Sadaf says she has gossip for us. I've never been on this side of gossip before. The very idea of it is thrilling.

At lunch, Sadaf tells Razia and me to meet in the girls' room. We wait patiently as everyone else files out. Finally, Sadaf has us huddle together, our heads bent. "Yesterday I saw something really strange," Sadaf says in a hoarse whisper. "You know Ravi Lala?"

I go cold at the name. Looking at Razia, I can tell that she doesn't know. How different would my life be if I had the privilege of not even knowing who he was? Sadaf lives not very far from the red-light area. She knows why her parents forbid her from crossing the referral hospital in the direction of my lane. But how much does she *really* know?

I listen as Sadaf tries her best to explain how Ravi Lala is the boss of Girls Bazaar, as if it is interesting and not terrifying. "He's a crime overlord, like in the TV serials. He lives in a house halfway between Heera and me . . ." Her voice trails off as she looks at me to add more, but I hesitate.

If I tell them everything, will they still want to be friends with me? They don't *really* know me, after all. They sort of do, of course, but only from glimpses of the life that I allow them to see or what Rini Di has told them. What am I supposed to say? That he is the single most powerful man in my lane? That he buys and sells girls like us? That my father works for him? That he's marked me to be sold and I only have one year to figure a way out?

I decide instead to keep it brief. "He's the worst kind of man. And he's not afraid to hurt, even kill, anyone who disobeys him."

Razia's face tightens with what I think must be fear.

To my surprise, Sadaf reaches for my hand. And for a moment I wonder if she knows everything. If maybe she's known all along and accepts me anyway. Half of me cannot really believe that sweet Sadaf has anything to say about Ravi Lala, but the other half of me is full of curiosity. I lean against the wall and wait.

"My house is on the other side of the road from his, just after the referral hospital," Sadaf says. "But I can see into his place from my roof, and last night I heard all this shouting and screaming, so I looked down and saw Manish leaving Ravi Lala's home with his dad. They practically ran out of there."

I think of what Mira Di said about Suraj Sharma being in business with Ravi Lala. But Manish? I instinctively begin to twirl Rosy's bracelet around my list.

"Did you hear anything they said?" I ask, desperately wanting to know more.

"Ravi Lala was shouting at them, so I did get to hear some of it," she says triumphantly. "It was about money. Ravi Lala wanted his money back. Suraj Sharma owed him."

My shoulders slump. The blood leaves my face. It's a story I've heard so many times before. But this time it involves Rosy's father and brother.

"You look like you've seen a ghost, Heera," Razia says.

I quickly shake my head and throw my backpack over my shoulder. For the first time, I allow the thought I've buried for so long come to the surface: I have escaped, for now, but what if Rosy hasn't?

I run to the kwoon as soon as the bell rings. I start moving slowly, deliberately through the routine Rini Di sets for us before I discover that Manish and his friend Rahul have joined practice.

I stumble.

Surely, nothing will happen under Rini Di's watchful eye.

I stop and take a few breaths, starting again at the top. I won't let them ruin the best hour of the day. I let the people around me fall away, as though the cracked cement beneath my feet doesn't exist. I concentrate on my breathing and let everything else click into place.

Rini Di's voice moves me through the horse stance, squat, and hold the position. Then it is the bow stance and drop stance. Each stance has a rhythm that I can feel in my bones.

Good, Heera! Back straighter.

Manish! Rahul! Next time I see you talking, you'll clean up the kwoon for a week!

I see Rahul scowl at Manish, but they stay quiet. As nice as Rini Di is, when it comes to class, there is no messing with her and everyone knows it.

If I'm to be better than the rest of the team, I have to listen to my body and activate my inner core. I tune out the students. I tune out the cawing crow. All I can hear is Rini's voice belting out instructions. All I can feel is my body responding, breaking through the surface of the air. Everything goes still for a moment, and it feels as if the air is lifting my body, easing me forward. I can feel the ground beneath me, but my legs are not pulled down by gravity. The earth is sending energy upward into them. I spread my arms wide and thrust forward with my chest, like a flying eagle with open wings. I feel more than alive. I can hear the rush of air. I can feel the universe as if it's all mine.

When Rini Di says time is up, Sadaf and Razia immediately run off to collect their bags and head home, but I hold my pose. Suddenly, I hear the sound of something moving behind me. I spin around to see

Manish and Rahul laughing as they run away. On the ground, I see a rock with paper wrapped around it. They must have thrown it at me, but I didn't feel its impact. I pick it up. Three little words.

Heera the whore

I ball up the note and shove it into my pocket.

Around me, everyone leaves, but I get back into position. I don't want to risk walking home at the same time as Manish. So I practice one more move. Then another. I will focus. I am like water. I can flow or crash. I choose to flow. If Salman can take Baba's wrath, I can certainly take Manish's.

I imagine what I will do to Manish next time I hear him approaching me from the back. I could do a backflip like I've seen in Bruce Lee's book and face him eye to eye. I would be as light as water against his heavy, plodding moves. I would glide like a swallow as I slipped punches and slaps on his face and chest. By the end, we would know who is worthy of being a hero.

"You aren't going home?" Rini Di asks, her hands clasped behind her back.

I shake my head. "A little more, if that is okay."

She nods and asks me to adjust my posture and try again. I do as I'm told.

"What does the note say?" Rini Di asks.

I'm not surprised that Rini Di noticed, but it doesn't make it any less embarrassing.

I show her. She takes her glasses off, massaging the bridge of her nose as she often does.

"Heera, why do you think Manish has chosen you to torment?" she finally asks, in the same way Salman asks me certain questions. So that I can arrive at the answer myself.

I have asked myself this question a thousand times. I can answer it with an infinite number of suppositions, in infinite number of ways. I'm well aware that nothing will be the complete answer, but one answer I'm sure of.

"I think he's jealous that I'm still in school and his sister, Rosy, is gone." My face puckers a little.

Rini Di gives me a minute to gather myself. She walks to the mango tree, and we sit down with our backs against the trunk. She looks at me, her mild eyes magnified and unblinking, her hands holding the stone and Manish's note in her lap. "Go on," she says.

"I think her dad forced her and her mother to go to Nepal. I think she knew she was never coming back. Manish has taken his anger out on me ever since," I continue, twisting my pigtail. I dither over the next thought that I want to share.

Rini Di nods, a stern expression on her face. "I'm glad you trusted your instincts and told me all of this. You might be right. This could be the reason for Manish's bad behavior, though it is no excuse."

I balance some stones lying in front of me on top of one another. I have more to say. "I think Ravi Lala has something to do with Rosy going to Nepal. Mira Di told me Suraj Sharma is in business with Ravi Lala. And Sadaf saw Manish and his father come out of Ravi Lala's house the other day. She heard Ravi Lala demanding money. Maybe Suraj Sharma owes Ravi Lala money. Maybe he's hiding his daughter from Ravi Lala in Nepal."

Rini Di crumples the note up in her fist before giving me a pat on the cheek.

The stones I have balanced on one another topple. I look at Rini Di. "Can you find out about Rosy?"

Rini nods, dusting her pants off as she gets up. "I will certainly try to find out where Rosy has disappeared to."

Rini Di kept her promise. She didn't give up on me. And if my instincts are right, if Rosy really is in danger, I won't give up on her either.

CHAPTER THIRTEEN

The front door of the hostel is open. As soon as I walk in, the sounds of laughter and singing spill out. The smell of boiling tea and clean laundry fills the air, along with a hint of smoldering sandalwood incense. Saturday is the day for deep cleaning. The corridors are shining. All the girls assist with the chores on a timetable under the watchful eye of the hostel's supervisor, Maya Didi. Clean sheets flutter off a clothesline in the tiny courtyard. A girl walks past with a bundle of sweet-smelling clothes. Besides Maya Didi, the hostel has a cook, a housekeeper, a security guard, and a cleaning lady. I can't help but daydream about what it would be like to live in a place with actual beds, proper blankets, no cold drafts, bathrooms with doors . . .

I pause with Sania at my hip. She plays with my pigtails as I savor the moment. Today is the day that I learn how to use a computer and send my letter off to Connie. I take a long breath as I imbibe the friendly atmosphere. Slowly, the knots in my stomach loosen.

As soon as I walk in, a group of girls who I've begun to recognize rush toward me.

Riddhima, who must be around eight years old, reaches for Sania. "Aww, cutie!"

"Don't worry, we'll watch her," Zehra says, putting out her hands to see if Sania will go to her instead.

Sania, who loves nothing more than being doted upon, stretches her little arms out and leaps into Zehra's arms. They offer to take her to the common room to play while I work on my letter. The cheerful chaos of the room is like something out of a fairy tale. Girls of all ages are on the colorful rugs, sprawled out, cross-legged, or resting against bolsters and cushions. Some are playing a board game called ludo; others are chatting; a few younger children have crayons and are drawing on large sheets of paper.

I wait for a moment to make sure she's fine before a short and plump girl with a mop of brown curls comes in and asks me to follow her. I know her name is Tania. I've seen her around, but she is one of the quieter girls.

This is my first trip upstairs. I've always thought it was just where everyone sleeps. But she leads me into a narrow room with a row of computers against one wall and a long window at the end.

"So, have you ever worked on one of these before?" she asks with a no-nonsense air about her.

I shake my head and try to act cool, but I can feel the worried crease between my eyes forming. I don't want her to think I'm stupid.

She sits down next to me and hits a switch. "Do you have what you need to type?"

I realize she's going to have to read what I've written and suddenly feel like disappearing into the gray wall. "Yes," I say, "but I don't know how to actually type it."

Tania gives me a warm look. Her gruff exterior disappears. "Most girls have never even seen a computer before they come here; it was the same for me. They all learn soon enough. And Rini Di tells me you're good at spelling and stuff, so this shouldn't be a problem for you."

I feel my shoulders begin to relax. I may not know *how* to use a computer, but I know what they're capable of. And with Rini Di's promise about finding Rosy echoing in my head, all I can think about is how this might be a way that I can reach her.

I stare at the machine, frozen with fear, as Tania talks me through the mysterious parts—monitor, keyboard, mouse. "And we're going to have to open you an email ID," Tania says. I don't have a clue what that is. But she explains that an email address is like having your own home address, but on a computer. Like an electronic mailbox that can send and receive messages. She gestures toward the tray with the alphabet and asks me to type. "Each letter is a key. This is the keyboard. Just look for the letters of the alphabet and press," Tania says. She types a sentence out to demonstrate. "Don't worry if you make mistakes. We can always go back and fix them later."

I take the letter out of my bag and look down at the jumbled alphabet on the keyboard in front of me. I press my first key, *D* for *Dear*, and a row of *D*s appear on the screen.

"Oh," I say after an idiotic pause.

Tania doesn't laugh, but simply erases the extra *D*s with another key and asks me to begin typing the rest of the letter. "You have to type very gently. Don't press too hard," she explains.

Once my panic recedes, I can see what Tania means—the keys are clear enough. I start looking for each letter. I know I'm slow, but I realize just *how* slow when I see Tania's fingers flying across the keyboard. For now, all I can manage is using my one right pointer finger. It takes me a painstakingly long time. So much longer than it took to write on a piece of paper, but I keep tapping away until I reach the end. Tania comes close to me again and helps me delete extra letters, gaps, and misspelled words.

"Now comes the fun part," says Tania, her curls falling onto her face as she leans forward to share my keyboard. She tells me we're ready to send the letter off to Connie. "It will be delivered to her inbox. So she'll be able to read it on *her* computer."

"Just like that?" My voice is a little too loud with excitement. "How many days will it take?"

"Seconds. It will reach her inbox almost immediately."

By the end, my notebook is completely full of instructions so that I don't forget later. My fingers are short and blunt, unlike Tania's, which are long and thin, stretching easily across the keyboard. She logs me out and then asks me to log in. I practice a few times. It had taken me days to think of what to say, half an hour to type it out, and now it will take only a single click and less than a second to travel halfway across the world. It's magic.

In the common room, Sania is holding a stuffed frog in one hand and banging a wooden block on the floor with another. She hasn't had a stuffed toy since the rag doll Mai made for her fell into the drain near our house. The younger girls have absorbed her as one of their group—they're playing too, beside her, with her. I listen to their giddy giggles as I squat on the floor and wait for her to see me. When she does, she quickly stands up and waddles over to me, holding up a little plastic cup.

"Dink," she commands.

"What is this?"

"Daal," she says, very seriously.

I pretend to sip. This game is an old favorite. I make loud noises. She chuckles.

"Sania is having fun?" I ask, grabbing her and giving her a squeeze. I'm not sure why, but I feel like crying. She doesn't bother to answer, but returns to her heap of toys and proceeds to ignore me. I smile to myself.

"So did you send it off?" Rini Di's voice catches me off guard.

I turn around to see her dressed, neatly but simply, in brown cotton pants and a loose white cotton shirt, her hair tied in a ponytail. She never wears any jewelry or makeup. Looking at her, you wouldn't think that she would take on someone like Ravi Lala or address a rally of hundreds of young women.

I nod.

"How exciting!" She sits down, cross-legged, near me. "While you're here, there's something I wanted to tell you."

I hold my breath, every muscle tense with the hope that she might, miraculously, already have news about Rosy.

Rini Di is looking at me with a smile on her face. "I want to sign you up for a martial arts competition at the Forbesganj High School in three weeks. Two girls from here, Nisha and Fatima, are going as well. And two seniors from school."

I look at her blankly as my heart flutters. "Why me?" This was everything I wanted. But now all I can think about is how I'm nowhere near ready.

Rini Di laughs out loud at my confusion. "Well, why not? There are all kinds of categories. One is for beginners."

I'm a little flustered. "But I've only just started. I'm not ready." What I don't say is that I don't want to fail the school. I don't want to fail *her*.

She watches me thoughtfully. "Yes, you are. Or you can be. There are three weeks still to practice. You've been spending so much time on the routines. If you keep it up, you will certainly be ready."

Her calm, businesslike tone is convincing.

She continues. "I can't promise anything, but you might have a shot at winning. In either case, you'll enjoy competing and preparing for the match. It's all part of the fun." She rests a hand briefly on my shoulder and I can see the conviction in her eyes.

I don't want to disappoint her, but I know anyone else would be better than me. All I can offer is a small smile, but she seems to know exactly what I'm thinking.

She lets out a sigh. "I will never make you do something you don't want. We'll just work together, practicing as though we are going to compete. Then it is up to you to decide if you want to go through with it or not."

I look at her suspiciously. "And if I say no . . ."

She thinks about it for a while. "We will simply continue as before. But I will ask that you at least attend the competition to watch the others. So you will be ready. For next time."

It's Sunday morning. The weekend might mean no school, but nothing changes in our home. Mai works a half day while I stay home to look after Sania and cook for the family. I want to try something new, something that we eat in school and at the hostel, something that will cheer Salman up. Or maybe I just want to distract myself from thinking about the competition and when, *if*, Rini Di might have news about Rosy.

I decide to be a little extravagant and make an egg biryani that Razia gave me the recipe for. Apparently, it's from Hyderabad. We still can't afford meat, but I do have spices, rice, cooking oil, onions, potatoes, and six whole eggs that I brought back from the hostel. I use up all six eggs so that I can share a portion with Mira Di. The smell of the biryani fills every corner of our hut as it roasts.

While we eat, the air clears. And to my surprise, everyone praises my meal. Even Baba. The golden-yellow rice with the crisp purple onion rings does seem to lift Salman's spirits. As usual, Baba gulps down half of it while Mai, Salman, Sania, and I share the rest.

Luckily, I set aside some for Mira Di, even before Baba walked into the hut.

As I begin to clear up, Salman picks up his books to head out.

"Where are you going?" Baba asks, accusation in his tone.

Instantly, the spell is broken. I brace for Salman's response. I can see Mai go still, Sania on her lap.

"I'm going to look for work," Salman says, loudly and firmly.

There is a pause before Baba replies. "The highway construction is on. You can go there with Mai," he says flatly.

"That's not the kind of work I mean," Salman says evenly.

I pretend I need to wash the dishes and take the bucket of water outside the hut. Not very far, though. I want to hear every word.

"Why don't you go to the farm and help there, then," Baba states again. There is menace in his voice.

"Yeah, maybe." I hear Salman take a half step toward the door of our hut.

"What, maybe? You can go there and start right now!"

"Because I want to work in an office, or a store. Maybe at the cash counter, or as an assistant. It will earn more money," Salman says respectfully.

Baba scoffs. "As if someone would hire you." I peer in through the window.

"Why not? I can read, write, and count." Salman takes another step, glancing at Baba, who is sprawled on a straw mat, ready to take an afternoon nap.

"And so can everyone else out there. They don't give jobs like that to people like us." It's as if I can suddenly see all of the insults and rejections that Baba has ever suffered written on his skin.

"Why don't you at least let me try?"

"Because you will try and try, and meanwhile your mother is working herself to the bone and you won't lift a finger to help!"

Salman turns fully to face Baba. "I'm still doing more than *you*! Why don't *you* go to the farm and ask for a job? You could, you know, even with your leg. Instead of just drinking and gambling away all the money she brings in."

My father gets to his feet, and I close my eyes. He might have a bad leg, but he's still strong. All morning, I had been steeling myself for an explosion. But Salman doesn't hang around to get hit again. He leaves, followed by a hailstorm of insults. And I'm left in his wake. If Baba feels that Salman trying to find a job is a waste of time, I can't even fathom what his reaction would be if I told him I might compete in a kung fu competition.

For the next two weeks, I do nothing but practice. On Wednesdays and Fridays, the other two students from school and I go through our routines. On Thursdays, there's an extra class at the hostel for all of us, including the girls from the home, Nisha and Fatima. When I'm not at school or at the kwoon, I practice in my head—spinning with the moves that I repeat again and again in my mind, the stances I try to perfect. The world lurches even when I stand still. Even breathing hurts.

Drop your weight.

Throw your shoulders back.

Center your gravity.

Hold your energy.

After practicing with the older students, I learn that everyone has tender points, that students of kung fu look for these vital points and apply pressure. They are fast, focused, and flexible. They can center their chi so that the softest parts of their bodies are unaffected by the strongest blows, their hands become like steel. I watch Fatima spin around, move back, and slice into Nisha as if her energy moves inside her body at will.

Within days I grasp that my kung fu lessons are a team affair. I would never have been able to train for a competition by myself. I see on display the lightness of technique and the centering of internal energy in each movement. Nisha dances around me, finding my pressure points. Within seconds I'm flat on my back just with the tap of her hand on my forehead. I observe, I try, and I learn.

Soon, my own muscle aches stop. I begin to feel weightless. My regular stride is firmer, more confident. I watch Nisha and Fatima with awe as they move through their routines with grace and power. They've both enrolled in the intermediate competition and have both already won gold medals. Nisha does a demonstration with a stick, which she swings through the air, crouching and moving with the grace of a cat. Her round and soft face, as gentle as the moon, never changes expression. She is thin to say the least, keeps her hair cut just below her ears, and has the strength of a tiger, ready to pounce on her sparring partner. Most of the time, that partner is Fatima.

In their categories, they'll need to fight an opponent. Fatima winds her hair back in a bun to keep it out of the way, showing off her long nose and elongated chin. She moves with precision, never wasting a single gesture.

My routine is very different. It contains the stances that are central to Shaolin wushu: kicking, punching, and animal movements. I'm not yet working with a partner, thank God, though Nisha and Fatima let me spar with them sometimes

At the end of the day's session, Rini Di gives me a pamphlet with the rules of the competition. They seem basic enough.

"So have you decided yet?" Nisha asks me.

I shake my head.

"What's the problem?"

I shrug, unable to put my thoughts into words. If I lose, which I likely will, I'll be labeled a loser, again. Baba will be right about our people, again. I don't think I can face another round of insults and sneers.

"I just don't know if I want to," I say noncommittally, doing one last stretch. "I have stuff going on at home."

"You know, I went for my first competition just last year," Nisha says.

Did she say one year? That's all it took! She always looks so confident; I had expected that she'd been doing this for her whole life. Politely, she doesn't probe into the home stuff, which I'm grateful for.

"Really? How was it?" I ask, pretending to be nonchalant. My hands slip into the pockets of my kameez to keep them out of the cold.

She grins. "I was *so* nervous. I'd never stood up in front of an audience like that. But it all fades away once you're up there. When you practice enough, like you have, you just know what you're supposed to do and you do it."

I take in this fact as I stomp my feet to keep warm. "And? Did you win?" My voice is cool and understated.

"Not the first time, no. But it prepared me for the next competition," she says.

"Weren't you disappointed?" I ask. Somehow, I never considered the fact that there might be another opportunity after this one.

"Yes, but it also made me more determined. You need to learn how to compete too. And you do get better at it," she says quietly, trying her best to make me understand what the joy of simply participating is.

"And did you win the next time?" I ask. When I glance at her, her face is serious, her eyebrows slightly bunched up.

"You bet," she says with a wink. "I've been to three competitions since and won at two."

I sigh. I'm not sure that people like me have the luxury of simply participating. If we don't win, we're out. Or worse, punished. I think of Salman at home, trying to appease my father as he looks for a way to earn money. I can see my father's face when I lose. The humiliation that will be piled on all of us—Mai, Salman, and me. Even little Sania.

"I'll think about it some more." I raise my chin in acknowledgment.

"I've seen you. You're ready." Nisha's eyes are sincere. She means it.

"You think so?" I do believe her. Somewhere deep down, I know I am ready to compete. To win? I'm not so sure.

"I know so. Did you know there's a cash prize for all the winners?" she asks.

My heart skips a beat. "No, I didn't."

She nods. "Five thousand rupees for first prize in each category."

My eyes widen. Why didn't Rini Di tell me? Somehow, I know there was a reason.

"Tempting, right?"

"But I will feel so bad now if I don't win!"

Nisha laughs. "Silly girl! Then imagine how bad you'd feel if you didn't even try."

I give her a wide grin.

The entire week goes by in a blur until there is only one day left.

It's Friday, and the competition is scheduled for Saturday afternoon. We've all been working so hard that I've memorized everyone else's routine along with my own. It's all anyone around me seems to care about: Will I compete or not? Sadaf and Razia grill me about it at least twice a day. Now that I've told Mai and Salman about it, they won't stop pushing me to go either. And they don't even know about the prize money yet.

There is one person who doesn't ask me, and that is Rini Di.

But suddenly, none of it seems to matter when Salman delivers his news.

The unimaginable has happened. He's been offered a job. Not a job breaking stones or threshing grain, but helping out at a grocery store close to home. The thing that was supposed to be impossible for people like us became possible. A thing so wonderful that it feels like it must be a sign that perhaps our time has finally come.

I come home to find him almost hopping around as he tells Mai. "Tell me again how you did it?" Mai asked, wide-eyed.

"The shop is owned by my classmate's father," Salman says proudly. "When I asked if he knew of any after-school jobs, he said I should try there! I start right after school, from four to nine when the store is most crowded. Weekends too."

"And money?" she asks.

"They'll pay me per day. The shop is closed on Mondays." He tells us how much. It's less than Mai brings home from the highway, even after she pays the contractor a kickback.

Wordlessly, we all share the same thought: *What will Baba say?* But it's not the time to ruin the moment. In the meantime, Mai wants to celebrate her smart son. She hugs him. They both sit on one of the mats. He lies down with his head in her lap and lets her ruffle his hair—something I haven't seen him do in a long time. Sania and I join them, soaking in the moment.

"This is good news," Mai says with a big smile that spreads from one ear to the other. "When do you start?"

"Tomorrow."

Later that night, when Baba returns for dinner and shifts the mood of our hut with his mere presence, Salman announces his big news.

"What will you do at this shop?" Baba asks, suspicious as always.

"Fetch the items from the shelves. Load things in bags."

"How much will they pay you?"

Salman tells him the figure.

"Less than your mother," he says, as we all expected him to. "How is that any better than working on a farm or on the highway?" His face is twisted in a strange way, as if he's thinking up a hurtful insult.

"This is what they're paying me for half a day's work. So, it's about the same. And this way, I can still go to school and study on weekends and during holidays."

A cruel smile forms across Baba's face. He's found his insult. "So, it's better for you because it is more *comfortable*." The way he says the word make it sound like a curse.

Salman's jaw clenches, but he doesn't reply.

I wish I were somewhere else.

Baba looks like he's about to start up again, but Mai's voice cuts through the tension. "So what if it is?" she asks. "If it helps us get by while allowing both Salman and Heera to study, what more can we ask for?"

Baba pivots his head toward Mai, taken aback by her candor.

I watch their eyes locked on each other in a kind of duel that I've never witnessed between them before, and feel a joy I've never felt before. I've heard of children—mostly in stories—who are used to their mothers standing up for them and placing their children above all else, but that isn't the way in our lane. Baba has always been first. He eats first. Sleeps most. Works the least. Yet his word is the final word.

I look toward Salman. His face is expressionless.

I wish I could bottle this moment. A firefly wanders inside. Its twinkling body shines a tiny happy light in our little hut. It's a bit like Mai's small acts of resistance to Baba, growing brighter and brighter since Chotu's death. Since then she's taken out a loan without consulting

Baba, tucked her earnings away with Jamila Bua, and continues to meet with Rini Di in the café near the hospital.

"I'll save it all till we pay back the loan," Salman says, always the peace-maker. "Should take two months. After that, Mai can take fewer shifts on the highway, maybe even go back to working on the farm. The farm isn't necessarily easier work, but it's safer for sure, especially for Sania."

By this time, Baba is done. He tosses his plate into a corner and leaves again.

When I take a nervous peek at Salman, I expect him to be angry. But instead, he looks sad. As incredible as his news is, it's not the same as boarding school. And now with an after-school job he'll have even less time to study. I wonder then if he's thinking the same thing I am: Will it all be worth it?

That night, as I lie on the floor, I reach into the pocket of my kameez and pull out the piece of paper that I have been afraid to open since Tania helped me print it from my inbox earlier today. Slowly, I read it by candlelight:

Hi, Heera!

I'm so excited. I've never had a pen pal before! That's so cool you do kung fu too. I've been practicing martial arts for a couple years now and I'm obsessed. My teacher is a complete badass. I love him so much. I competed for the first time last year and met a girl from your village named Nisha. Do you know her?

I used to live with my mom. She's from Korea. But I was moved to a foster home about a year ago. It was a whole mess there, so now I'm in this group home and doing okay. No, I don't have any sisters or brothers. It was just me and my mom for years. No pets either, which sucked lol. I have two roommates now at the hostel, Anna and Jameela. It can be annoying to have them in my face ALL the time, but it's mostly cool.

I guess the worst part of staying at the hostel is that I miss my mom. I get to see her once in a while, but it was just the two of us for so long. So not having her around feels weird.

Tell me about yourself. Do you like your older brother? I always wanted one. Your little sister sounds adorable.

Okay, bye for now!

Love,

Connie XO

PS I'd love to read some books about India. Feel free to pass on any recs!

I want to read it all again. To absorb it. To *understand* it. What is "lol"? What is "XO"? Did Nisha win her gold medals in New York? I picture myself wearing my uniform and standing onstage. Just like Nisha, Fatima, and Connie. The world suddenly feels a little bit different. I am no longer Heera, who is destined to be sold at the fair. I am Heera, whose brother has a job at the grocery store. Who lives in a house with four walls and a roof. Who goes to school and has friends. Who has a pen pal across the world. And tomorrow, I might become a champion.

CHAPTER FOURTEEN

The next morning, I wake up to the sound of the train whistle, feeling unusually well rested. The competition is at noon and I'm supposed to get to the hostel early to have a protein-filled meal with the other girls before we head to the venue together. When I sit up, Salman raises his eyebrows at me. We're the only ones in the hut this morning.

I nod, the beginnings of a smile at the corners of my mouth as I throw my bag onto my back.

He knows what my decision is. And he knows better than to wish me good luck. It'll either go wrong or right, but I know I'm prepared. There's no such thing as luck.

Today, for the first time, I won't be the girl from the red-light area but a girl in a kung fu uniform, onstage in a beginner's competition.

I demonstrate the moves behind my eyelids as I wash up outside.

Before I can stop it, the dark thoughts find their way in. What if luck *is* real? What if *fate* is real and my destiny as a Nat is already laid out for me?

As I plait my hair, I begin to second-guess myself more and more. What if I slip? What if my pants tear? What if someone says a girl from a red-light area isn't allowed to enter the competition? What if Baba shows up and starts hurling insults? What if Ravi Lala's men burn down the stage?

The sound of a motorcycle floats in.

I close my eyes and make myself go through a list of things I need to do until the match. Wash, eat, change, practice, perform. I will bow in the four directions. I will bend gracefully, deep and low, when everyone applauds, like the white egret bird bends its long neck in the rice fields to catch a fish.

. . . Water, the softest substance in the world, which could be contained in the smallest jar, only seems weak. In reality, it can penetrate the hardest substance in the world . . .

I repeat to myself, *I am like water. I will flow, not crash.*

At the hostel, the girls have nearly finished breakfast when I walk in and am greeted with a symphony of cheers and hellos as if they'd been waiting for me, expecting me. I didn't think that my face was capable of smiling as hard as it is. That I would feel as much a part of their efforts as my own.

Nisha and Fatima clap me on the back and tell me they knew I'd come all along.

Maya Didi sits me down and makes me a plate. There is puffed rice poha with peas, potatoes, and yogurt on the side. I also get a shining clean apple. Maya Didi hovers. "Eat slowly!" she says. "You'll feel sick if you stuff yourself before the competition! Not to mention the disaster it will be if you spill food on your clean uniforms." The free end of her blue sari billows out as she turns, revealing a gorgeous peacock motif. She has a stern face but a soft heart, always looking out to see what each girl needs. And I realize that I've become one of the girls she cares for as well.

I eat slowly, watching all the others, listening to the familiar sounds as I practice the stances and the moves in my head again and again. The horse stance. The dragon stance. I imagine my front leg dangling soft and light for a quick kick, my hips relaxed and my back leg bent ready to spring forward like a cat. I imagine myself crouched on the floor with my front foot turned outward and the back foot resting on its ball, arms at my waist. I end my mental exercises with my favorite stance. I lift one knee high into the air, keeping one foot on the floor. I balance as gracefully as a crane as I relax down to the ground beneath my foot. I look ahead in my mind's eye and see an open blue sky with a bird flying toward the sun.

At that moment, a hard-boiled egg plops onto my steel plate. Maya Didi seems like she might be nervous too, with the amount she is fussing. "You have to eat the egg! You too, Nisha!"

Nisha makes a face. She really hates hard-boiled eggs. I suddenly remember Connie's letter and remember to ask, "Nisha, did you go on the exchange to New York?"

"Yes, last year," she responds with an expectant half smile. "You want to see photos? I'll show them to you after the competition."

I nod vigorously. I want to ask her what Connie's like. I want to know what New York is like. But suddenly there's no time.

I'm about to ride in a car for the first time in my life.

After Maya Didi issues a set of orders, we're packed up and lined up outside the school gate when Rini Di's white car pulls up. "Pile in, girls," she calls out. "How are you all feeling today?"

Nisha and Fatima are pumped, and they say it. Fatima and I sit in the back and let Nisha grab the front seat. Both seem to be taking this car development in stride. I brush the tips of my fingers against the smooth leather of the seat.

"How about you, Heera?" Rini Di asks, looking at me through her rearview mirror.

I watch her press down on a pedal under her right leg. The car picks up speed. She presses another pedal and shifts a stick near the steering wheel. I imagine myself in the driver's seat controlling the powerful engine with a turn of the wrist and the pressure of my foot.

"I'm okay," I say softly.

I stick my neck out the window. The wind rushes through my hair. We whiz past the shops, the passersby, and the cows, dogs, and goats. I wave at some children standing at a corner. I never thought I'd be the one inside the car.

"You know, it's okay to feel nervous. We all do sometimes. Well, maybe not Nisha."

We all laugh, and I realize that I'm suddenly not as afraid anymore.

But as our car slows down and we stop in front of a massive, neatly painted, sparkling building, something shifts and I instantly become more terrified than I've ever felt in my life. At the heart of the fear is something unexpected. I've forgotten every single move and stance. I can't even remember their names, let alone the positions. I sit, frozen in panic as I hear the car engine die down.

Nothing about the prim and proper atmosphere does anything to settle my stomach. The lawns stretch for miles. I've never seen such well-maintained green grass before. The driveway is longer than our entire lane—six big yellow school buses, the kind that never come near our house, are lined on one side. Even the government referral hospital near us only has two rickety ambulances.

The children look as well turned out as the lawns in their crisp, starched uniforms. They look as if they do everything with military precision. Our ragtag bunch with our peeling shoes, wearing the only kung fu uniform we own, are a world apart. There is no way we can compete with these healthy, bouncing kids.

Fatima's eyes are as round as mine. "It's a private school," she whispers, holding my hand as she helps me out of the car. I don't even know how to unlock a car door; how will I compete in a public competition? All I can think about is how I might get home from here if I drop out now. But before I can say anything, as soon as we're out of the car, Rini Di makes a beeline for the registration counter.

"Di!" I yell after her. I break into a run to catch up. "I changed my mind. I don't want to compete. I think I'll just watch this one," I say, out of breath.

It had started out feeling like a good day, a great day actually. But now I remember I'm not supposed to be here. As I see the vast numbers of students from other schools getting out in their kung fu uniforms from buses and cars, the full impact of the event thumps down on me. I can't imagine exchanging cheery waves with these perfect students with their perfect postures in their perfect clothes. I've never been good at anything. That's Salman. I'm just a scrawny, patched-up girl, who cuts her own hair in awkward angles and tries to read books, even in English, because she loves a good story. *Is a crow trying to walk like a swan?* I can hear my father say scornfully.

Rini Di stops and looks down at me. "Heera—"

I'm sure I'm white-faced. I know my jaw is as tight as a fist as I bite down on my lips. The tall building looks menacing, as if it will swallow me up.

"No, Di. I thought I could. But it's too much right now."

"Heera," she says gently, putting her hands on my shoulders. "Look around you."

I take a deep breath and do as I am told. There's a buzz in the air of students and parents and instructors. Everywhere, there are students in uniforms.

"Students just like you," she says.

"No, but—"

Rini Di's face is kind. "I know I gave you my word that you could change your mind if you wanted to. But I want you to stop thinking for a second. Take a deep breath and ask yourself something. Do you really want to walk away? You've worked so hard for all these weeks. You deserve to be here just like anyone else."

I feel a hand on my back. Nisha and Fatima are at my side.

"Go ahead, Di," Fatima says. "Put her name down."

Rini Di looks at me. She won't go back on her promise: If I want to back out, I still can. But I find myself nodding, and before I can change my mind once again, the girls sweep me toward the entrance hall.

I'm registered. I'm a competitor. There is no escape. I don't know how I'll get through the forty-five minutes that I have to wait. All I know is that it will pass.

Inside, the arena is slightly raised in the center of a big hall. A banner with the name of the competition and the school hangs in the background.

"It's called a dais," Fatima whispers.

The judges, teachers, and parents sit on chairs facing the competitors while we take our places, sitting on both sides on benches. It never crossed my mind to invite my parents. But in a way, I'm glad. I don't have to worry about Baba mocking me when I fail. Maybe it's my imagination, but some of the other kids look nervous too. One girl twists her hanky into a knot, while another moves her left toe along her right ankle, up and down, up and down. Another boy paces around and around the hall, refusing to sit.

All day I've been steeling myself for the big moment, observing the nerves traveling up and down, from my stomach to my throat. And now that it's almost here, I'm not sure if I desire it or want to run away. But as time passes, as I watch the first three competitions, my stomach seems to settle. I'm as good as any of them and I know it. I remember the moves; I have not forgotten.

As soon as the nerves begin to fade, I start to feel something else.

The energy in the hall is electric. Suddenly, I'm a kid again, watching my uncle take down his opponent. It's in my blood. I picture Baba's beaming face when he watched Chote Mama pin his opponent to the red-ocher floor. I'm pulled in. The sea of kung fu uniforms, the confusing announcements, the referees with their terrifying expressions—it all becomes part of the experience.

I closely watch the hand and arm strikes, the various kicks, observing what each person brings to their own unique style. One girl's butterfly kick is superb. I get up and cheer at a particularly elegant elbow strike.

And then I hear my name. It's my turn.

I look for Rini Di, sitting near the judges. She gestures with her chin toward the arena, her thumb up in a gesture of good luck. But I don't need luck. I'm prepared. Nisha gives me a nudge and I get up.

The hall is buzzing. There must be two hundred people here, young and old. It's a two-minute walk to the arena, but it feels like two years. I feel that all two hundred pairs of eyes are on me. I tell myself I'm my mother's daughter. She hasn't given in to the superstitious chattering of the women in our lane, or the evil Ravi Lala, not even to Baba's fists, so how can I give in to this momentary panic? I come from a line of pehelwans.

Somebody claps, and then more students join in. They don't know where I come from. They don't know who I am, or perhaps they do. I am a girl in a kung fu uniform about to exhibit some classy moves. The buzz that I hear is a symphony of hoots and cheers. Of anticipation and encouragement.

And then I'm standing on the blue mat, soft and slippery

underneath my feet, unlike the hard ground of the school kwoon. I push away all thoughts to focus on my body as I begin.

There's no music, but I have a beat in my head. I pull my feet together, my hands on my hips. I bow to Rini Di and the judges in all four directions. I start as taut as a bow, my left foot pointed straight, my left thigh parallel to the earth, my right leg stretched all the way back. My right hand punches out while my left forms a fist against my side. My back is straight while my breasts and hips share my weight with my thighs and knees.

As I hold the pose in front of the judges in perfect balance, I get a sudden flash of realization—that every part of my body is equally valuable and linked to the other. I don't feel ashamed of it anymore, because I value every cell and know I will keep it safe.

I finally understand another one of Bruce Lee's wisdoms:

You must accept the fact that there is no help but self-help. I cannot tell you how to gain freedom since freedom exists within you.

The judges lean forward as I hold the pose longer than most advanced competitors.

Then I move to the horse stance, demonstrating the fist thrusts as I hold my body in a low squat. In the crouch stance, I lean in with one leg bent at the knee, the other stretched out, almost flat to the ground. I hold both my feet and go even lower.

Every pore of my skin breathes in unison. My body sings and I'm in tune with it. I can't see or hear anyone anymore—the judges, the hall, the students, the teachers. My mind is still.

I stand straight and adopt the empty stance, one foot pointed, arms swinging through the air. I cycle through the various kinds of kicks, ending with the one that's gotten me into the most trouble—the side kick.

And then it's over.

I get off the mat and head to the changing area, feeling as though I may float away. The applause fades. I return to Planet Earth when I hear a voice and see Rini Di coming toward me.

"You did it!" shouts Rini Di. "You were flawless!"

I'm smiling so hard my cheeks hurt. We hold each other in a tight hug. I repeat to myself what Rini Di just said. I did it.

A familiar form bursts into the hallway outside the changing area.

"Sadaf! You came!"

My spirited friend throws her arms around me. "Duh! That was *amazing*, Heera!"

Goose bumps spread across my arms and legs as we walk back out to the competition area to watch the rest of the students.

Sadaf's eyes shift excitedly. I know her well enough to know when she has gossip to share.

She leans in close and lowers her voice. "I also wanted to warn you that Manish is here, and he's with some girl with a nose ring," Sadaf whispers.

My heart sinks. A girl with a nose ring can only mean one thing. She will be married off to a banana tree at a Bisi Bele just like Mira Di's, if she hasn't been already. My mind immediately fears the worst: What if Manish has started helping his father and Ravi Lala in some way? But at this moment, I forbid myself from dwelling on it.

Sadaf and I find our seats toward the back among the cheers and screams of laughter. The audience stomps their feet and shuffles their chairs over the announcements. We cheer as Fatima and Nisha ace their routines and the judges study their sheets, whispering to one another. A group of boys chant someone's name loud enough that the announcer asks them to tone it down. It's a mad scene. A stranger pats me on the back, saying, "Good execution. Well done." A wide grin spreads across my face.

And then I spot Manish sitting a few rows in front of us with an older girl, her nose as red as an apple. I try my best to get a look as she tilts her head to talk to him, but an announcement pours through the speakers, scratchy and loud. It's time to declare the winners.

We jump to our feet, scurrying over to huddle around Rini Di while they announce all the winners in the younger age groups, in all categories.

Then they come to mine.

No matter how many times I've told myself it doesn't matter, in this moment it does. More than anything else.

"In third place," declares the announcer, "in beginners' Shaolin kung fu, is Kushal Gupta of Forbesganj High School!"

We all clap. I grab Sadaf's hand and squeeze so hard I must be hurting her, but she smiles and squeezes right back.

"In second place is Heera Kumari of KGBV Secondary School!"

It's as though time has stopped. My heart skips a beat.

I'm deafened by the cheers and applause of my friends, by the blood pumping in my ears. Instantly, I'm engulfed by arms, showered with backslaps. Rini Di hugs me. I don't even hear the name of the first-prize winner as I go onstage to collect my medal, certificate, and an envelope.

And just then, as I walk back and glance up at the cheering crowd, I see her.

The girl sitting next to Manish is Rosy.

She looks a little plumper. Her round cheeks are redder and rounder. Her clothes are tighter. Her salwar kameez is not cotton, but some kind of shiny fabric. Her eyelashes look mascaraed; her lips look reddened. Different colored plastic bangles line her arms all the way to her elbow. Earrings dangle against her cheeks.

When did she come back from Nepal? Why has she not come and said hello? I didn't necessarily expect her to find me the moment she returned, but I at least expected her to come and say hello when we're in the same room.

Manish's arm hangs lazily around her. They stand quietly in between the cheering audience, but then they start talking. Arguing.

If I'm any bit unsure, Sadaf confirms it. "Oh my God. That's Manish's sister!"

The adrenaline I felt only a moment ago turns suddenly into a fist of anxiety in my throat.

"Is she crying?" Sadaf asks softly. "It looks like it."

CHAPTER FIFTEEN

There was one night, years ago, when Rosy convinced Manish and me to spend the night under the school mango tree. We stayed up until the stars disappeared. The moon went behind a cloud and the leaves of the mango began to form strange, dark patterns. Then, just as we fell asleep, Rosy changed into a black dress to blend in with the night, jumped out from behind the tree, and scared us half to death. We all shook with laughter in the darkness.

I miss her mischief, her joy, her laughter, her zest for life. She always knew the latest fashions, the most popular movie, the bestselling songs. Now she is near enough to touch but miles out of reach.

I'm still in a daze when Rini Di says she'll drop me off on the way back to the hostel, though I know it's completely in the wrong direction.

"This is the first time I have three champions on my team, in any competition," says Rini Di after she eases herself into the driver's seat.

The back seat is all smiles. Nisha won gold in her category, while Fatima also scored a silver.

"So how does it feel, rookie?" Nisha asks.

"Really good," I say.

"Better than good, judging by the look on your face," Fatima says with a laugh.

We discuss what worked and what could be improved upon. But I'm not listening as closely as I should. I have other things on my mind.

As soon as Nisha and Fatima are let out at the hostel and Rini Di and I are alone in the car, everything comes out in word vomit. The nose ring. The tears. Manish's arm dangling over Rosy's shoulder. Rini Di slows down. She turns toward me, a worried look in her eyes.

I look over to her from the passenger seat. "What if Suraj Sharma owes Ravi Lala money and has given him Rosy instead? That's what my father wanted to do. What if her Bisi Bele is around the corner?"

I wonder if Rini Di will think my suggestion is ridiculous, that I overthink things, that I think everyone has the same terrible life that I have.

But Rini Di's eyes sharpen. "It's possible. I'll have to go to higher-ups in the police since she's Suraj Sharma's daughter. If I thought I could trust Manish, perhaps he could have been an ally."

Finally, we pull up outside Girls Bazaar. There are the usual sounds of Bollywood music, drunken brawls, barking dogs, haggling women, yelling vendors. I wish Rini Di hadn't stopped just here. She gets out of the car and holds the door open while I climb out.

"Congratulations again, Heera," she says, her arm outstretched. "For now, I don't want you to worry. I want you to be proud."

I had known that there was a cash prize for the winner, but I hadn't expected to win, and I had not expected to be handed money for my second position either. But here I am, holding an envelope with twenty-five thousand rupees in cash, and I don't quite know what to do with myself. The envelope feels hot in my hand.

I hand it back to her. "Rini Di," I say quietly, "please take this."

"For safekeeping?" she asks.

I shake my head. "It's for you. For the loan. We'll give you the rest by next month."

Her face goes blank, and I can't tell what she's thinking. "I can't take this from you, Heera. You won this money. It's yours," she says after a beat.

"Yes, and the best thing I can do with it is pay back half that loan. This way Salman won't have to work so hard."

She looks even more perplexed. "What does this have to do with Salman?"

"Salman has a new job after school. First, he'll pay back the loan we took from you, so Mai doesn't have to work so hard. And then he'll save for supplies for the school in Siliguri."

She sighs. "Oh, Heera, what can I say? I don't want you to pay me back. I've already told you that until the pending money comes from the school authorities, I don't need this. Here," she says, pushing the envelope toward me. "Please take this back."

I just look at it there between us. "If I take it home," I say, "it will be gone before tomorrow. And it will be better for Salman—and me—if they think the loan is being paid off."

Rini Di gives me a little nod and puts the money in her pocket. "I understand. I will take it and keep it safe for you. It will be my honor to return it to you once this is all over."

The following morning, after Baba leaves for the station, I pull my prize out from my schoolbag. "I won a medal," I say softly. The pink satin ribbon swings back and forth in between all of us in the pink light of dawn. I held my secret in for the whole night, waiting for the right moment to tell Mai and Salman. I wanted to see and feel their reactions so I could remember them forever.

It's Sunday, so Mai is home earlier than normal and Mira Di has come over to help us with chores. Mai covers her mouth with her hands, her eyes lit with joy and amazement. Mira Di grabs the medal and then me, engulfing me in a big hug. I garland Mai with the medal, skipping around her.

"This is for you, Mai," I say.

She pats my back as I watch her absorb it all. "Well. We must celebrate."

Salman makes khichdi, a mixture of rice, daal, and some vegetables. As the khichdi stews, we gather around in the mild morning sun. Mai sits on the bamboo stool that used to be exclusively for Baba, turning the medal over in her hands several times. Its shining silver glints in the sun's rays. Silver and gold mix in the light. Mira Di and I play with Sania on the straw mat, pretending the ball Salman gave her is a doll and trying to feed it the potato skins.

I think of the feeling I had onstage—of loving every part of my body—and realize that I want more than anything for Mira Di to know that feeling. To know that she can feel safe in her own skin too. But what if it's too late for her? What if that moment was only just that? A moment.

The calm that I felt only a second ago seems to dissipate and the reality of Girls Bazaar feels crushing once again. The familiar morning sounds of the lane cloud my eardrums. Nothing has changed just because I won a medal or had a flash of realization. Nothing has changed for Rosy. And despite Rini Di's urgings, I know there is something much more vital that I should be focusing my attention on.

"Mira Di, remember what you told me about Suraj Sharma?" I ask. "What exactly does he do with Ravi Lala?"

Mira Di's eyes flick up to mine. "Why do you ask?"

Mai and Salman turn their heads to me as well in a gesture of curiosity.

"You said he's in business with Ravi Lala. But how, exactly?"

Mira Di sighs in disgust. "He gets girls for him from Nepal, for the fair, for other places. That's what I've heard, at least."

I probe further with my newfound confidence. "Heard from who?"

"The other girls in the dance party. They were brought by him from villages in Nepal and Bihar. He told them he had jobs for them in homes in Delhi and Mumbai. And as a cop he's able to transport people easily, even across the border. No questions asked."

"And the girls believed him?" Salman asks.

"Why wouldn't they?" Mira Di says. "They don't know any better. He's a police officer. But then he never takes them to either city. Just this piece-of-crap slum before they're sold at the fair. He uses Forbesganj as a kind of depot, where he stores the girls and then Ravi Lala sells them. Sometimes he even allows abandoned girl babies at the referral hospital to be sold to the brothels."

"But Suraj Sharma has a nice house near the market," I wonder aloud. "He's a policeman. He has land in the village. Why would he do this?"

"Maybe this is how he's made most of his money after all," says Mira Di cynically.

I shake my head and remember being inside Rosy's home. It was the only time I'd ever seen a computer before going to the hostel. "But he's from an upper-caste landed family. He has two wives and lots of farming land in the village. Rosy's mother has always been so kind to me, offering books for me to read since I was a child," I respond with the information I have.

Mai's ears prick up. "Are you talking about Roopa Ji?" she asks.

I realize that I don't actually know Rosy's mother's name.

"They live two doors down from the referral hospital, no? Oh, Heera. I'm so sorry. I didn't put it together until just now," Mai says.

"Mai, what are you talking about?"

"I went to get Sania checked at the hospital yesterday and saw Roopa Ji there with her sister. She was there for an ointment. She had a big bruise on her cheek." Mai takes a deep breath. "They were talking about plans for a Bisi Bele. Of course, they didn't call it that because they aren't Nats. She didn't recognize me, but I knew she was Rosy's mother."

"Go on," I urge. Mira Di and Salman are all ears too.

"They were talking about the menu. Biryani and firni. Roopa Ji was crying. Her eyes were swollen and her right cheek was an ugly red. It was clear she did not want the wedding. Her sister promised to take care of everything."

"When is it?" I ask as I get to my feet.

"Soon. If not today then tomorrow. And from what they were talking about, it doesn't sound like Rosy's being sold to the fair," Mai continues. "They spoke about sending her to Mumbai."

I finger my medal absentmindedly as I begin to pace. "Why would he do this to his own daughter if he traffics other girls? They have never gone to bed hungry. They used to skip the school lunch because their breakfast at home was too heavy!"

"You think my father didn't know exactly what I was in for?" Mira Di interjects. "You think your father doesn't? They may have a slightly blurrier picture than Suraj Sharma about the cities, but all of them know what the girls go through. These men don't care."

I nod. My face is tight. I can feel my teeth clench.

Mira Di shakes her head and says, "Even the rich can have empty pockets, Heera."

I wake up early on Monday morning to get the kwoon to myself. My magic hour. Today I'll be able to tell Rini Di even more about what I've learned about Rosy before it's too late.

Girls Bazaar is finally quiet at 5:00 a.m. The dense winter mist covers our lane like a shroud. At the railway station, I have the water pump all to myself.

There are footsteps behind me and I assume it must be Salman—the only other soul who stirs in our lane at this hour. He's begun to study at dawn now that he works at the shop in the evenings.

Suddenly, a hazy figure darts near the huts in the white eerie light of the morning moon, and I know at once that it's not Salman. The winter condensation is as thick as a brick. I turn around and can make out that it's a man, much larger than my brother, enveloped in the foggy universe. I hear his breath and realize that the blur is getting closer, following me as I begin to run.

Sweat breaks though my skin even in the freezing cold. My feet take off in the opposite direction and I scream as loud as I can.

His footsteps become louder.

A hand comes down over my mouth. Another arm holds me in an iron grip.

The man is strong, but so am I.

I do a back kick into his groin as hard as I can. He yells in pain. Even if I can't break free, I can slow him down.

Another set of footsteps get louder and louder, and the next thing I know my mother is shouting, "Let her go! What are you doing! Let her go now!"

"Get out of my way!" the man yells back. He's still holding me tight.

I jab him with a back elbow thrust and we stumble onto the uneven earth. The cold ground gives me some relief. I've put up enough of a fight to prevent him from dragging me too far away from my hut.

More voices take up the space around us, people who have come out of their homes—my aunt, a neighbor or two.

"What's happening here?" another woman yells.

"What's going on!" It's Salman's voice. I can see his fury through the fingers spanning my face and use the distraction to open my mouth and bite as hard as I can.

The man lets out a yelp. He stinks—a body odor of country liquor, sweat, and grease. Finally, his grip loosens enough that I squirm away. As soon as I'm free, I take gulps of clean air.

A crowd has formed, and it is formidable. I'm safe. My lane feels different even in the short time since I got the medal. As if the medal is for all of us—a source of pride.

Someone holds a lantern up and I run to my brother's side, turning to get a good look at the man who grabbed me: Gainul, one of Ravi Lala's enforcers. I should have known as soon as I smelled him. Somehow, I had known deep down that he wouldn't leave me be.

Gainul's arm moves swiftly as he whips a knife out of his pocket. "Let me through."

The crowd wants to protect me, but no one dares touch him. At the same time, I know that no one plans to leave. They're here for me, despite the cold and the fear.

Mai pulls me close to her. We stand with our arms around each other in an unspoken challenge to him. "What do you think you're doing, coming here and manhandling my daughter?" she screams. Fear has given her courage.

"Just following orders," he says. And at once, we all know who he means.

My mother's rage turns to confusion. "But why does Ravi Lala want Heera? We have paid our debts!"

Gainul's voice comes out as if someone has scraped his throat. "I don't ask questions; I just do as I am told. Now let me pass, or there will be trouble."

We all know that his threat is not hollow.

CHAPTER SIXTEEN

Once we're safely back inside our hut, Mai alternates between scolding me for being out alone in the dark and thanking her stars that I'm safe.

"Why would he come here and try to take Heera!" she asks for the third time.

Baba answers. "This is what they do. How many times have you seen it? Why does it surprise you now all of a sudden?"

Mai turns to him, outraged. "They almost took Heera today, and this is all you can say!"

But there is something new in Baba's voice—perhaps it's resignation. Perhaps it's even concern.

"It's my fault now, is it?" His insensitive, cruel tone is gone. "Who was it who thought they could take a loan from that man and get away with it?" he asks.

"I paid him back, didn't I!"

I wipe the tears from my face with my palms. I don't think she realizes, but Mai is still holding me.

"Not before he decided it was Heera's time!" I can hear a note of fear alongside Baba's acquiescence to our fate.

"Who does he think he is?" she says.

"If you don't lower your voice, I can guarantee you will find out," Baba warns her softly.

"Stop it! Both of you!" I yell. They both look at me, surprised. We all look silently at one another, unsure and afraid.

"Look," Baba says at last, explaining the mind of the man he works for. "Ravi Lala is used to getting his way. He thought he would get Heera for that money that he loaned you. That's what he thought he was due, and then you went and foiled his plan by paying him back. So, this is his revenge. He's trying to uphold his reputation. Prove to the community that he never lets a single girl go."

Mai shudders at the truth in his words. "He won't stop, will he?"

Baba lets out a sigh. "No. He won't. Not as long as we live here on his soil," he says with finality as he gathers his shawl around him to walk to the water pump.

"We can't let him do this," I say. I realize I'm shivering. "Not when we've fought so hard to turn things around."

Baba looks at me and shakes his head. "It's time for you to accept that people like us don't always get what we want." The venom has left his voice since Rini Di repaid our loan, but he still refuses to believe that our fate can be different.

I have dirt all over me. My hair is in tangles. My legs feel wobbly. I know that I need to wash and get to school, but the thought of the walk to the railway platform is terrifying.

But as Baba reaches the door, he surprises me with an unexpected gesture. "Do you want to walk to the pump with me?" he asks, his hand outstretched. "We can't have you going alone."

Later that morning, Salman leaves for school. But I'm forced to miss a day for the first time since I was allowed back. Mai and Mira Di take turns staying with me, huddling around me, not allowing me to leave their sight.

"You got away. I can't believe you got away," says Mira Di, eyes ablaze. "The kushti is helping."

"Kung fu," I say, correcting her for the millionth time, but no one cares. "Mai nearly screamed his ear off," I boast with a touch of pride in my mother's newly found courage.

"You were pretty effective too," Mira Di says with laughter bubbling in her throat. "I saw those kicks."

"Side kicks," I say with great satisfaction. "I bit him too," I add with glee.

Mai and Mira Di both chuckle.

After Mira Di leaves, Mai goes to take a bath. "Don't go anywhere," she says. "We don't know if those people are still around."

Jamila Bula, Mai, Mira Di—they keep saying I'm lucky. But all I can think of is how I failed. At some point over the past twenty-four hours, while I lay pinned beneath Gainul or confined to my hut, Rosy was likely wed to a banana tree. Her fate was sealed and I did nothing to stop it. I lie on the straw mat with Sania climbing all over me. I tickle her and she laughs, her plump cheeks brimming with joy. But my mind is elsewhere. Not for the first time, I dream about leaving Girls Bazaar. With Mai and Salman both working, the money coming in for sending me to school, and whatever I can win at competitions, maybe, just maybe, there is a way of saving enough money to get a place in another part of Forbesganj. A place where Mai could own her betel paan leaf shop and Mira Di could be freed from Chacha's back room.

And then suddenly, a shadow falls over me. Someone is on the other side of the door. I jump up with fright, my whole system clammy and weak in seconds. But as the shadow's voice introduces itself, I relax. It's only Rini Di.

"I heard what happened," she says, entering our hut. She's in her black track pants and sneakers, a black hoodie over her white shirt. And I realize she's come right from kung fu class. Before I know it, I'm crying. I don't know how long it takes for the tension to subside, turning into intermittent sobs, and finally just to shaking. I take deep gulps of air, the impact of what happened finally hitting me.

After a while she pats my back. And then, just as suddenly, I stop. "Who told you?" I ask, wiping my tears away.

"Mira Di," she says softly, bringing with her the same unflustered and peaceful air that hangs over the kwoon and the hostel.

We both sit down on the floor, and without invitation Sania crawls into our guest's lap. Rini Di gives her a cuddle, but Sania isn't interested—she grabs hold of her glasses and tugs. Meanwhile, Rini Di extracts a packet of cookies from her bag and hands Sania one. Immediately, her glasses are free.

"You should eat one too," she suggests, with a smile.

"You are always trying to feed me."

"I suppose I am," she says, pulling one out of the packet to hand to me.

The cookie tastes delicious and I realize I haven't eaten anything all day.

"So. You've had a fright," she says, perhaps sensing that I'm ready to talk at last.

"It wasn't so bad. I could at least put up a fight thanks to the kung fu classes," I say reassuringly, hoping to chase the worry from her eyes.

"Yes, you might look like you are all skin and bones, but you're strong. Did he hurt you?" she asks, darting a quick glance at my face and arms.

I shake my head as I take another cookie. But the pain from Gainul's grip has spread to my ribs. A spot behind my right temple throbs from when we fell to the ground.

Mai comes back and I can see she's not surprised to see our guest. She folds her hand in a namaste and lets out a sigh. "I didn't think he would do this after I paid back his money." She puts on some water to boil for tea and sits down with us.

"He had no right. And he'd have had no right even if you still owed him money," Rini Di says in a grim tone.

Mai looks at her, measuring these words. "Did you think this would happen?"

Rini Di purses her lips. "I wouldn't say that, but I wasn't surprised."

"I didn't grow up here," Mai says with a sigh. "My brothers never wanted me to have to sell my body to anyone. That's why they married me off to Heera's father. I was barely older than she is now. God knows we've had our struggles, and my husband may have his faults, but he never wanted me to lie down with other men to make ends meet."

The sunlight spreads across the brown mud walls of our hut, making the room look much bigger than it is. For once the Bollywood music isn't blaring and I can hear the faint sounds of pigeons cooing on the electric poles near the railways. As Mai speaks, I can recall a different version of my father—the man who used to play the flute.

"In all the years we have lived here, I have seen a lot of things," Mai continues, "but this is the first time I've seen them try to kidnap a girl over whom they have no claim."

Rini Di takes a deep breath. "It might be a sign of things to come. I've learned from some colleagues that the fair is short of girls. Many have begun to fall sick with AIDS-related complications and the owners are willing to pay a premium. Ravi Lala has been busy doing whatever he can to maximize his profits. It's also very possible that he feels he has to prove something with Heera—that he gets what he wants."

I look at Rini Di in awe. How does she know all this? Mai's slim shoulders are rigid as she pours the tea into glasses, and a sapping sense of doom rises from deep inside my stomach.

"There are options," Rini Di says softly. "Heera could come and stay at the hostel."

I realize with certainty that this is why she's come today, to take me away from all this. Just as I secretly wanted. Just as my baba feared. But then I'm surprised at my own feeling: I don't want to go. Our family is finally becoming a family, at long last. Something has shifted, even in Baba.

Mai looks from her to me and back again. "For good?" she asks, her voice quivering.

A loud noise pounds in my head as the trucks from the highway thunder past. I want to hug Mai and tell her I won't go. I'll stay and help with Sania, stand up to Baba, do the cooking and cleaning when she's at the highway and nestle into her arms when she comes back.

"At least for now to begin with, until the fair goes away. Just to keep her safe." Rini Di looks at Mai steadily with compassionate and understanding eyes.

"How would that work?" Mai asks. "Would we have to pay you?" Worry flickers across her face.

"No, not at all. The home raises money from people to support children in need," Rini Di promises, patting Mai's hand reassuringly. "It's clear how loved and cared for Heera is. I wouldn't have suggested this had it not been for the physical threat."

Mai is quiet and I know that some vague part of her doesn't want to let me go—we have not lived a day without each other since I was born—but a bigger part knows what's right. I watch her doubts vanish as she seizes on Rini Di's last two words: *physical threat*. She nods in vigorous assent, blinking away her tears.

"She will be so close by," Rini Di adds. "She can come home for weekends and come and go during daylight hours. Perhaps Salman or Sadaf can escort her. You can come to the hostel when you like too, perhaps drop Sania off on your way to work?"

I close my eyes. This isn't supposed to be happening. Things at home were supposed to get better. I wasn't supposed to leave.

"But if those men want to get her, they can find her at the hostel too," Mai says, an invisible weight pressing her down. For a moment, it feels as if I'm watching her lose Chotu all over again. But she leans forward, gathering her sari into her waist in a businesslike way, as if she needs to understand every aspect of my stay in the hostel now that she has decided I am going.

Rini Di squeezes her shoulder comfortingly. I listen carefully but can't bring myself to speak. "Ravi Lala and I have had our own run-ins. He won't mess with me at the hostel. And hopefully, if she's out of sight for a while, they will forget about her—or the fair will move farther away, and it will be safe again."

I want to pick Sania up and bounce her on my hip, but I'm too sore. So I snuggle my cheek against hers instead. My stomach turns over. How will I live without Sania? How will she survive without me? She's already lost one sister this year. A day without her babbling or her chubby hands reaching out for me is unthinkable.

Rini Di puts one hand over one of Mai's as she gets up to leave. She tickles Sania under the chin one last time before waving goodbye.

I'm sure they've both noticed that I haven't said a word. That's because I haven't been asked a single question. Deep down, I know it's not my choice. And even if it were, I know what the answer would have to be. But I can't help it. I feel like the little girl who hid behind Mai's sari whenever she saw a stranger. The little girl who never hugged anyone, who was grateful not to be picked for anyone's kho-kho team, who sat in the dirt at the entrance of her hut at twilight, waiting for her mother to come home. I want to stay as close to Mai and Sania as possible.

After the door shuts behind Rini Di, I turn to Mai. "Don't send me away, Mai. Please!"

"Listen to me," she says, more determined than I've ever seen her. "I would never send you anywhere if I wasn't sure it was for your own good. I don't care what your father says. You are going to go to that home." She reaches out to put a calloused hand on my cheek, gentle and warm.

I let out a sob. "But I'll miss you too much. I can't do it."

"You aren't safe here," says Mai firmly. She kneads her thumb against her palm, the telltale sign that she's worried. I've seen her do it hundreds of times—when she left for the hospital with Chotu, when Shaukat was taken away in the police van, when I told her that the principal had thrown me out of school, when Baba said it was time to sell me to Ravi Lala, when Gainul stood with a knife.

My heart skips a beat when I realize there is no arguing. And for a moment, I can hear Chotu's laugh. Mai isn't going to risk the safety of one of her children ever again.

I stifle a sob. "Will Baba agree? He didn't even agree to send Salman to the Siliguri school."

Mai nods. "If I have to, I'll do the one thing he's afraid of more than anything else." Finally, her shoulders relax. "I'll stop giving him a single rupee."

I gasp at the words I never thought I'd hear Mai say.

My mother is a new woman. She is a pehelwan too.

A gunny-bag that contains all of my meager possessions swings from Salman's shoulder. It's late evening by the time we finally arrive at the hostel, bathed in the golden glow of the last rays of sun. Small electric bulbs twinkle through the windows of the rooms above, where I'll soon find a bed of my own. I have a fleeting moment of heartache for Mai and Sania, but I force it back down.

The entire walk over was spent fighting with Salman.

I wanted to be the one to explain to Baba why it was best for me to go, so that maybe it would spare Mai an argument. I would use logic to explain why this was the best decision for everyone, that if I lived at the hostel there would be one less mouth to feed. That perhaps there would be even one less than that if he decided to let Salman go to boarding school. In the end, Salman and Mai both felt it was best for me to sneak away before Baba returned. I tried to argue it, but Salman's warning look beseeched me into silence. I obeyed the code. He wanted to handle it himself.

As we walked, even though all I wanted was to take his hand in gratitude, I could only manage to feel anger toward him. Once we reached the referral hospital, I began scolding him. "Your faith in me, in a future where I will be a champion, is ridiculous. I may not amount to anything, whereas you are actually *good* in school. You could become a scientist. You should be at the Siliguri school. In proper science classes with a science lab."

He stayed quiet as I berated him. Salman doesn't open his mouth when he doesn't want to. It's easily the most annoying thing about him. "How could you have given up on that school so easily?" I asked. Still, not a word. I fumed. "I won't go to school if you don't, and that's that."

We were near the bus stop, halfway to the hostel, when he slipped his hand into mine.

Salman has deserted the tradition of the Nat men in our family, just as I have deserted the tradition of Nat girls in my family. We are two of a kind, unmistakably brother and sister. And I am immeasurably proud of him.

I clutch on to him at the hostel gate, which is probably a little ridiculous because I will see him in less than a week. He seems to feel the same way because he hugs me for a long time too. I balance myself on my toes as I give him a kiss on his forehead.

Finally, he speaks. "You mean more to me than a science lab," he says matter-of-factly. He holds up his hand when he sees I am about to protest. "Let's do this for now. When your school money comes and we repay Rini Di's loan, we'll plan again."

I nod.

"We are in a much better place than we were when you were thrown out of school. Our roof is not leaking, we have more food than before, I have a job, and you have a medal," he says, not unreasonably.

His words loosen the knot in my chest. "I just wish we still had

Chotu," I say, allowing myself to speak aloud the unsaid. My voice is a bit uneven.

A frown robs Salman's face of its boyishness as he hands me the gunny-bag. In Girls Bazaar, we've all had to grow up faster. There is nothing left to say.

I leave the cold smoky air behind, outside the high walls that surround the hostel. Ravi Lala and Gainul certainly can't jump over this. I never noticed how high they really are until now.

It's quieter than normal. All the girls have gone up to their rooms after dinner. The sound of flying footsteps echoes through the hall, followed by a thud. It's Tania. The exertion of her flight downstairs has brought on a bad bout of coughing.

"Your room's all ready. I saw you come in through the window," Tania says through heavy breaths.

Maya Didi follows soon after, laying a hand on her back. Over the weeks, I've learned that Tania has never known her parents and was brought into the hostel as a sickly child, recovering from pneumonia. Her health is a constant worry.

"One thing at a time," Maya Didi says. "We have some dinner left over in the kitchen with a plate covering it. Once you're done, Tania can take you up. Your bed is ready."

I gulp down my food as fast as I can, eager to see my room. Maya Didi walks me down the long passage upstairs to a room at the end and taps at the door. The room is long and narrow, with cupboards along one wall and bunk beds along the other for four of us girls. There are long French windows that open onto the wraparound veranda outside, but in the darkness all I can see is the stars outside. The bamboo blinds have been rolled up. The two bulbs on the wall are covered in a pretty blue cloth, casting a warm yellow light in the room. I have never been in such a cozy room.

My gunny-bag is in front of a cupboard. "That cupboard is for your things and that bottom bed is for you," Tania explains. All the beds have crisp white sheets, a pillow, and a blanket. I realize that I will sleep on a bed with a warm blanket to cover me for the first time in my life and swallow a sob thinking of everyone at home shivering on the mud floor.

"The toilets are just across the corridor. You have to take your towel and toothbrush with you. Maya Didi left pajamas for you to change into and there's a towel and soap on your bed." Tania grins, introducing me to my roommates. They're already in bed, reading books. They tell me their names and greet me with friendly smiles, but I'm too exhausted and overwhelmed to chat and thankfully they don't ask me many questions.

"Tomorrow, Maya Didi will give you a list of all the rules and regulations, but today she said we're not supposed to tire you out. We're switching off the lights but will leave one on near your bed, so you can switch it off when you get back." A light that switches on and off. I've never had that either.

The room is silent by the time I get back from washing up. I get into bed, pull the blanket over me. But strangely, it's a struggle to get comfortable. The pillow makes my neck hurt. The bed is too soft. I toss and turn, wishing I had come tomorrow morning instead. I miss Mai and little Sania with every breath.

My mind races until it lands right back where it started only a day ago when I was headed to school to catch Rini Di: Rosy. Her Bisi Bele has probably already happened. If there was anything I could do, it would be too late now. I wonder where she's sleeping—if she has a mattress or a pillow.

I take the blanket and a sheet and shift to the floor near my bed, pretending the pillow is Sania. By the time I get up the next morning, the room is empty.

I quickly get ready. I bathe in a bathroom by merely turning on a tap, with water that's not freezing cold. Going to the toilet with four walls is a novelty. But I have no time to linger or savor these moments. Everything is according to a timetable.

I arrange my few possessions in the cupboard. I have nothing to keep in the drawers except my Bruce Lee book. I hang my two kameezes and put some smallclothes on the shelf. I fold my two salwars neatly and head downstairs with my schoolbag. The girls come down to breakfast in a trickle and then in a flood. Many of them are so used to seeing me at the hostel that they greet me and move on as though it's any other day.

At that moment, it dawns on me that what feels like an extraordinary day in my life is only a day like any other for the rest of them. And that each and every girl here has had a day such as this of their own. They come in as frightened, nervous creatures, doing as they are bid with a painful readiness, and gradually become high-spirited, healthy girls. I've seen it happen even among the girls who came in since I started eating at the hostel.

My tutor, Zehra, comes down and knows instantly that this is an unscheduled appearance. I'm never here before school. "Heera! What are you doing here?" she says, taking the seat next to me.

"I've come here to stay," I say, my voice barely above a whisper.

A smile slowly creeps across her face. "Really? For good?"

"For now."

She puts an arm around me. "Welcome."

I learn later that there's an unwritten rule in the hostel: Don't ask anyone their story. If they want to tell you, they will. Until then, mind your own business.

It's a good rule.

CHAPTER SEVENTEEN

At school, Sadaf and Razia notice my bruises right away. I can't help but act more quiet and withdrawn and they pick up on that right away too. But unlike the girls in the hostel, they waste no time in asking me what happened. To my surprise, it's a relief to be asked. I need to share my burden with someone. And I can only hope that they know enough about Girls Bazaar, Ravi Lala, and Rosy at this point that my aborted kidnapping attempt won't scare them away.

As I narrate the details of the kidnapping at lunchtime, of everything that's happened in the past day, I almost can't believe myself. Just a few weeks ago, I was so ashamed of my life, my family, my lane. I wouldn't have ever talked to anyone about it. And here I am relating a blow-by-blow account to my two new friends.

"You bit him, eh?" Sadaf says with a smile.

I grin with relief. "By that time, he was cornered by so many people, he had no choice but to let me go. I think screaming at the top of my lungs helped too."

"Wow, Heera. You should be beating your chest and boasting about your superhero moment. Here you are making it sound like it was no big deal," Razia says.

I barely get a minute to bask in the glory when the lunch bell rings. It isn't until the end of the day that I realize that Manish isn't there.

"Was Manish in school yesterday?" I ask Sadaf.

Sadaf takes a second to think. "I don't think so. Why?"

It feels like the conversation I had with Mira Di and Mai about Rosy's wedding ceremony happened a million years ago.

"I think Rosy's Bisi Bele was yesterday," I say. I can hear the guilt in my own voice as the words exit my mouth. Again, I'm the one who's safe while Rosy's fate is unknown.

There's a moment of silence between all of us as Sadaf and Razia absorb what I tell them about what Mai overheard at the hospital. The reality of it seems to crush all of us at once. One of our former classmates, my friend, will actually be sold, and her brother is still in class with us.

"So he didn't sell her to the fair?" Sadaf says, after a long pause.

"I don't know for sure, but we think that she's headed for Mumbai."

"Why would they take her to Mumbai instead of somewhere closer to home?" Sadaf asks, nibbling her lower lip.

"Mumbai, Dharamganj, Forbesganj, it all boils down to the same thing. The only difference is the size of the price tag. They will auction her off to the highest bidder," I say, trying to explain it as best as I can. Sadaf and Razia will never understand quite how desperate I and everyone in Girls Bazaar really are, but they have at least begun to see how dangerous Ravi Lala is.

The difference between their life and mine is night and day. A writhing spiral of fear twists in my stomach—that they may recoil from me. But I see that the fear in their eyes is replaced by a sorrow, a compassion. More than that, a desire to do something about it.

Going back to the hostel after school feels strange. The walk home usually takes over twenty minutes. Now the hostel is barely two minutes away, but I find myself practically sprinting to its doors. The noise of laughter and chatter floats through the windows. But I can't shake the feeling of sadness and guilt that I'm protected, and Rosy is not.

The girls line up for afternoon tea as I walk by them and head straight for Rini Di in the library. At long last, I will finally be able to tell her what I've learned about Rosy.

Rini Di sits behind her desk, her head bowed over her keyboard. "Namaste, Heera. How was your first night?" she asks, lifting her head up.

"Namaste, Rini Di. It was fine," I say, sliding into the chair in front of her, adding, "A little muddled. Getting used to all the new things." I think of the blanket and pillow, the water, the pajamas. I don't know why I feel stupidly close to tears.

She seems to understand. "Missing home is a natural part of this," she says gently. "You'll see them in a few days. I know life might feel overwhelming to you right now, but it won't always be so," she says, shutting her computer. "It's a bit like your bruises. The purple will become black and then brown and finally it will be gone. Are they still hurting?"

"Much less," I say with a nod to indicate that I understand.

She walks me through some of the hostel rules. Nothing too bad or unexpected. No fights, no bullying, no damaging property. My name is being added to the meal roster and she will take into account my kung fu training schedule as well, alongside the weekly home visits. "And if for any reason you won't be going home for the weekend, just tell us on Friday morning so we can plan meals and work accordingly. But never feel you *must* go home for the weekend, or that you must stay there from Friday afternoon to Sunday morning. The most important rule right now for you is that you can't be out alone on the street, especially not after dark."

My skin bristles. "Do you really think they will come for me again?"

"I don't know, Heera, but I want to make sure we do everything possible to ensure your safety. The rules are comparatively few but must be obeyed. Any questions?" she asks finally.

"Yes," I say. "But it doesn't have anything to do with this. Not really."

"Ask away," she says, pushing her glasses back up to the bridge of her nose.

"You remember what I told you about Rosy?" I feel my pulse in my neck as Rini Di leans forward, her elbows on the table. "I think her Bisi Bele was yesterday. And now they plan to take her to Mumbai."

Rini Di looks at me with alarm. "Where did you hear this?"

"Mai overheard her mother talking at the hospital about the Bisi Bele. I wanted to come to you right away. I tried to, but Gainul . . ."

Rini Di takes notes furiously as I relate what my mother heard. Her eyes narrow. "This is not your fault, Heera. Even if you had come to me with this information before, the problem is that Rosy is Suraj Sharma's daughter and Suraj Sharma is a police officer. Rosy's Bisi Bele was surely in a very secret location, not like the ones in Girls Bazaar where the whole community comes and the girl is sold with so much fanfare. I have been trying to find out as much as I can."

"What can we do *now*, though? Can I help you?" My voice is sharp with anxiety.

"Thank you, Heera. You already are. But for now, you must concentrate on getting better, your studies, and kung fu. I will certainly remember your kind offer, but these are dangerous people and we must be careful." Rini Di looks at me intently.

I don't press further. I know her priority right now is keeping me safe.

"Run along, Heera. Make friends and enjoy yourself at the hostel. There's lots to do."

But the only thing I can think about is how to find Rosy. The hostel is an explosion of noise—girls chatting and playing games. My head feels as if it might explode. I think about going up to the bedroom, but I'm not sure I will be alone there either.

So, I head to the computer room and find a free station. I think of everything Connie shared with me in her short email. I haven't told her much by comparison. But today, I have so much to share. I'm miserably slow at typing, so it takes me forever to say it, but there are things that feel so much easier to share with Connie than with people sitting right in front of me.

Dear Connie,

So much has happened since I wrote last.

Yesterday morning, a man tried to kidnap me near my house. He works for a crime boss who controls our neighborhood and sells girls into prostitution. Everyone's concerned that he'll come back, so I'm living in the hostel where Nisha lives for now. It's for vulnerable girls and orphans, a bit like the hostel home that you live in I guess.

Last night was my first time away from home and I really missed my mom. I understand what you meant now—no matter how difficult things can be sometimes, my mom is my mom. I feel like I've abandoned her. Especially since it has only been a couple of months since my little sister died.

I didn't tell you about her before. I'm not sure why. We couldn't bring her fever down and couldn't afford a doctor. I miss her all the time and I know my mother does too and I hate not being there for her. My older brother is a much better student than me, but he's the one stuck working when he should be studying. I've tried to tell him, but he won't have it any other way. If he doesn't work, my mother will have to work longer.

I'm safe here and I know I will see my family again every weekend, so I hope I get used to it fast. But I'm worried that my friend Rosy is in trouble. The same man who came for me still has his eye on her and I'm worried that I'm too late and she could already be on her way to Mumbai. I don't know why I didn't tell you about her either.

I'll write more later.

Your friend,

Heera

Over the next few weeks, I'm somehow able to fall into a routine. I learn to sleep in a bed. I'm cleaner and more rested. I go to school. I have kung fu lessons. On the weekends, I go back to the earthen floor of our house. I always take eggs, fruits, and cereals for the family. Sania is all mine—from the moment I enter on Friday afternoon until the time I leave on Sunday afternoon, when she has to be pulled from my arms as I leave for the hostel.

From week to week, I watch Salman become thinner and the circles under his eyes grow darker as he walks me to and from the hostel. He works through the weekend, mornings with his books, evenings at the store. I study, practice kung fu, chat with Mira Di, and help Mai cook. I warily answer their questions about life in the hostel. I watch Baba's anger about me leaving fade over time.

There's been no sign of Ravi Lala's men, for which we're all relieved. But none of us are fools. As the fair continues on, all we can do is watch and wait. I try as hard as I can to forget and move on. I'm getting good at forgetting, or at least ignoring whole sections of my life. Like I do when I'm at the hostel and I try to close off the part of my brain that contains memories of home. It seems to keep my guilt in check every time I eat a proper meal, every night that I sleep in comfort.

The only thing I cannot forget is Rosy. I have visions of her in Mumbai, nightmares about what's happening to her. I try to prod Rini Di for information, but she has nothing to share yet. She went to Suraj Sharma's house the day I told her about the Bisi Bele, but neither Rosy nor her mother were there, so all I can do is continue on.

School, miraculously, begins to feel normal. I can feel myself doing better, like I can actually concentrate. Zehra says the same thing happened to her when she first started living at the hostel and learned what getting eight hours of sleep feels like. But most of all, Zehra thinks it's about having enough food. "How can anyone remember what they learn at school when they're hungry?" she asks. I'm not sure she's right, though, and tell her that Salman seems to do just fine. She scoffs at this. "He probably gets fed more than you. Just like my brother does at home." I don't think so, because I know Salman. If he had extra food, he would share it with us. But then I remember all the times that the last bit of khichdi has gone to him or my father. Or the money Mira Di gives him for meals when he's studying late.

"Maybe a bit more," I admit.

But staying at the hostel comes with its distractions too. There are chores and there's a TV. We talk, play badminton, kho-kho, and kabaddi. We watch TV together. I learn to jump rope. As the days roll by, I seem to find my voice again and begin chatting and making friends. But not all distractions are so pleasant. There are fights, almost daily. Sometimes fistfights too. I try to stay away the moment I sense trouble, and so far, I have. The days I've spent here before, studying and eating with the girls, have prepared me. I know that some of the girls have problems controlling themselves when they get upset. I can be the same way. And oddly enough, it's a bit of a relief to me that the hostel is not a magic place where people are always kind to one another. I know how to handle that, and Maya Didi and Rini Di know how to defuse a conflict—when to get involved and when to let the girls sort out their problems themselves.

Then the biggest distraction arrives three weeks after my arrival at the home. Another kung fu competition.

"This one is a big one—it's a district-level meet," Rini Di tells us one day in school. "Would you all like to participate again?" There's a little rustle at this, and everyone looks up, clapping and cheering. She has asked the same group as last time to stay back, with one rude and unpleasant addition: Manish.

Everyone is enthusiastic, but I can't imagine practicing as hard as I did last time with Manish breathing down my neck. Everyone has enthusiastically agreed, but I haven't moved a muscle. Rini Di looks at me then.

"Can I think about it?" I say. "We have exams coming up, so . . ." I can barely hear myself by the end of it.

"Of course," Rini Di says. "We'll be running through similar routines as last time, but this is a more competitive stage. So we'll have to up our game and practice even harder." There's a fresh outburst of clapping. Rini Di contents herself with a few final remarks about the need to work hard, observe the rules, and study, and then dismisses everyone with a reminder to clean not just the kwoon but the entire area around it. But she asks me to stay back.

"What's the problem, Heera?" Rini Di says, probing me with her kind eyes. "I thought we went through the jitters already and overcame them."

I look at the floor. Surely she knows the real reason.

"Is it because Manish is in the competition now?" Her face fills with dismay. "Is he still bothering you?"

I pull a long face, embarrassed that I'm still afraid of him. "No! I mean, a little, but it isn't anything major and please don't say anything."

"Look, Heera, I know it can be hard to stand tall when someone is trying to put you down," she says, placing her hand gently on my shoulder. "But remember what we learned. Water is the softest substance in the world, yet it can penetrate the hardest. It's impossible to grasp a handful of it, yet it does not suffer hurt. Stab it, and it is not wounded. Sever it, yet it is not divided. It has no shape of its own but molds itself to the receptacle that contains it."

I look at her blankly.

"Think about it," she says, walking away, mindful of the fact that I need to think this through alone.

Feeling restless, I head to the computer room. Today, I'm not in the mood for metaphors. My letters to Connie have become more frequent. My English has gotten better and better. It's much easier to share everything with a friend who doesn't know anyone in my immediate environment. There's no fear, no expectation, no judgment.

I get better at typing, more detailed. She was full of questions about the episode with Gainul, how I got away, my new life at the hostel, and especially about Rosy. She's been telling me more about her life too: how her mother had let her go with a strange man who told her he would get her a job. About the first hostel she went to, where she wasn't looked after very well, but the caretaker was arrested soon after she arrived. That was how she moved to Phoenix Group Home, which she said is much better.

Hey!

Just wanted to say we went to our sister hostel, Sunshine House, for a play they put up. I met a girl there named Azra. She's originally from Nepal but was brought over here by traffickers about a year ago from Mumbai. I know Mumbai is a huge city, but it made me think of your friend Rosy. Azra was sold to a brothel they run out of a massage parlor in New York, but she managed to escape—incredible, right? That's how she wound up at the hostel.

I know this sounds stupid, but I wasn't sure where Nepal was. So, I looked at the map and that's when I realized that it's right next to Bihar in India! (Isn't Nepal where Mount Everest is?) Azra told me that her mother was tricked by a man who told her he had a job for her in Mumbai and she chose to trust him. She said it was because he had a tattoo of the god Krishna on the back of his hand. That's what happened to my mother too. She was tricked by a man with a job offer here in the US. I guess what I'm trying to say is that I didn't realize how wide this trafficking system really is. And I think you're right to be worried about Rosy.

XO

Connie

My stomach drops. I remember what Mira told me about Ravi Lala's agents. How they're part of a trafficking ring that brings girls from all over. But I never imagined that they would end up in the United States. Again and again, my thoughts come back to Rosy. I know Mai thinks that she's being taken to Mumbai, but what about after that? She could be anywhere.

I go back downstairs and two of the girls are screaming about who cheated at ludo, so I quickly head to the library. I pull out the atlas. Is this girl from Nepal my age? Is she a Nat too? It's as if I can feel Gainul's hands on me all over again. I can't even begin to imagine how terrified Azra must have been. I look at the world map to see how far Nepal is from the United States. It's oceans away—nine countries in between, from the route my finger has taken. Despite everything Mira Di has told me about how this world works, I still feel like I don't understand anything.

Rini Di catches me studying the map and walks over from her desk.

"Heera?" she asks. "You look upset."

My head is bent, a pencil in hand. I debate keeping it to myself. I've already burdened her with so much, but I can't help it—the words exit my mouth in one breath. I tell her what Connie has written about Azra and finally ask, "How does a girl from Nepal end up so far away from home? All the way to the US?"

Rini Di exhales deeply and takes a seat next to me. She doesn't even know Azra. Neither do I. But somehow, I realize that I don't need to explain where my worries came from.

"You ask good questions, Heera. There are many possible answers, but the easiest way to explain it is that a girl from Nepal ends up in the US in much the same way that a girl in Girls Bazaar ends up in a dance party that takes her all over the country."

If that was supposed to clarify anything for me, it doesn't. Of course I've witnessed far too much of what Mira Di has had to go through, but there's so much more.

"How do they even get to *America* from here? Won't someone stop them on the way?" I drag my finger along the map again, across the nine countries between here and there, genuinely perplexed.

Rini Di takes a deep breath. "Unfortunately, there are many ways in which girls can be smuggled to foreign countries. She may have been told she would be doing some other work and then pushed into the sex trade once she arrived there. Or given a false passport to travel. Or even snuck in on a ship."

Instead of despair, I only feel anger. "Is this something that could happen to Rosy?" I ask.

"It's possible," Rini Di replies. My stomach sinks. "We went to her home the day you told us about her Bisi Bele and she wasn't there. The family isn't cooperating, so it's been very difficult for us to track her down without more information. But I've alerted all of our partner organizations in Mumbai and the authorities that we know we can trust. Now we must hope that we'll hear some news if that is where she is headed."

I can't stop myself from asking question after question. What happens if they find her? Will they bring her back to her family? Where else would she live? Something between hope and trepidation makes my voice quiver. My eyes focus in on Rini Di's face, studying the details of her expressions to determine whether there really is a chance. But as she answers each question in the careful and methodical way that she does best, I realize that I already know the answers. It might not be possible to bring her back to her family. Not when it was her own father who put her in this situation and who could very likely do it again. So she might very well live in a home just like this one. If she's found, that is.

I close the atlas and find my thoughts drifting to a different place—another part of my brain that I've learned to shut off. I picture Mira Di scooping me up in her arms, swimming in the pond among the water lilies with us, sewing the holes in our clothes with utmost concentration, climbing trees and eating raw mangoes. And then I see her swaying her hips—a frozen smile and glazed eyes glued to her face, cigarette marks on her skin.

"What about Mira Di?" I say at last. "Why not rescue her too?"

Rini Di gives me a long look. I know there has to be a way out for her. Rini Di had a solution for me. She must have one for Mira Di too. I wait for her to tell me a plan for her, but that doesn't happen. She folds her hands in her lap, then pushes her glasses back up to the bridge of her nose—a habit when she's thinking hard. "That's another good question. It's different when the person involved is an adult. When it comes to children, it's our responsibility to help. But when the people involved are adults, they need to make the choice themselves."

"But Mira Di hates her life!"

"I understand what you're saying," Rini Di says, a hand on my arm. "And maybe you can ask Mira Di these things yourself. I can't speak for her; that isn't right. I can get her medical help. I can get her a bank loan to start a small business. I can even try to get her a government grant to build her own simple low-cost hut. Trust me when I tell you that I've had these conversations with her myself. But ultimately, it's her decision."

I listen with respect. As much as I don't want to admit it, she has a point. And I wonder why my headstrong cousin hasn't asked for help for herself. "Mira Di has always told me not to believe in the superstition that our people are destined for prostitution. But part of me thinks that she believes it's true for herself." I pause, noticing that Rini Di has given me the floor to continue. "She would have been an incredible seamstress."

Rini Di nods, adjusting her glasses once again. "Did you know that I grew up in Forbesganj?" she says out of nowhere. "I never even knew about Girls Bazaar then, or about the kind of suffering the women here are forced to endure, or about the girls brought from Nepal to be sold here and beyond. No one wrote about it in the newspapers. So I started to write about it myself. And then I started to teach people about it. And then I started working with the hostel, teaching girls like you how to defend themselves," she replies seriously. "You did me proud against Gainul. Better than any medal."

Now it's time for me to give her the floor.

"I've seen things start to change," Rini Di continues. "I've watched people become aware of what's happening here. And when people become aware, they start to act. Maybe they'll take action against traffickers like Ravi Lala. Or force the police to become more active. Or invest more in their child's education. Or help women start businesses and have their own bank accounts. Maybe one day they won't blame women for their own exploitation."

I swallow the lump in my throat and nod solemnly. I know exactly who and what she's talking about, after all.

"You, your mother, your brother. You've all sent a message in your lane. This is not about destiny. It's about control—who controls whom and why. Remember that your body is your own, and no one should be able to tell you what to do with it."

I close my eyes, just for a moment, and find myself at the kwoon. Finally, Bruce Lee's words make sense.

I can live in Girls Bazaar, but that doesn't define me.

I can live in the hostel, but that doesn't define me.

I can fight with Manish, but his words don't define me.

What's on the outside might change the way I appear, but I'm still the same, because I am defined only by what is within me.

I am like water. I will compete. And I won't give up on Rosy.

CHAPTER EIGHTEEN

The next two weeks before the competition are filled with activity and preparation.

I go to school; return to the hostel; study, study, study for exams; practice, practice, practice for the competition; collapse into bed; wake up; and do it all over again.

The week before exams, we're allowed to stay up late to study. That weekend is the first one I spend in the hostel and not at home. In the home stretch before summer break, I feel like I've never worked so hard in my life. And by the end of exams, I'm bone tired but content knowing that I couldn't have done any more. I've inhaled as much of the English material as I could, and with Zehra's help, I pray that I've at least passed math and science. But until report cards come, the only thing I let myself focus on is the tournament.

Without the pressure of school or books, we get lost in the routines, the practices, the sparring. The structure is soothing. I've become an expert at blocking out Manish. When we're training, I feel like he's in my territory. Nisha, Fatima, and I are a team. The winning team. In these sessions, the kwoon is mine, and Manish is the new entrant. And in class I am always with Sadaf and Razia.

As it happens, the tournament falls on the same day that our report cards will be distributed in school. But Sunil Sir has forbidden any of us from seeing them until after the competition. "Your exams are over, and you can't change the results now, so focus on what you *can* do."

The morning of the tournament, I wake up with a muddle of jumbled impressions from my dreams throughout the night and the constant vision I have of our stack of report cards tucked away in Rini Di's drawer. In my dream, I'm flying with Bruce Lee in the sky. I've kicked Gainul's butt and somebody has garlanded me with my favorite potato fritters—samosa. Sania is eating them one by one. Then, suddenly, Salman and I are running to Rini Di, but the closer we get, the harder it is to see her—her form slowly disappears into the dark space behind her. I wake up in a sweat. The girls are making their beds. The sunlight is streaming through the window. I rub my eyes. There's no one following me, no dark space, just friendly chatter and the easy morning light. I take a sip of water from the glass near my bed.

"Morning, Heera," Tania chirps. "Feeling ready?" And I realize I am.

Last time, all I wanted was to survive—to be able to go through all the stances without completely forgetting them. But this time, I want the gold. I want to win. I've asked Rini Di to invite my family, including Baba. The thing that occupies my mind more than anything is showing him what I am capable of.

Downstairs, the girls are buzzing with excitement. With exams over, they're all coming to the tournament to support those of us competing. We hurry through our morning chores—airing out the beds, cleaning the floor, throwing out the trash, dusting the shelves—before we wash up and go down for breakfast.

The competition girls sit at one table, gobbling down the omelets, orange juice, and apples that Maya Didi has prepared. "Eat slowly, Heera," she says. "Give your stomach time to digest the food."

But there is no time. In what feels like a heartbeat, we're already piling into Rini Di's car. At that very moment, I know that Sunil Sir is fetching my parents from Girls Bazaar while the other hostel girls take a bus with Maya Didi.

I roll the window down. Spring is not quite in the air, but everything glows in the mellow warmth of the sun, the bitter cold of winter behind us. Nisha, Fatima, and I look sprightly in our white uniforms and bare brown arms and legs.

A busload of wedding passengers drive by, all dressed in glittering finery.

Nisha leans out the window. "Good luck!" she yells.

We giggle as they wave back.

"Actually, *we* need all the luck," Fatima says.

"You will be fine. You are well prepared," Rini Di says in a calm, unruffled tone as she steers the car through a herd of goats crossing the road.

The venue is much bigger than the last one. It's not a school, but a local stadium. As soon as my feet hit the pavement, all the same nerves from last time rush back. As we're led to the waiting area for participants, the seats fill up more and more. But this time, I don't think about making a run for it. Not with Baba here. Not when I know it would give Manish too much satisfaction to see me freak out.

We're divided into our groups and just like that, I'm separated from my friends as I wait with the others in my category. Luckily, no one talks much. Hunching my shoulders and compressing my lips, I shut my eyes and practice in my head. I repeat to myself—the horse stance, the front stance, the cat stance, and the fighting stances. I punch. I jab. I block. I kick.

When I pull myself back into my surroundings, the stadium is full and the quality of the participants is higher than I ever thought possible. I rest my hand on my brow, searching for my family in the audience—Baba's bright orange bandanna or the top of Salman's head. But there are too many people to search through. Why on earth did I ask Rini Di to invite my family? It would have been so much easier to fail away from the sneering eyes of Baba. Or the crestfallen faces of Mai and Salman. Winning means more today than any other day. I want to prove that I'm not just a Nat girl. I'm a pehelwan.

I'm not afraid in the same way I was last time. I have faith in my ability. Rini Di says that both my balance and flexibility, the most essential attributes in kung fu, are superb. And those are attributes we learned as Nat babies. My cousins would just tie rope on two bamboo poles and perform. Naturally, Salman and I learned to walk the tight-rope with them.

But I'm afraid in a different way. I'm afraid of not winning the gold. This is the competition that Nisha had her break in last year, I remind myself. But I'm nowhere near as good as her. The doubts come hurtling back.

One by one, the line in front of me gets shorter as the girls in my category are called. I look to the crowd once again. This time, I find myself looking for Rosy to be there, miraculously, in the front row—standing up and applauding, her nose free of piercings. But of course I know, deep down, that she won't be there.

And then my number is called over the loudspeaker. My thoughts cease. I've learned something from last time. I tune out the sounds, the surroundings, and the audience. And as soon as I'm out on that blue mat once again, it all fades away. I can't even see Rini Di or the judges this time. They must be too far away. It's only me and my opponent.

I feel my body move without thinking. My competitors don't matter. The prize doesn't matter. I widen my legs and bend my knees. I snap out my wrist in a jab. I form my hands into claws, moving into the dragon stance. And then I come out of my squat and plant a side kick into the stomach of my opponent. I'm too fast to be blocked, too agile to be attacked. She tries to hit me in the chest with her left hand but I duck out of the way. I slap my palms together as my opponent tumbles to the ground. She rebounds to her feet and leaps forward. I dodge, throwing another punch, quick and hard, my elbows close to my sides, my hands thrust forward in iron fists. She makes as if to hit me in the chest but I deflect with my elbows. She spins. And then, like the sarus cranes in our rice fields, I spread my arms to the sides, pull my right foot up, point my toe down, and hold my neck straight. I kick and I fly.

In the blink of an eye, it's over. The force of my kick strikes my opponent's hip. She howls as she falls. She forgot to spin or stabilize her core to keep her balance. Sweat pours down her forehead. Her energy leaves her and I wait while she remains on the mat, defeated.

I don't remember the applause in the stadium, or the feeling of my uniform growing increasingly wet with sweat. I don't remember Nisha and Fatima carrying me away on their shoulders, or the look on Manish's face the moment my name is called over the speakers. I don't remember going up to collect my medal.

But I remember the feeling of the cool, solid gold in my palms.

I, Heera of Girls Bazaar, have won a gold medal at a kung fu tournament.

And then I see them. "Look who's here to congratulate you." Rini Di gestures next to her and at last I see Salman and my parents. I didn't even notice that she was standing next to me, a lump in her throat as she tells me I've done my school proud. Mai is crying. Salman is patting me on the back. I don't even recognize the expression on Baba's face—a mix of pride, respect, and awe. It's the expression he wore when we watched my uncle win. He reaches out and pats me on the head.

"My daughter, a Nat girl," Baba says, shaking his head in disbelief. "You won a medal in a stadium full of people. From the entire district of Araria." He reaches out for the medal hanging around my neck.

I realize then that I've been waiting for this moment all my life.

At the hostel, Rini Di has laid out a celebratory meal for the winners and our families in the library. Nisha has won gold too, though Fatima missed it this time. But with our classmate Sanjay's bronze, the medal haul is still three.

Baba is very quiet as we walk the halls of the hostel, almost timid.

"Maybe he's intimidated by the brick walls. Or the furniture. Or the all-round cleanliness," I whisper to Salman as we fall behind the rest of the group.

"Or he's not himself without the drink," Salman retorts. "He actually came to the match without a single drop of alcohol in his body. He was a mess on the drive over, but once he saw you onstage, he actually started cheering."

Baba cheering, instead of jeering. I can hardly picture it.

In the library, the table is set with a spread of Chinese food—chow mein, fried rice, spring rolls, and chicken Manchurian as a tribute to the origins of kung fu. I've never eaten Chinese food before, but I imagine Bruce Lee having exactly what we are eating. Rini Di asks us to put what we like on our plates and eat with either our fingers, spoons, or two sticks she calls chopsticks. She asks Mai and Baba to take the food first.

Hesitantly, they take a little rice and chicken, choosing to sit in the far corner and eat with their fingers. My heart nearly bursts as I watch Rini Di make her way over to sit with my parents in the hostel, my second home. She says something and Baba nods, without his usual bitterness. Tania, who has been looking after little Sania, pokes her head in to deliver the bathed, fed, and gurgling child, who promptly jumps into Mai's arms.

Salman and I fill our plates. The noodles keep slipping out of our fingers. The spices are different but delicious, an orchestra on my tongue. Rini Di eats with the chopsticks, moving them up and down like a pro, taking in big mouthfuls. I try but I can't hold them together. She finally shows me how to wrap the noodles around a spoon with three prongs called a fork. Finally, Salman has managed to balance the chopsticks. We end with scoops of vanilla ice cream—another treat that I've never experienced, and I wonder if it's the closest I can get to heaven as a living being.

When our bellies are full, Mai asks me to sit next to her, pulling me close into her sari. I give Baba the gold medal. He holds it with one hand while he continues to eat. He's hardly spoken a word through dinner, but a small smile remains on his face the entire time. It's the most wonderful meal we've eaten together as a family since the feast we shared after my uncle's victory.

At last, Sunil Sir gets up to drive them home.

Baba stands, placing the medal back around my neck. "I am the father of a gold medalist," he says at last, thumping me on the back.

I don't even know how to respond.

"Maybe this really is the beginning of a different Baba," Salman whispers.

I cross my fingers as I wave them goodbye.

When we finish cleaning up, we return to the common room, where Rini Di pulls out a stack of booklets and all my joy evaporates. Report cards. I'd almost forgotten. This is not something where balance and flexibility will matter.

I take mine with trembling hands. At first, I don't want to look, but the suspense gets the better of me and I open it. My eyes go to the exam marks first. I have passed—decently—in all subjects. I can see from everyone's expressions that they have all passed as well. Well, *almost* everyone. I can read the look on Manish's face—dread, disappointment, rage. Even though the meal is over, he and the other boys in the tournament have been allowed to stay in the hostel this one time to celebrate and receive their grades.

"The hostel kwoon is charmed this year," Rini Di says, before announcing that a movie night is in order. While the hostel girls argue between *Enter the Dragon* and a romance, I can't keep my eyes off the anger that is emanating from Manish's brow.

"Before we watch, I do have one more announcement," Rini Di says.

We're all huddled together—the common room is just a little too small to accommodate all of us girls, plus the boys who have been allowed in today.

"Those of you who were here last year probably know what's coming, especially you, Nisha," Rini Di says.

Everyone is smiling, and suddenly I feel a few sets of eyes on me.

"As many of you know," Rini Di continues, "our hostel has an exchange program that began last year, where we get the chance to nominate one of our leading kung fu students for a four-week boot camp in New York. Last year, Nisha took part in the international martial arts competition, won a medal, and even gave a talk at a hostel like ours called Sunshine House. This year, I'm thrilled to announce that the student who has won this award is Heera!"

I look around me. Surely I haven't heard correctly.

"What?" I say.

"You'll be going to the US to study kung fu! And you'll be able to meet Connie in person, as well as many other girls like you who have been studying martial arts," Rini Di says, grinning from ear to ear. "I already have your baba's consent. I asked him at dinner."

I can't believe it. Bruce Lee practiced in America. My heart jumps with excitement.

"It's an award for being so kick-ass at kung fu!" Nisha says.

But then the jumping in my heart turns to a quake. America is *oceans* away. Everyone there is rich. Well, maybe not everyone. Not Connie. I try to think through the riotous cheers around me. I feel that I don't deserve so much happiness. My life has been spent knowing that something bad could happen to me at any time. Because it had. Expulsion. Chotu. Baba's addiction. Constant hunger. The threat of being sold. And now I have been surrounded by cheers for the second time in one day. As I look around, I realize that Manish is missing from the crowd. Suddenly, it's all too much.

I run from the room into the garden.

Within a minute, Nisha is by my side. We sit on the stones that ring the mango tree. The moon disappears behind a cloud. The shadows of the leaves change shape and the air smells of the possibility of spring. She has a few peanuts in a newspaper that she offers to me. I peel one brown skin off and pop the nut in my mouth. I notice some raw green mangoes on the ground and wonder how I can collect them and get them to Mira Di.

When my breathing returns to normal, Nisha speaks. "I know how you might be feeling," she says, placing a hand on my knee. Her skinny body turns in an arc toward me.

"How's that?" I look at her intently.

"Fear of how different it will be there? The sense that you don't deserve it?" Nisha's smooth moon face is expressive for a change.

I nod to let her know that she's nailed it. But there's more. I feel as though the universe will punish me if I take too much happiness from it. I squeeze her hand.

"The feeling will come back, again and again," she says sympathetically. "But it isn't true. This is bigger than anything you could have ever imagined happening to you. Anyone in your shoes would be overwhelmed."

"So how did you deal with it?" My left foot beats a nervous rhythm on the earth.

"I dove right into the work. And it's hard, hard work. You'll collapse in bed every night, but the structure is good."

"What are the people like over there? Is the English we've learned good enough? Could you even understand them?" I spew.

"You'll learn that they aren't so different from us. I'm still in touch with a couple of the kids I met. And you *do* understand English. You can write it. Don't forget you have a friend there."

I still don't know what to say. But my foot stops tapping. The fear subsides just enough for some of the excitement to resurface.

"And I'll help you prepare," she says, getting to her feet. "Come inside?"

"In a bit. You carry on." I want to take a moment alone with my thoughts.

When Nisha leaves, I take my medal out from my pocket, turning it over in my palm. I think of Salman and how I wish I could share this moment with him. If I'm here, it's only because of Salman. He's the first person who ever told me not to give up. He gave up his dream for the dream I never even knew I had. Somehow, I had hoped that there was a way we could both come out of this better, together. Though the medal is shiny and gold, I know it's worthless to save Salman from his drudgery. There was no cash award at this competition.

Despite all the comforts and the camaraderie of the hostel, living here has been hard. I miss Mai and Sania. I feel guilty when I eat, when I sleep, even when I watch a movie with my friends. How will I possibly manage the homesickness and the guilt all the way in America?

The moon comes out from behind the clouds, filtering through the leaves. I hear a squirrel scamper, maybe a rat. The shadows are longer.

Suddenly, a voice hisses in the dark. "What have you got there?"

I jump up at the sudden interruption. My eyes adjust to the gloom. Manish.

Nausea stirs in my stomach and the tree seems to spin for a moment. "Why are you still here?" I say with a scowl.

"What? You scared?" he sneers.

Unexpectedly, I realize that I'm not. I'm just outside the hostel. I have friends. I've just won a gold medal. I've passed my exams. And now I'm going to America. Manish no longer has the power to make me afraid. "No," I say. "But you can't be here. It's a girls' hostel."

"Don't get so excited, I was on my way out," he says. Sweat has broken out on his upper lip.

"Why are you so sour? Did you fail your exams?" I shoot at him.

He scoffs. "As if our school fails anyone ever. Even scum like you can pass here."

I feel the anger rise in my throat, but I refuse to let it show. Not today. Instead, I get up to leave, and am about to put the medal in my pocket when he lunges at me, making a grab at it. I snatch it back in time, but he lunges again. As I begin to run toward the hostel, he stretches his leg out and I feel myself flying headlong, hitting the ground with a thud.

I shoot up to my feet, unwounded now that I know how to break a fall.

"What's wrong, Manish?" I yell. "Can't stand that a girl—a Nat, no less—won and you didn't?"

"No," he shouts back, arms crossed across his body, eyes fiery. "You're a loser, and your stupid gold medal doesn't change that."

I laugh. "Winning sort of does change that. But you wouldn't know that now, would you? Because you'll never win in your life!"

He comes at me again, but I easily pin him down with an arm against his throat. All his kung fu is forgotten as he lashes out, punching and hitting the air. I hold him down with my right palm on his forehead at the exact pressure point that makes him lose control. My left knee is on his chest and my left palm pins his wrist down. He can't move.

"You stinking whore! If it wasn't for all the charity you get from everyone, you would have been passed around from man to man by now!" His insults hit me harder than I expect them to.

I retaliate. "What—you mean like your sister?"

As soon the words leave my mouth, I want to take them back. How could I say this about my best friend? About any girl? I let go of my grip.

A shout of rage leaves his throat as he pushes me off. "Actually, she's going to be getting a *real* job doing housework. Not that you would know what a real job is."

I get up as quickly as I can, ground myself on two feet, slightly bent at the knees. I want to punch him so badly, but I know that it's better not to. As I look him in the eyes, I see his anger. But there is something else in his gaze—sadness, grief, betrayal.

I feel the same emotions mirrored in me.

The other girls begin to rush out and we jump away from each other, startled by the noise. Manish runs toward the main gate while I head back into the building, even though all I want to do is go home—to my own home, where Mai is. But I know that what I really want is to get away from is my own shame for what I've said. And for that, I know, there will be no escape.

CHAPTER NINETEEN

In what feels like a blink of an eye, it's the last day of school before summer break. This morning, I snuggle down under my blanket just a little bit longer—my head nestled into my pillow, my gold medal under it. I let myself dream of Connie and America. At school, teachers set our final readings for the summer. I sit between Sadaf and Razia at lunch, who are still so delighted about my medal they can hardly stop crowing. The bullying boys avoid my eyes. As for Manish, I'm too ashamed to look at him. When the final bell rings, schoolbags fly through the air, the sound of car horns blare as parents wait for children, shrieks of laughter echo across the courtyard, and goodbyes are passed between kids.

I search for some peace from the choir of celebration in the quiet of the library, where, at last, there is an email from Connie in response to my flurry of good news.

Dear Heera,

Congraaaaaats!! A gold medal!!!! That's HUGE. I'm so psyched for you.

I have some pretty cool news for you as well. I'll be at the same boot camp! My teacher is a friend of your kung fu teacher. I guess that's how our pen pal program was set up. Anyway, she told me that we both got in. Isn't that amazing?! We're finally going to meet! And I CAN'T WAIT to see you perform.

If you're interested in reading any American books before your trip, my two favorites are *Little Women* and *To Kill a Mockingbird*. That might give you some clues into American life, maybe a little in the past, though, but a lot of things are still the same.

Hugs,

Connie

PS What does it feel like to be a champ?

Something between excitement and relief rushes over me. I will have a friend in New York by my side. Instinctively, I look to Rini Di as she studies something intently behind her own computer screen. Whether she notices my eyes on her or can hear my heart thumping, she looks up and catches my gaze.

"Rini Di," I say, pointing to the letter on my screen as if she can read it. "It's not a coincidence that Connie and I are both going for this boot camp, is it?"

Rini Di stifles a laugh. "There are no coincidences," she says. "But it worked out nicely, did it not? When we paired you as pen pals, we only knew you were both good enough to win the nomination. But we had no control over the rest. We might have known that you were both standouts, but there was no guarantee you'd both get through."

I nod thoughtfully, relieved to hear it. I realize then that I could easily spend the rest of the holiday before New York relaxing at the hostel. But I can't shake the feeling that I shouldn't be here.

"I think I'd like to spend some time at home," I say before I can think better of it. "If that's all right."

Rini Di pushes her glasses up to the bridge of her nose, a look of concern on her face. "Is everything okay?"

"Everything's fine. I just feel like I need to be home. To help Mai. It's getting warmer and Sania is getting bigger. It's a lot for Mai to carry her around all day." I wonder then how much Sania might grow in the four weeks that I'm away in America.

Rini Di pushes her chair back. "It's wonderful how much you think of others, but I'm still concerned about Ravi Lala. He's the reason why we brought you here in the first place. If he tried to take you once, what's to stop him from trying it again?"

I'm ready for this question. "With no school to get to, I won't be doing much except staying at home. I'll go to the railway platform with Mai, Mira Di, or Salman. And the fair is gone now anyway. And all the dance parties have gone with it. There's no one for Ravi Lala to sell me to. I'll be more careful this time. No wandering around alone."

Rini Di looks like she's considering this. "You'll also need to come to the kwoon to start training for the competition, starting this weekend. So Salman would need to walk you to and from."

She's right. I'm going to need as much practice as I can get. The competition in New York is going to be a Shaolin weapon demonstration, alongside the floor routine. My weapon is the only one that is readily available—the bo staff. But I can use anything like it to practice. Even a piece of bamboo of approximately the same dimensions.

"I'll practice every day. And come back a few days before New York," I say.

"So basically, the entire holiday?"

I realize she's right. "Yes, is that okay?"

"Of course it is, Heera. I might not be completely comfortable with it, but you should go if that's what you want. Your mother is lucky to have such a considerate child."

"And there's one more thing." I pull the envelope I've been guarding out of my pocket and hand it to her. "The rest of the money we owe you. Salman saved it up. He gave it to me last time I went home."

Rini Di takes it, a smile on her face "What would you like me to do with this?"

"Keep it," I say. "Then if the school gives us the money, you can return this to us."

She nods. "I will hold on to it for you."

"Thank you. Now Salman can tell Baba this is paid off, and he won't be under so much pressure. Mai might even be able to take it a little easier."

Rini Di's eyes glisten with what look like unshed tears. "You kids sometimes take my breath away. You know I will not touch the money and I don't like taking it from you."

"You're not taking it from us. Just keeping it safe," I say.

Before I start packing my things, I know there's one more email I need to send.

Dear Connie,

I can't believe this is all happening. Rini Di told me that the judges happened to choose both of us. She also said there are no coincidences. There's a lot about fate that I don't believe in, but I think this might qualify.

I did want to ask you something else. I've been thinking a lot about Azra. What did her mother believe she would be doing for work? Is there a way you could ask her?

And thank you so much for the book recommendations. I need all the help I can get.

XOXO
Heera

To my surprise, Connie writes back immediately:

I did ask her that, actually. They told her she'd be doing housework, working at a palace as nice as the Taj Mahal.

—C

Home is the same, but somehow it's not. Baba treats me with new respect. He's stopped taunting Salman. He's stopped going to the liquor shop with Mai's money. He's even started going to the railway station to see if he can get some odd jobs loading or cleaning. Even though he wears his struggle with alcohol on his skin, slowly it begins to feel like the old times before we came to Girls Bazaar.

Mai says he's been much quieter since the day at the stadium. "I think he has hope again, Heera," she says softly, her eyes wet.

Salman takes it even further. "I think his pride in you has made him look for his own self-respect," he says in one of the rare moments that I see him between the shop, his friends, football, and studying. He's been far too busy to have our usual heart-to-hearts.

Day after day, Mai leaves Sania with me while she works the highway site and seems a little less exhausted when she comes home at the end of the day. Baba grumbles about me being idle, because he seems to have no idea how much work it is to have a two-year-old hanging off you all day. But it's worth it for Mai. I train in the mornings at the kwoon three times a week, and practice at home with a slender piece of bamboo as a bo staff. Our house is far too small to be swinging it around and I keep hitting myself with it. Each night, I read the copy of *Little Women* that Zehra lent me. Marmee seems so much like Mai. Jo is tall, thin, reckless, and clumsy like me. But as the time between now and New York narrows, I wonder what will happen when I'm no longer there to watch Sania. Mai is trying to find other work apart from the highway construction that will pay money and not some paltry amount of grain, but so far, she's had no success.

Finally, one morning, Mira Di shows up outside our door after she wakes up. She'd been fighting a fever for a week before Jamila Bua and I convinced her to go to the local clinic. After moving to the hostel, it feels like I've hardly spent any time with Mira Di, since I've only gone back on the weekends when she's the busiest. It's not until I see her again that I realize just how much I've missed her.

She takes one of the pills that the doctors prescribed her in addition to rest. "Let's see how long my brother listens to me and holds off on clients," she tells me with a tired smile, exhausted and overworked.

"Why wouldn't he?" I declare forcefully. "Shaukat might be a pimp, but he's still your brother."

"The moneymaker is never allowed to take a break," Mira Di says with a shuddering sigh. She begins to walk with her hand on my shoulder and I realize that she needs to take the weight off her legs.

"Can you even work when you are so sick?" I ask with alarm as I wrap an arm around her waist to give her more support until we reach the door.

"It hardly makes a difference really," she says with resignation.

I roll out a mat for her and she lies down when we get inside. Slowly, she sips her water.

I kneel beside her. "Mira Di, if you want to leave the line, maybe Rini Di can help you."

Her eyes are closed. "How would she?" she mumbles.

"Maybe she could give you a job?"

"Yes, she could, but would my father and brother let me go? It would be one thing if Rini Di could give me work that would earn as much money as this job, but they wouldn't settle for less. They wouldn't *survive* with less," she says with a weak smile. "They have to support their habits plus the weekly payoff to Ravi Lala."

I hate feeling so helpless. A cold block of fear settles in my chest, slowly replaced by anger and something else. A will to resist. "Is there no other way?"

"No way that wouldn't send me straight to hell."

I remember what Rini Di had said she could do.

"There are other ways." I try to remember everything just as Rini Di told me. "You can start a small business. Rini Di can get you a loan. And a low-cost house from the government on some land allocated for poor single women. Chacha's land is mortgaged to Ravi Lala anyway."

"What business, Heera? I didn't even finish school," Mira Di says tiredly, as if I'm wasting her time.

I put her head on my lap and massage her temples, hoping to relieve some of the pain. "You could be a seamstress. You are so gifted, Mira Di. With the loan you can buy a sewing machine and some supplies," I say, struggling to stay calm.

She gives me a vague, noncommittal smile. "They will never let me leave."

"How could they stop you?"

She opens her eyes slowly. "What do you think? They will let me walk out of here just like that? They will bring me back even if they have to drag me every step of the way. And then what happens if Rini Di brings in the police to rescue me? They will arrest Shaukat again. I couldn't live with that."

I dig my fingers into my palms and suppress a shudder. As hard as Mira Di has fought to help both Salman and me, somehow, she can't seem to find it in her to do it for herself.

One morning, on the playground after practice, Sadaf surprises me with a visit. Right away, I can see in her eyes that she has news. But the look on her face leads me to believe that it's not good. We take Sania for a walk away from Girls Bazaar, mindful of the fact that Sadaf's parents don't want her to go there, and that Ravi Lala is still a threat.

"I have something to tell you," she says in a hushed tone as we walk into the children's park near the hospital. I put Sania down to play with a wooden puzzle on the grass while we sit on the swings, our legs dangling toward the ground.

"What is it?" I ask, a little abruptly.

Sadaf swivels her head from side to side, but we're alone. "Rosy hasn't left for Mumbai after all," she says rapidly. "She's still here!" she nearly yells before clasping her hand over her mouth.

My mouth falls open. I nearly fall off the swing. "Where is she!" I gasp.

"She's at home," Sadaf breathes out. "Yesterday, I swear I saw her face in the window when I was going to the market with my mother."

"But they said she had gone!" I exclaim. My cheeks flush with excitement. My friend is still at home. That means she's still safe. "Did you say anything to her? Are you *sure* it was her?"

"Of course I'm sure!" Sadaf says expressively, a little offended. "But I didn't speak to her. She moved away as soon as she saw me."

"This doesn't feel right," I say, relapsing into silence. I think of Azra. How they had taken her from Nepal to Mumbai and then all the way to America. "Now that Rosy has had her Bisi Bele, she should be on her way."

"You want to speak to Rini Di again?" Sadaf asks in a panic.

I think for a moment and shake my head. "Rosy's family will just lie to Rini Di again."

"Well, we could ask Manish," Sadaf says through a cringe.

"Yeah, right."

"Heera, he might be horrible, but he's her brother. Don't you think he'll want to help her?" Sadaf reasons.

"Like every other girl in Girls Bazaar is helped by her brother?" I say, thinking of Shaukat and Mira Di. I pretend to think, but I've already decided on what I need to do. "What if we were to speak to her directly, get the truth, and then go to Rini Di? You saw her through the window, didn't you? Is she ever alone?"

"Her father does go out in the morning. I think Manish does too. I've seen others in the house, though. Are you sure you want to risk it?"

How can I explain to her how it feels to be the girl in school while Rosy is the girl locked up? That the words that I said to Manish during our fight after I won the gold medal haunt me every night? That even though I hate Manish, I can't stand that he believes his sister will only be doing housework. I can't take back the words, but I can do everything in my power to stop it from happening. That is my only redemption. My friend is here, and I won't let her slip through my fingers again.

CHAPTER TWENTY

The next day, I knock on Sadaf's door and realize it's the first time that I've knocked on any friend's door. She opens it and ushers me in. I feel awkward—I don't know her parents, and I don't know if they'd consider me welcome. Nats like me most often are not, according to my father.

"I've been watching, and everyone is gone, even the mother," she says in a whisper, gesturing in the direction of Rosy's house.

I look around.

"No one's home," she assures me.

We head down the street toward Rosy's house, down a lane lined with small homes, some bigger than others. It's a massive step up from Girls Bazaar—no more benches outside homes with back rooms here, no illicit booze being sold.

"There it is," Sadaf says, pointing to the small green house that I haven't seen in what feels like years. Somehow, it looks entirely different. The little window beside the front door is clouded with a frosted glass windowpane, protected by pink-painted iron bars. I notice that the rosebush is completely neglected.

"That's where I saw her," Sadaf says.

"What should we do?" I ask.

Sadaf opens her palm—revealing a bunch of small pebbles. Gently, she tosses one at the glass. Nothing. Then another. And another.

At last, a form appears on the other side. We can't see who it is, but we certainly have an idea. Sadaf and I hold our breath. The person inside hesitates for a moment.

Sadaf waves tentatively.

"I don't think she can see you," I hiss.

And then the window opens. Rosy's eyes are wide with fright.

"You're still here!" Sadaf exclaims in a whisper, stepping closer.

"What are you doing here?" Rosy breathes out, darting worried looks up and down the road.

"We wanted to know how you were!" I say.

"I'm okay," Rosy says, so soft I can hardly hear her. "But if someone sees you here, I'll be beaten black and blue!"

"Do you know if you're going to Mumbai?" asks Sadaf. "Or *when* you're going to Mumbai?"

Rosy hesitates.

I lean in closer. "Do you even know if that's where you're going?"

"I'm not sure," Rosy confesses. "I just know that I'll be doing housework. For a rich family with a big home." Even she doesn't look like she believes it.

"Then why did you have a Bisi Bele?" I ask.

Rosy looks into my eyes as if she is wondering who I am. It feels like we were never friends, that we don't know each other at all.

"I know someone who can help you," I say.

And then her eyes widen with horror. She closes the window with a bang. I spin around. Standing in front of me are Ravi Lala and Manish's father, Suraj Sharma. I turn to Sadaf but she has somehow managed to bolt away.

"What are you doing here?" Ravi Lala snarls.

"Nothing," I say, voice shaky. "I was just going to the market."

Suraj Sharma blocks my way. "Who are you?" he asks, looking at me, eyes narrowed. And at that moment, I recognize something that I've never thought to notice before. A Krishna tattoo on the back of his hand.

"Heera, isn't it?" Ravi Lala answers him.

Suraj Sharma's lips curl into a cruel smile. "Mira's cousin Heera? The one who fights with everyone?"

In a flash, I see Sadaf hiding in the bushes. I turn to run, but Suraj Sharma grabs my dress from behind. I scream but there is no one around to bat an eye before a hand muffles my mouth. A bolt of searing pain cuts through the back of my head. And everything goes black.

I wake up in a small room with dirty brick walls and a broken plank of wood on four legs for a bed. It's dark except for the scraps of daylight that creep through the cracks in the wooden window and door. I stand up and the world reels. My hand goes to the back of my head and I feel a lump there, but it doesn't seem to be bleeding.

Tentatively, I steady myself and take a step toward the door. I push it as hard as I can. It rattles but it doesn't give way, and I can see a chain on the other side. I'm locked in.

Through the crack, I can only see a small sliver of a wall. I could be anywhere. I feel the panic rise but don't give in to it. I slide down to the floor and try to slow my breathing.

How long have I been here? If it's still daylight, maybe a few hours. I close my eyes and try to pay attention to what I can hear. Soon, the azaan starts, and I realize it's evening, around 5:00 p.m., and the prayer is the same one I hear every day from my own home. I'm not that far away after all.

I look around the room again now that my eyes have adjusted to the darkness. There's a naked light bulb in a corner, so there must be a switch somewhere. I grope around and finally find it behind the bed. The light bulb goes on. And suddenly I know where I am, or at least the sort of place—I am in a brothel. Even if someone could hear me scream, they wouldn't care.

It's only then that I begin to feel the terror. I empty my mind of all fear.

I am like water, I tell myself over and over again. *I am like water.*

It's dark when I hear the chain rattle outside.

I freeze as the door swings open. Standing there is Ravi Lala.

I'm cowering in the corner when he stretches his hand out toward me once again.

"Get up," he says.

I don't move a muscle.

"Get up," he repeats more harshly.

I put my hand in his and do as I am told. I consider trying to fight, but I am trembling with fear and know I won't get very far. Ravi Lala is smart and there is nowhere to run.

"There is nothing to be afraid of, Heera," he says. "We'll take care of you. Good care of you."

"I want to go home."

"I'm afraid that won't be possible."

I will not show this man my fear, I tell myself. "Why?"

"Because you are meant for bigger things," he says, and from the look on his face, behind his henna-dyed beard, he actually believes it.

A man walks in bearing what looks to be a bowl of khichdi and a glass of water.

"Eat," Ravi Lala says. "In thirty minutes, we'll send someone to take you to the bathroom."

"I need to go now."

Ravi Lala looks at the other man, and then nods. "Take her."

The bathroom is a few doors down. I try to get a look at my surroundings, and it seems as though I was right. I couldn't be more than five hundred meters from my home. But I've never felt farther away.

I hear voices now—the guard and another man that I don't recognize as Ravi Lala.

"Door is open? Where is she?" asks the new voice.

"Bathroom."

"When will Raja be here?"

"In an hour."

"He'll take her today?"

"Not till we get the other one."

"Suraj's girl? Mumbai again?"

"Taj Mahal!"

My entire body flinches. The sound of their laughter echoes through the hall before Ravi Lala shouts at them all to shut up. My guard takes me back to the room and I am locked in again. Alone, I wonder what to do. On the one hand, I'm famished. On the other hand, I'm sure the food has been drugged. Or is it the water? I don't see that I have a choice. The drugs might make me sleep and I'd rather sleep than be beaten. But if I don't eat it, I might have a chance to fight. Time is running out.

The chain outside rattles again. There's a sound of metal on metal—the key turning in the padlock. And then that creaky hinge again.

I take my stance. The cat stance. I bend my back leg to put my weight on it and let my front toe dangle down, my front knee bent and ready to kick. I form a fist and draw one arm close to my side, the other posed toward the front.

I can see the silhouette of a man against the dim light outside. As the door opens, I swing a kick and strike his groin. He doubles over in pain as he falls.

I punch hard into his eye, which is now at the level of my fist. One hand automatically reaches out to protect the other eye as he yelps in pain, the other hand between his legs. I jam an elbow into his back and jump over him out the door. He lets out a surprised yelp. .

I slither into the small space behind him, even before he has time to straighten, and push him down again with a back kick. He lets out another sharp cry. I'm faster and nimbler than he can ever hope to be. I make up in speed and balance what I lack in size and strength. I jam the door shut on him quickly, bolting it from the outside. My body is covered in sweat. It's all just a few seconds, less than a minute, but it feels like a lifetime. I realize I'm panting hard and try with all my might to quiet my breathing.

I can hear him curse and kick the door, but I don't look back. The door rattles. I know he's about to start shouting soon. There's no one in the courtyard, so I run as fast as I can toward the boundary. But I can hear banging against the door, shouts for help. I hoist myself up the wall, but before I can clear it to the other side, I'm pulled back, down, down into the darkness. I kick and claw but now the tears start because I know there will be no more chance for escape.

Ravi Lala hits me across the face, and I fly to the ground. The guard takes a step toward me, but Ravi Lala puts out his hand to stop him.

"Enough, you fool. You'll only reduce her value."

I awaken again, this time to footsteps and loud voices outside. I curl up on the plank of a bed, waiting for the door to burst open. They'll take me away now, and I'll never see my family again.

But when it does open, it's a police officer, and behind her, Rini Di. And Salman.

They rush in, and for a moment I wonder if I'm dreaming. Salman scoops me up and rushes me out of the complex and over to a van. Rini Di stays with me while Salman goes back in again.

"What's happening?" I ask. I take deep breaths of air through the open window.

"Shh," whispers Rini Di. "Don't worry about a thing."

Salman returns at last, supporting the form of a man. Badly hurt, limping. It isn't until they get close that I can see who it is.

"Baba!" I shout, struggling to get out of the van to run to him, but Rini Di holds me back. My father whimpers as Salman lifts him onto the bench. The door is closed behind them. "Where are we going?" I ask.

"To the hospital first, and then to the police station."

At the hospital, Baba and I are examined by doctors. All I know is that Baba has been badly beaten. If not for the adrenaline, I would have no energy at all. They take me to a separate room with Rini Di.

"Heera, did they hurt you?" asks Rini Di.

"They hit me."

"Did they try to assault you, sexually?"

I shake my head.

"Are you sure?"

"Yes, Rini Di."

They complete their physical exam, and Rini Di takes pictures of my injuries. Baba's too. What happens next is a blur. I go with Baba and Salman to the police station. There is an officer. He shouts an awful lot, though I think that's just how he speaks all the time. Rini Di tells me which questions to answer and responds herself to others.

Through the course of it, though, I get an idea of what happened last evening after they grabbed me. Sadaf had run off in search of Salman, and not finding him at home, tracked down my father at one of his usual dens.

After he heard what had happened, he went charging off, but none of his friends were brave enough to take on Ravi Lala, so he was left to face the goons all by himself. He never had a chance. When he arrived at Ravi Lala's house, Gainul beat him to a pulp, and then they locked him up. He had been three doors down from me the whole time.

Thankfully, Sadaf found Salman eventually. She told him everything, and my brother called Rini Di. By the time she rounded up the police and convinced them to come and conduct the rescue, several hours had elapsed.

"Will they arrest Ravi Lala?" is all I ask her.

"I don't know, Heera, but we have done all we can for now," she replies.

CHAPTER TWENTY-ONE

I know I'll have to go back to the hostel, but first I want Mai. For at least a day. Rini Di isn't happy about it, but I think she sees the desperation in my eyes and reluctantly takes me home. But the relief of having my mother by my side for a few hours disappears when I see how distraught she is. It's clear that she hasn't slept. Her eyes are swollen with tears. And that's more than I can take.

I crumple in a heap at her feet as she runs a gentle hand over my hair. Finally, Salman brings me a glass of water and a towel to clean myself up.

"What did you think was going to happen when you went to Suraj Sharma's house?" Salman says once I've stopped whimpering.

"I wanted to see if Rosy was home, that's it." But the fight has gone out of me.

"Why?" asks Mai.

"To see if I could help her get away."

Mai wipes away my tears, and then her own.

"How could—" Salman voices his frustration.

"Hush," Mai says to Salman, pulling my head onto her lap. Salman covers me with a blanket and, eventually, I manage to fall asleep.

The next morning, Baba comes home after spending a night in the hospital, and the guilt washes over me in waves—one of his ribs is cracked and his lip is split. His face is covered with dark bruises, a line of stitches running down his cheek. He walks with even more difficulty than usual.

He sits down on a chair Salman has borrowed from somewhere. I stand next to him while his eyes focus on the ground. And then he reaches out, takes hold of my hand, and lets out a strangled sob. It's the first time I've heard Baba cry.

I don't know what hurts more, my ribs or his sadness. "I'm sorry, Baba," I say.

"You have nothing to be sorry for. I should be sorry. They had three girls there who they were going to send away, and they thought they'd add you to the list." His body is stiff with anger at himself.

I feel sorry for the man in front of me, but it's not the Baba I know—the man who growled when he spoke, took Mai's money to gamble. The one who was so ready to sell me just a short time ago. A rush of anger comes over me as I remember it all.

"You were going to sell me yourself," I say. "What changed?"

He closes his eyes and seems to deflate. "There was a time when I believed that being a part of Ravi Lala's gang was the safest thing for all of us. I thought if I sold one daughter, I could keep the three other children safe. And I drank to stop myself from caring."

Somehow, his confession only makes the pain worse. "Why me, Baba? Why were you prepared to sacrifice me for the rest of the family?" I ask, unable to look him in the eye. "Why am I the least loved?" I didn't know how much I actually believed the words until they exited my mouth.

Baba grips his hands on his lap. "That's all I knew, Heera. That's what I saw around me, with my own sisters, with Mira Di, with every hut down the whole lane. You are not the least loved. I was harshest with you because I thought you had to be the one to go." Baba's voice is choked, nearly cracking. Then he rubs a hand across his face and adds so softly that I almost don't hear him, "But you've made me see things differently. I know you've been saying it all along, but I didn't really understand until I saw you that day at the stadium. You did us proud. You are such a fierce little thing, Heera. You made it impossible for me not to see you." He looks at me then, his eyes glassy.

His words cut into the icy wall of anger I've made around my heart, and I let a tear escape down my cheek. Next to me, Mai and Salman are also wiping their eyes.

Then Baba frowns, shaking his head slowly. "If you hadn't been in front of Manish's house, they would have come for you here once again. There is no escaping them. You must return to the hostel tonight." He looks tired all of a sudden.

I can still see Rosy's face in the window, tired and frightened. He's right: If they're willing to trade Rosy, a police officer's daughter, how will I escape them? Especially now that I've embarrassed them once again. And yet here I am. Safe. For now.

After Salman walks me to the hostel, I go straight to my room and climb into bed. But every time I close my eyes, I can see Ravi Lala's angry face, and my father's beaten one. Is what Baba said really true? Will it ever be safe at home again?

The answer to that seems to be no, as I discover the next morning when Rini Di calls me to her office after breakfast. To my surprise, Mai is there when I enter. I sit down next to her. After the morning spent recounting my misadventures to all the girls, I am worn out and her presence calms me.

"Heera, I asked your mother to come as there are a few things we need to discuss," Rini Di says. I look from her to Mai, and it seems that they've already been talking for a while. "The police have arrested Gainul," Rini Di continues, "but they have not yet arrested Ravi Lala."

A wave of fear shoots through me. "How can that be? After what he did to me? To my father?"

"We're trying to push the police but, as you know, he's very powerful in this town."

Somehow, I knew this would be the result. "What about the other girls? What about Rosy?"

Rini Di adjusts her glasses. "The three other girls have been rescued. But Rosy is at home, and there's no way to prove that she's in danger."

I look back and forth at my mother and Rini Di, looking for some sort of explanation. "How could that possibly be? Her mother won't speak up?"

Rini Di and Mai share a look. "I'm afraid not," Rini Di says.

"So it was all for nothing," I cry out.

"Didn't you hear me? You helped save three girls from being sold. That is amazing, Heera! And there's more good news," Rini Di says with a smile at Mai. "The school has finally agreed to transfer the total money you're owed for the years of your schooling."

Mai's eyes widen.

Rini Di hands me a piece of paper. It has my name on it, and what seems to me to be a giant sum of money. "That's a check, Heera. We'll need to open you a bank account so you can deposit this."

I quickly do the math. "But this is much more than we should be getting," I say.

Rini Di shoots me a grin. "Quick calculation there. I must confess that this past year, the school hadn't started the payments, so I have been pitching in."

"We are going to give that back, along with the loan," Mai says quickly as my mouth hangs open. "You've already done so much for our family, giving Heera a place here, getting our voter cards and ration cards made."

Rini Di shoots me a look, and I shake my head, hoping she understands that I don't want her to say anything about the money Salman and I have already paid her for the loan. "Fine, I will accept it, but I want to see you use the rest of the money well, Heera."

Once again, I'm somehow safe while Rosy is behind bars. I look at the number again. "Wouldn't this be enough to move to a proper house? Farther away from Ravi Lala?"

"What is the need?" asks Mai. "We have a house now."

"None of us are safe here now," I say. "Think of Sania."

Rini Di nods. "There are one-room homes you can rent. You'll have to pay up front for a number of years, but you can manage that with less than what you now have as a deposit."

And then it hits me. "Now Salman can go to boarding school!"

I can tell by Mai's face that she is wondering if Baba will agree to this scheme—moving out, Salman going away. I wonder the same thing.

When we reach home, for the first time since I can remember, Baba is playing with Sania. His hands are trembling and I know it's because he hasn't had anything to drink in some days. I've seen it happen to enough drunks around Girls Bazaar to know the signs.

As Mai recounts what Rini Di has shared, Baba looks back and forth between the two of us, bewildered. A tired Salman tries to process it all as well after a long shift.

"The money will be transferred to a bank account in my name," I say quickly. And then I tell him about the plan to move out. "Even after paying for the deposit, we'll have enough from the monthly payments and what Mai makes to run the house for a while. If we can reduce our expenses just a little."

Baba frowns at first, but then begins to nod, processing it all.

I soldier on. "If we move to the other side of the tracks, there's an anganwadi center that Rini Di says Mai can drop Sania to when she goes to work. Sania will get lunch there. She might even learn some things that will help her in school."

"Slow down. For free?" he asks, brow raised. "How long will they keep her there?"

"Yes, for free," explains Mai. "They'll keep her until we can pick her up in the afternoon. Rini Di says it's very small and crowded, but it's better than Sania hanging out at the highway every day."

"And what will you do?" Baba asks me.

"I will go back to the hostel until school starts again," I declare.

Baba raises his eyebrows, and then grimaces when the stitches bite back. "What about the competition in the US?"

"Maybe next time," I say, looking at my feet.

"What?" Salman chirps. "Why wouldn't you go this year? How do you even know you'll get the chance next year?"

"I want to stay here," I say, observing the bags under Salman's eyes. "There's far too much to do between finding a new house and getting settled there."

"You don't seem to understand that even on the other side of the tracks, we won't be out of the grasp of Ravi Lala," Baba says as he struggles to get to his feet. "Yes, we will be better off the farther from here we go, but they can come for you there as well. If there is any way to get away from all of this and away from the fair for good, it's this competition."

"How will it make a difference?"

"Who knows," Mai interjects. "You are good at this, just like your grandfather and uncles were."

"But what about finding a place to move into?"

"We can handle it without you," says Salman with a roll of his eyes.

I rest a hand on my hip and roll my eyes right back at him. "But you won't be here either."

"How's that?" Salman says.

"Because I'm only going to the competition if you get to go to boarding school."

I see Salman's jaw clench. Mai stiffens and Baba instinctively rolls his head back in annoyance, so I launch into the argument I've been putting together the whole way home. I turn to Baba. "You know what will really make a difference to this family? Sending Salman away to study. With this money, you don't need what he's bringing in to put food on our plates every night. It will mean one less mouth to feed as well. It'll just be the three of you, and even Sania will be getting lunch at the daycare. And next year, she'll be going off to school herself."

"You've really worked this all out, haven't you?" Baba says, his arms crossed. I can't tell if he's angry or impressed. But our family would not be our family if someone didn't put a spoke in the wheels.

"Only one problem," Salman says. "I'm not going anywhere. I'm going to stay here and take care of you both."

If there's one thing you can predict about Baba, it's that if you say one thing, he'll say the opposite. "Like hell you will," he says. "Heera, tell Mira Di right now to speak to the school. If they'll have him, Salman will leave right away."

The next few days are filled with things I have never imagined doing, including passport applications and shopping. It appears that my current collection of two tattered dresses isn't appropriate for this trip. I have one gi already, with two more being tailored for me, and I think that should do it, but Rini Di seems to have other ideas. Some clothes come from the home's donation bin—a pair of track pants, a couple of T-shirts. But much of it Rini Di deems inappropriate.

I've never been shopping—not like this. Buying clothes has always been a once-a-year affair for us, if that. I wear the same dress until it's threadbare, and then we buy another. Same for everyone in the family. But I quickly discover that this is not what Rini Di has in mind.

We go to one store, and then another, and another. "There will be all sorts of events for you to attend—you're there for a month," she says. "Having the right kind of clothes for the right occasions will make you feel more at ease."

But "at ease" is far from how I feel. I try on shirts and pants and dresses, one after the other. I put on something I'm told is a formal outfit, then a beautiful blue salwar kameez, T-shirts and track pants, a couple of dresses, and even a pair of jeans—which I'm super excited about until I try them on and realize it feels like someone has bound my legs together. Rini Di laughs when I complain and suggests I try on a different style, something that is less "skinny," which is only marginally better. She buys them for me anyway and tells me if I don't like them, we can return them to the store.

Finally, it's down to the last day. The following morning, I am due to leave for the Bagdogra Airport, close to the town of Siliguri, from where we will board a flight to New Delhi and then New York. So that day, I go home to say my goodbyes.

I've never seen Mai and Baba so emotional.

"I'll only be gone a month," I say, playing with Sania's little pigtails.

"Do you realize what a big deal this is for our family? None of us have ever even imagined going abroad," Baba says.

With his stitches out, he looks better than the last time I saw him, even though his ribs are still healing. Salman told me that he hasn't had a drink since he returned from the hospital. He hasn't even played cards. "It's clearly been rough on him, but he seems determined. He mopes a bit, goes and sits by himself, but he doesn't give in. Maybe you inherited your determination from him."

We both smiled at that.

"Thanks, Baba," I whisper. And since I can't remember the last time I hugged my father, I grab my baby sister and hold on tight. She paws at my cheek. "I'll miss you, Sania," I say.

"Heera go. Heera go," she says.

"Heera come back soon," I tell her.

I give Mai all the details of my journey again, for the tenth time. I tell her that I have Mira Di's phone, and that she can call from Jamila Bua's shop if there's an emergency. I tell her that Salman has my email address, and he can write to me from the hostel home. I will be sending emails as well.

When Salman walks me back to the hostel, I ask him if he's done any shopping of his own yet, now that we've found out that the boarding school in Siliguri still has a seat open for him in the new school year.

He shakes his head. "There's still time for that."

"You'll be leaving for school before you know it. Just a few weeks after I return," I say. Luckily, Rini Di had returned his earnings and my prize money, and I forced him to promise that he'd take all of it to buy the things he'd need for school. "The right clothes will help you fit in," I told him.

"What rubbish," he replied. "I'll be using most of it for books."

"Have you started looking for the house?" I ask now.

"Yes, I've seen one or two. It won't be much bigger than what we have now, but it will have brick walls and a bathroom."

I slow down our pace just before we reach the referral hospital. "There's somewhere I need to go before we get to the hostel," I say. Rather, there's one more person I need to see before I leave. It's what I want to do least of all, which is probably why I leave it for the last possible minute.

"Where?" Salman raises his brow, immediately suspicious.

When I explain it to him, he scolds me the entire way, but I know he'll stay by my side to make sure I don't do anything stupid on my own. We reach the pond and I pace nervously as we wait. Suddenly, I don't know why I'm here. It feels like a pure waste of time. And if I'm not back at the hostel by sunset, there will be explanations to give, maybe even a search party.

Just then, they arrive: Sadaf, trailed by a reluctant Manish.

He stands before me and Salman, resentment on every inch of his face.

"You came," I say, no idea how to bridge the gap between us.

Manish grunts. The only reason he's here is because Sadaf went to fetch him with the message that we had information about his sister. It was a long shot, but it worked.

"There was no need to drag me all the way out here, was there?" Manish says.

"Well, I couldn't exactly show up at your doorstep again, could I?" I snap. And then I replay where the guards said they're taking Rosy. *Taj Mahal.* The same thing the traffickers told Azra's mother. I remember I need his help, so I soften my tone. "Has Rosy left?"

He offers us a nod.

"Do you know where she is?"

"No," Manish barks. "I thought you did."

I don't believe him. "If you can tell us anything at all, we can get help for her."

"How would you do that?"

"Rini Di can help."

He sneers. "No, she can't."

"Why not? She helped me, didn't she?"

Manish traces a pattern in the dirt with his toe. "My sister has gone far away."

"I know," I say. "Mumbai. But Rini Di—"

"Not Mumbai, you fool. She's—" He stops abruptly. We wait for him to continue, but nothing is forthcoming.

"What, Manish, you can tell us," says Sadaf gently.

"What good will it do! She has been taken abroad! That's all I know," Manish yells. Salman takes an instinctive step closer to me.

"Where? To the Taj Mahal, right?" I ask. "That's what I overheard the guards say. I assume it's a code word for something."

Manish crinkles his brow. "What do you think it's a code word for?" he says, and I realize that he knows the answer.

"The US?" I can't believe it. But then I picture the Krishna tattoo on the back of Manish's father's hand. I turn to Sadaf. "What if she's following the same route as Azra?"

Manish narrows his eyes. "How do you know Azra?"

"What do you mean? How do *you* know Azra?"

Manish's shoulders seem to relax just a bit. "I also know someone named Azra. That's all. I met her over a year ago. She came from Nepal and stayed at our house."

"And now she's in the US. In New York." If it's the same Azra, I can hardly believe it. But then I think of what Rini Di says: There are no coincidences.

"I don't know about that!" Manish breathes out in frustration. "Do you think my father tells me anything? He said she was a friend of the family on her way to New York. She stayed for a while and then they took her away again."

"Do you know if Rosy is going to the same place that Azra went?"

"I don't know. Maybe. Ravi Lala said he had big plans for my sister. That she was too beautiful to be wasted on small things."

Sadaf and I look at each other. I realize that Manish never truly believed Rosy would just be doing housework.

"What happened, Manish?" asks Sadaf. "Between Ravi Lala and your father?"

"What difference is it to you?"

"Rosy was my friend. *Is* my friend." I stare into his eyes, begging him to remember.

Manish kicks the ground. "He didn't give my dad a choice. There were some photographs he had of my father with very young girls. He said he would send them to my father's bosses if my father didn't join the gang. And that was it. About a year ago Ravi Lala told him he wanted Rosy. My father tried to protect her by sending her to Nepal, but Ravi Lala never lets a girl go once he sets his eyes on her. He made my father bring her back."

"I'm so sorry, Manish," I mumble.

He laughs a cold hard laugh. "That's rich. For what?"

"For what happened. And for what I said about Rosy."

He grunts again. "Don't know how you think you'll help. Last time you tried, you made it worse."

"Worse?"

"Rosy was at home, wasn't she? And then you two heroes show up and she was gone before I knew it."

"That wasn't our fault!" says Sadaf.

"Yeah, whatever." He leaves, stalking off.

Sadaf turns to me. "What are we going to do?"

"Nothing," Salman says. "You two are doing nothing. Who made you think you can meddle in such things and get away with it?"

Sadaf looks put out by Salman, and the last thing I want to do is worry him right before I leave. All I know is that if I can somehow find out more, if I could talk to Azra and find out what route she took, maybe it would be enough information for Rini Di to find Rosy.

Sadaf shakes her head slowly. "I can't imagine what Rosy is going through. She isn't strong like you, Heera."

"You mean she won't knock people's teeth out?" Salman says.

I take a stab at him with my elbow, but he jumps out of reach.

242

Sadaf smiles. "Kung fu will save you, Heera. Don't doubt it for a second."

That night, I say my goodbyes to all the girls. There's no celebration, but there are a million questions as the girls continue to make me feel special.

Which is why what I do next makes me feel so much worse.

I'm packed and ready, and there is nothing left to do except go to sleep. We're scheduled to leave before dawn the next morning. Instead, I wait until I'm sure my roommates are sleeping and creep downstairs, tiptoeing through the darkness as I walk past the staff quarters.

I go into the library, closing it behind me as softly as possible. I feel my way along the wall to Rini Di's desk. Once I'm sure there's no one around, I switch on the flashlight Sadaf brought me, searching for the set of keys I've seen Rini Di slip into her desk drawer countless times. I go to the filing cabinet and open it up. There's a creak in one of the floorboards in the hallway as I open the drawer to the filing cabinet. I hold my breath. *One, two, three seconds.* But no one's there.

I have no idea what I'm looking for. There's no file labeled ROSY in bold letters. All I know is that if I can find something, anything about where Ravi Lala takes these girls in the US, I could try to find some way to help Rosy.

I flip through as many documents as I can—there are files on all the girls at the hostel home, which I skip through. Then there are files on administrative affairs. I open the bottom drawer and finally seem to be getting warmer. There are police reports, copies of the complaint I signed about Ravi Lala. That is of no use to me; I already know what it says. I flip through a few folders and come to one that mentions Suraj Sharma. But as I go a little further, there are more complaints. My eyes skim over the words in my haste. *Nepal. Coercion. Prostitution.* I take out the phone Mira Di gave me and begin to take photos. I haven't used a phone like this before, and my hands are shaking terribly. But I manage to steady myself as I take photo after photo, unsure about what might be useful, eager to not leave anything behind.

And then I freeze as I hear footsteps in the hallway. I remember the flashlight and quickly switch it off. I'm afraid to move any more than that. If someone were to open the door, they would immediately see me crouched on the floor over the file cabinet. All I can hear is my own breathing. A light goes on and the footsteps are back. I see them pass right in front of the office, moving shadows that flicker through the crack under the door.

And then the light goes out again.

It's a while before I work up the courage to turn the flashlight back on.

I get up, returning the file and the keys to their original locations, and creep back into bed once again, my cell phone tucked safely into my backpack sitting atop the big black suitcase beside my bed.

Water is the softest substance in the world, yet it can penetrate the hardest.

PART III

I exist for the world, and the
world exists for me.
~Bruce Lee

CHAPTER TWENTY-TWO

No one told me that I would float among the clouds when I was on the plane. That the world would look like a magical faraway land that slowly disappeared as I soared higher. That the blue of the sky would pierce my eyes with an intensity that merged blue and white. That I would actually feel closer to the stars.

And then I realize that for some people, such as Rini Di, this is an ordinary experience. For once I'm grateful that I've never done this before so I can feel every second of it now. But that isn't all I feel. My cell phone burns in my pocket while I battle the guilt I have about going through Rini Di's private files. So much so that when she asks if I would like to speak to a group of trafficking survivors in the US, I instantly say yes, even though the idea of speaking to a crowd—of foreigners, whose native language is *English*—terrifies me. But Rini Di promises to coach me.

"Your English is already good because of all the books you read. All the years of classes and your letters to Connie. You just need some practice in public speaking. I want girls like you in the US to know that the problem is global, that the criminal rings are big and work across countries," Rini Di says, and then adds with a smile, "I want them to know about your courage and your heroism."

As I sit next to Rini Di, still digesting the belly full of juicy chicken momos with red-hot chili sauce that we ate at the airport café, it dawns on me that I—a girl who had no knowledge of anything outside Forbesganj—am heading halfway around the world.

Rini Di looks up from her laptop, glancing in my direction. I think she wants to make sure I'm okay. How can I tell her that I'm not okay at all? That I'm so far beyond okay that I don't know how I'll ever come down to earth ever again? I'm so wildly excited that I can hear my heartbeat.

We land in Delhi and I look down on buildings that look like toys but are bigger and taller than anything I've seen before. As expected, Rini Di is right: Bagdogra has left me completely unprepared for the Delhi Airport. It must be as big as our entire town. I've never seen so many well-dressed people, so many shops. But we have no time to linger as we hurry through endless queues, check our bags in again, eat a snack, use the restroom, and swap the tiny plane for the giant one.

This plane is so much more deluxe than our earlier one—the seats go far enough back to become a bed, with a movie screen for each passenger, and a lady called a flight attendant who serves us strange food on a tray. I stare at everything, wide-eyed, trying to concentrate on the English shows through the teeny-tiny TV I have all to myself. I try to memorize the words just in case they come in handy when I land: *Oh my God, cool cool, jackass, awesome.* But my eyes continue to drift out to the sky streaked with rays of the setting sun until it becomes dark.

I'm strangely awake when we land. Rini Di explained that I might feel this way. She's shown me pictures of New York and I've seen enough movies, so I think I know what to expect, but as we work our way through the madness of the airport, the anxiety rises from my chest. Rini Di is in control of it all; I can tell she's done this a million times before as she herds me gently by the elbow. We show our passports, the man at the counter compares the photos to our faces, stamps our booklets. We collect our bags, and we are out.

I'm in America, oceans away from Forbesganj. And now I know that Rosy is too, our paths inexplicably linked once again.

So far, the one thing I can say for certain is that people in this country like to walk fast. Everyone is in a hurry. There are fewer porters here than even the Forbesganj station and most people take care of their own luggage. Even six-year-olds are pulling their own bags. Everything smells different. Everyone looks different. Everything feels different. More skin colors. More languages. A mother anxiously clutches her daughter's hand, telling her not to walk too far away. A young man rushes forward to help an old lady with her bags. A couple shares food. These are so similar to the sights on the Forbesganj railway platform that I smile to myself. People are the same everywhere.

It's still morning, around 10:00 a.m., when we get to the bus station, and Rini Di tells me that we'll reach our destination by 1:00 p.m. I've been on a bus before, but not like this—with seats just as cushioned and comfortable as the plane. By the time we're properly boarded and take our seats, I realize that, at last, I'm tired enough to sleep even beneath the overhead lights and the low-toned chatter of other passengers.

When Rini Di gently awakens me, we're already at our next stop, which is still not our final destination. Waiting for us as we get off the bus with our bags is a dark-haired, tall, graceful woman in blue jeans and a simple white button-down cotton shirt.

"Rini!" says the woman with a broad smile.

"Sue!" Rini Di responds. They hug and then erupt into a volley of conversation so rapid that I can hardly understand them at all. And suddenly I'm filled with a fear that has recurred a few times in the past weeks: that I won't understand anyone, and that they won't understand me. I shrink a little toward the back of the group.

"This is Heera," Rini Di says, turning toward me. Sue looks at me with warm brown eyes framed by square brown glasses.

"Welcome," she says, holding her hand out.

I begin to fold my hands in a namaste, but then I awkwardly change the gesture to a handshake. I return her smile with a shaky one of my own. This is the first time I've touched a foreigner.

"We are going to have a fabulous time, just like we did with Nisha."

Rini Di and Sue load our suitcases in the back of a huge black car and I get into the back, fastening my seat belt like I did in Rini Di's car on the way to the competition. As we whirl through the streets, I look out and take it all in—the tree-lined avenues, taller buildings than I have ever seen, children in strollers, dogs on leashes pulling their owners, men and women in suits walking briskly on broad sidewalks, shining shops, food trucks, cars of all different colors, shapes. While we drive, Rini Di explains that Sue is also a trained kung fu instructor and lived in a shaolin temple in China for years, immersing herself in all the aspects of the art. That's where she and Rini Di met, and how our Forbesganj hostel became included in the scholarship program. She runs the whole camp out of the house we're headed to, willed to Sue by her grandfather, who always loved her spunky spirit and desire to do good. It's since become a reputable kung fu academy where instructors from all over the world join her to teach students, who flock here.

"How is Nisha doing?" Sue asks.

"Oh, just wonderful. She's winning medal after medal and her confidence levels are just . . ." Rini Di's hand shoots up like a rocket.

Sue laughs. "Wow! She was so shy when she got here!"

Nisha, shy? Is such a thing even possible?

Rini Di nods. "Really something, isn't it?"

At last, we pull off the road and drive toward a square, two-storied building with a green door and gabled windows, a tiled sloping roof, and two, maybe even three chimneys. The house is surrounded by neatly trimmed grass lawns, enclosed by leafy hedges. Somehow, the house doesn't look intimidating. Maybe it's because of its well-worn air, like our hostel. Or maybe it's because of the trees that surround it. Or because of all the pictures Nisha showed me.

A pebbled stone path leads up to the porch, flagged by two giant flowerpots filled with a jumble of colorful flowers. Fallen leaves fill the front yard. A swing hangs from the branches of a tree. There's a garden full of roses at one end near a stone water fountain.

I'm struck by the silence.

I've never experienced such noiselessness in my life. Even during exam time or the holidays, there's something going on in our school compound. And there's never a minute when the music isn't on in Girls Bazaar. I inhale the peacefulness.

It's still light. The white bricks of the house look clean and restful in the sunlight filtering through the green leaves of the surrounding trees. I've never seen such tall windows. Their green shutters match the green leaves.

"You're the first ones to arrive," Sue says as we enter. "Everyone else will be coming in tomorrow."

She helps us lug our four suitcases into a big wood-paneled hall with high ceilings. Again, there is a stillness I've never felt before. I look around, absorbing it all. There's no Maya Didi who rushes forward. But there is artwork by children hanging on the walls, and a series of framed photos of laughing children in various martial arts poses.

"Those are our students, some of whom you'll meet," Sue explains with a look of pride.

We head up the grand wooden staircase with our heavy suitcases and Sue shows us into a room that feels like it could be part of a movie set. There are two beds with floral bedspreads, a window that looks out onto the garden, tiny tables capped with blue lamps, a wooden desk with a blue vase full of the roses, and a blue rug so thick that I feel like I could sink into it. A curtain with tiny blue flowers is drawn across half the window, letting some of the sun filter in.

"Same room as Nisha's last time," Sue says. "Yours is across the corridor."

"Yes," says Rini Di with a smile. "And it is just as perfect as I remember. I will stay in this room tonight in case Heera needs any help and move to my room when her roommate arrives."

Sue nods and then leaves us alone. Rini Di shows me the closet, which has towels and extra blankets.

"Your roommate will come soon, so we must keep the room tidy. I'll sleep here with you tonight, so you don't feel alone, if that's all right," Rini Di says reassuringly.

My roommate. I feel a jolt of fear. What will she be like?

Rini Di explains how I should hang my clothes and store the rest of my things. She shows me how to use the shower—that the hot water comes straight out of the faucet and that I'll need it because it gets cold here, even in May. She shows me where the towels and soaps are and then leaves me to my own devises. I shower beneath the gush of water. Curls of steam fill the air. I've only ever taken bucket baths so far, but this feels like a waterfall.

I can barely recognize myself when I'm dressed, wearing my new V-necked blue dress, cinched at the waist. I'm not skin and bones anymore, thanks to the food and exercise, and the dress actually fits. My body looks different—shapelier, healthier, like the girls I used to see in school. I never knew my body had any contours at all inside those perpetually baggy kameezes.

All these years I've had clothes stitched two sized bigger than I am, so that they would outlast my growth. My hair is cut, thanks to Rini Di, who took me to the salon for the first time ever. I have bangs that fall to my eyebrows, and my straight black hair ends near my ears. My mother was appalled that I cut it off, but I love it. I know the word that Razia used when she saw my dress. Smart. That's how I look today.

Downstairs, I breathe in the crisp air and walk through each room, alive with a mixture of nerves and excitement. I push through a tall wooden door into a vast room that I feel must be a from a palace. I've never seen such a graceful and stylish space. A gleaming wood dinner table sits in the middle with a white bowl full of fruits, surrounded by four matching, carved chairs.

I want to pinch myself to see if I'm dreaming. The evening sun, shining through the windows that overlook the backyard, reminds me that this is real enough. I'm still the urchin from Girls Bazaar, but I'm also Heera, who is here because she won a kung fu competition.

A door opens and Sue finds me in my bewildered state. "Rini Di is in the kitchen. Come with me," she says with a kind smile and a wave of her hand.

We walk down a short hallway with posters of women and girls lining the wall with the words:

Freedom Is an Everyday Struggle.
Girl Power.
Yes We Can.

In the kitchen, Rini Di is cooking up a storm. She has a couple of pots on the go and is chopping vegetables with lightning speed. I go over to see if I can help, and she hands me a knife and some tomatoes to chop while Sue peels potatoes.

"Tomorrow, there will be a full house and a cafeteria going," Rini Di explains, "but today I thought I'd cook a nice Indian meal for us."

She's told me to expect different kinds of foods than what I'm used to back home. She's shown me pictures and made me try some of the things she said I might be fed. Roasts and vegetables. Sandwiches. Pizzas. Pasta. I've been using a knife and fork at every meal to get used to it, though she tells me to use my hands if I like. I know how hard she's worked to make me feel comfortable here, just as she did with Nisha last year. Just as I know that this meal, a little piece of home, is meant to help me ease into it all.

The three of us sit down at the long wooden table. As soon as we serve ourselves the rice, daal, and vegetables, a wave of homesickness sweeps over me, so strong that I squeeze my eyes shut for a second. It doesn't feel right that I'm here in this grand house, eating this delicious meal, while Mira Di is suffering so much. While Rosy is missing.

Rini Di turns to me then, as if she can feel my anxiety in her own skin. "I'm sure you feel tired and overwhelmed. It's past midnight in Forbesganj, and our bodies are still on India time," she says. "After dinner, I want to show you something."

Sue says she'll clean up while Rini Di and I get some fresh air. We head toward the back of the house and walk into one massive open space, spilling out into a deck on the garden.

"What's this?" I ask.

"This is where the training will take place," she says with a grin.

It's utterly serene. I try to imagine what it'll look like with the other students, the teacher. But all I can picture in my head is the kwoon in the school courtyard back home with all my friends.

We spend the rest of the evening walking around. Rini Di says after today, there won't be much time to relax.

"The house is away from the city, so it's quieter out here," she says.

We walk to a park by the river, and I can hardly believe how beautiful it is as it weaves through walkways and flower gardens. Rini Di gets her camera out and takes some pictures.

"You'll want to remember your first day," she says.

When we return, I follow Rini Di through another hallway and up the flight of stairs. Luckily, she knows which of the dozen doors is ours. "I'm setting an alarm so that we wake up in the morning," she says. "It'll be bedtime in India when it's time to get up here, so our bodies won't want to get out of bed." None of this makes sense to me, but I nod obediently.

I sink into the too-soft mattress and drift off in no time. But later in the night, I wake up with a start, forgetting where I am. The bed feels like it's sinking under me. The blankets are too heavy. Too warm. After tossing and turning for what feels like hours, I decide that it's useless. So I pull my cell phone out from under my pillow.

It's the first time I allow myself to look at the pictures I took in Rini Di's office. They all seem to be legible, which is a miracle given how much my hands were shaking. But there are so many parts that I don't understand. For now, what I can tell is that several complaints have been made against Ravi Lala and Suraj Sharma. But they were able to evade all charges against them, just like the case of my abduction. Again, it feels as though Ravi Lala truly is untouchable.

There's no mention of Azra in any of the files, but I do find a complaint from a year ago, filed by another family from Nepal about their daughter, who had been lured away from the village and sent to New York. I read the email their daughter sent them, and my eyes immediately lock onto the names that I recognize. She names Suraj Sharma as the man who lured her and Ravi Lala as the man who sold her.

Somehow, even as my heart beats fast with rage, my eyes still manage to drift off into sleep.

I jump out of bed, sure that I hear someone scream. And then I realize it's only Rini Di's alarm on her phone, which she fumbles with in a daze of her own. She finally manages to turn it off and looks at me as we both burst out laughing.

"How are you feeling now?" she asks.

"Like I'm still asleep," I reply in a drowsy voice, my eyelids still stuck together.

"Same. Let's get out of here," she says, peeling the curtains open. "Some fresh air and exercise will help."

I get ready in a haze and change into my gi for practice. Just as I get to the top of the stairs, a slender girl walks in clutching her bag. Her straight black hair is tied loosely back from a clear-skinned, pointed face. Her dark eyes shine and her tiny wiry body is turned toward me.

I know at once who she is.

She looks up and sees me, and sort of squints as if she's inspecting me. I know I look nothing like the picture I sent her, with my new haircut and my sparkling white gi.

"Heera?" she says eagerly.

I give her a shy smile. When I reach the bottom of the steps, she's ready with her arms open wide, practically running toward me.

"Hey, roomie!" Connie says. And somehow I feel just a bit more at home.

CHAPTER TWENTY-THREE

The house is transformed in the space of a morning.

Students pour in and the bustle and noise feel comforting. Snatches of conversation echo up and down the stairs. Animated groups of friends exchange holiday news. The doors of rooms are open as girls unpack. A matron walks around with an eagle eye—she has the same air of authority as Maya Didi and most likely a heart of gold too, otherwise the enormous noise of talking and laughter around us would have earned a severe reprimand.

The kitchen has been taken over by professionals, and breakfast is a variety of foods that Rini Di has tried to make me appreciate over the past few days: cornflakes, fruits, milk, porridge of some kind, eggs, and toast. So, eggs it is for me.

Connie walks me to a room outside the kitchen where there's a sprinkling of small tables decorated with flowered tablecloths. Some of the other girls are already sitting and eating their breakfasts. They nod and smile as we walk in and find an empty table.

"So, what's it like—your first trip to America?" Connie asks as she spoons cereal into her mouth.

I pause. "I haven't seen anything really except the airport and this house, but it's very different. So quiet," I say mildly.

That seems to surprise her. "New York, quiet?!"

I shrug. "For me." I don't know how to explain the incessant, unceasing noise in our lane of bus horns, Bollywood music, and haggling customers.

"I guess. I've never been to India. But I hear cows are allowed on the road, right next to cars and bikes."

"And in our village even goats, and chickens, and pigs," I respond with a laugh. I try to reply with short words while I feel my way through English with someone who not only speaks with a different accent but also speaks much faster than I do. I think she understands that a long conversation in English is beyond me at this stage.

"Better hustle," she says. "I have to go up and change before we start. But first, did you finish *Little Women*?"

I smile, relieved that she's chosen a topic we can both talk about.

Outside, the empty space from yesterday has been transformed into a kwoon, with mats covering the floors and other pieces of equipment that I've never seen before along the sides. The camp here is for a variety of martial art forms. I watch as some of the other students, who seem *way* bigger than me, chat as though they know one another already.

"These people have all paid money to be here," Connie says as we take our places on the mat. "This is, like, their job. They're what we call pros."

"Do you know anyone here?" I ask hesitantly.

"Nope. I've only been to local competitions before. Too small for these people."

And then a man walks in—short, bald, expressionless. In his spotless white gi, he is unmistakably the teacher.

"My name is Zhang Yi. You may call me Master Yi," he says. "There are fifteen students here, from all parts of the country, and a few from other countries as well. You are all here for one reason and one reason alone—to compete. We will focus all our energy and attention for the next month on this. Got it?"

We all nod as he looks around at us and finally cracks a smile. "I've been told that people like talking about themselves, so that's how we'll begin, with introductions."

We sit down in a circle. Everyone says their name, age, discipline, and something about themselves. I instantly forget each name, most of which I've never heard before. But I won't forget their stories. One boy with the reddest hair I've ever seen has been practicing Jeet Kune Do for ten years. Another boy named Aiko from Japan says he wants to make it to the Olympics.

Then it's my turn.

"My name is Heera. I'm from India, and I'm competing in the

beginner's category. I won gold at the district competition in Bihar, where I live."

I see the group smile in approval. I've never been somewhere where no one knows me from before. And I realize that there's fear in that, but also power. Everyone takes me at face value and greets me as a peer.

Master Yi introduces us to four other teachers who will help all the students in their various disciplines. He breaks us up into our various disciplines and age groups. And then we get down to business. The warm-up routine feels familiar enough. We begin with breathing exercises. "This is to center our chi," Master Yi explains. But as we move on to the strength-building workout, I'm more out of breath than I thought was even possible in such a short period of time. My arms ache and my thighs burn. I look around at everyone else, who all seem to be able keep up, suddenly feeling small and weak compared to the others, including Connie, who is wiry but fit. I pant and stumble through the rest of the set, thinking of Rini Di telling me to eat more protein.

Master Yi comes over to me and I stiffen. "Pace yourself. Do as much as you can. Listen to your body and be the judge—you won't be doing as many burpees as Shawn over there," he says with a toss of his head toward a boy who is so tall and broad that three of Salman could fit inside him.

At the end of the session, I'm fully aware of how much harder I'll have to work to even have a chance in this competition, or even to make it to the end of the month of training. Nisha warned me to expect this feeling. "But don't give up. Go prepared to work harder than you've ever worked in your life," she said. "Get everything you can out of that

one month. If you don't, you'll only cheat yourself." I didn't understand what she meant until now. Rini Di has done her best with us
scrawny lot in Forbesganj. But this is something else altogether.

It's lunchtime, and we haven't even started with the actual routines yet.
I'm both famished and too tired to eat all at once. In the cafeteria, I try
to take everything I see Connie taking. She puts something like the
Chinese noodles we ate when I won the gold medal on her plate, so
I take that too. She adds a red sauce made of tomatoes to it. I do too. She
takes two pieces of grilled chicken. I take one. She takes a pile of broc-
coli. I skip that. We sit with a couple of the other younger students. I
watch them eat and try to follow what they do.

"That was brutal," Connie says.

I nod. My sentiments are as much about eating with a fork and knife
as the workout.

"But you all were making it look so easy," I say, with some admira-
tion and a twinge of jealousy. I try to spin the noodles around my fork
in the same way Connie does.

"Are you nuts? I didn't think my butt was capable of sweating that
much. Did you not hear me gasping for air?" says Connie.

"No! And you were right next to me." But I'm relieved to hear that
Connie found it hard too.

"I had a teacher who used to tell me pain was all in my mind," a girl
named Bornani says, another international student here from Nigeria.
"And that if I ignored it, it would go away. I always felt like flicking her
in the nose."

We all laugh. Even sitting down, Bornani is still a full head taller than us.

"I don't mind the pain," Aiko says. "I like challenging my body."

"But you still feel it, right?" asks Bornani.

"Yes, but I am its boss," Aiko says. "It's not the boss of me."

Connie rolls her eyes, but I think it's pretty cool. If I could get away from Gainul, what are a few push-ups?

Later that night, Connie and I return to our room, aching from the tops of our heads to the soles of our feet. I've never trained so hard in my life, and it's only day one. In the scurry of activity, no one even asked me about my jet lag, but it seems to have vanished. In this boot camp, no one wastes a day. Master Yi, the Shaolin instructor, has already showed me the kind of routine he plans to build for me by the end of our first week, and I broke into a sweat just watching him. Months ago, Rini Di showed us some videos of moves that I'd dismissed as impossible, at least for me. But today, I saw people perform those moves right in front of my eyes.

I can feel my body begging me to rest as my mind continues to practice the routine that Master Yi has in store for me. But my mind and body can't seem to connect.

"Ready to go back home yet?" Connie asks, collapsing onto her bed.

"If I lived an hour away, maybe I would," I say wishfully.

"Everything hurts," Connie moans. But she gets up again, clearly with more energy left in her body than I have in mine, and begins to unpack.

"Have you ever traveled to a different country?" I ask her.

She shakes her head. "My mom always said we'd go to Mexico. To chill by the beach, just over the border. But it hasn't happened yet." She puts her last things away and sits back down. "I still can't believe you kicked a sex trafficker in the nuts."

We both share a laugh.

"I know. But honestly, if it weren't for Rini Di, I could have wound up wherever Rosy is now," I say solemnly.

Connie's face becomes more serious. "You still haven't told me if you got the stuff."

"What stuff?" I ask, accepting the sticky piece of chocolate that she offers me.

"From the office at the shelter home. In your email you said you would try!"

"I did," I whisper with a smile, my eyes round with excitement.

"You're kidding," she exclaims in a hushed tone. "Those are some secret agent skills you got there."

From her expression, I assume that this is a compliment and find myself grinning from ear to ear. "I managed to get pictures of some papers, and I've barely had a chance to go through them. But there's something in there about a girl trafficked from Nepal."

"Okay, tomorrow you explain it all to me," she says approvingly as she settles into her bed, her blanket pulled to her chin. "I need to be wide awake to understand it all."

My own eyes begin drooping too.

"But seriously, first thing you do when you get your hands on a cell phone is break into a filing cabinet." Connie chuckles.

I feel a fresh wave of shame.

"Hey, I'm just kidding," she says, stretching out and putting a hand on my arm. "You're doing it to help your friend. I've done far worse, for no good reason at all."

By lunchtime the following day, after another morning of strength training, my body feels like it needs an excavator to scoop me off the ground. Yet somehow, I stay upright.

But during our hour break, Connie signals for me to come upstairs.

"Let's talk now. Otherwise, we're going to get to the end of the day again and both pass out," she says. I shut the door quietly behind us and begin flipping through the documents on my phone.

"I don't understand a word of any of it. You'll have to explain it to me," she says.

I scan my eyes over the documents once again. "I'm struggling too. It's all police and lawyer talk. But I think the girl you met at the shelter, Azra, stopped in Forbesganj on her way from Nepal to New York. I think she was trafficked by the same people who nearly got me. The same people who got Rosy."

"You're kidding?" Connie says, her eyes round. "What are the chances of that?"

Suddenly I can see the tattoo of Krishna on Suraj Sharma's dirty hand as he lunged forward to grab me outside his house. I imagine him doing the same to Azra. To the girls in the cells next to mine. To Rosy. Just how many girls has he helped Ravi Lala kidnap? "I know," I say. "Unfortunately, it's a much smaller world than anyone would like to think. She stayed at one of the trafficker's houses before she came to New York. His son, Manish, told me."

Connie sits up straighter, shaking her head and rubbing her temples. She's heard all about Manish through my letters.

"From what I could find, Azra's family didn't go to the police, at least not in Forbesganj," I say. "But there's another girl who ended up in our neighborhood from Nepal a year before in exactly the same way. Her parents tracked her down and filed a complaint, and this is it." I pull up the blurry document and read out the bits that make sense. "She was lured away from her home in Nepal with the promise of work in a hotel in the US. She was kept in someone's home in Forbesganj by traffickers, who then took her to the US with fake papers. She says the man who brought her was Suraj Sharma and the man whose home she was kept in was Ravi Lala. She managed to somehow send a message to her family, and they filed this complaint."

Connie leans over to try to read the files on my phone. "What did the message say?"

"That she was in danger, somewhere in New York," I tell her. "I don't know if they found her, but at least it confirms that this is a trade route for girls from Nepal."

"And nothing happened to the traffickers?"

"Nothing," I say, knowing the reality of it all too well. "They keep all the politicians and cops happy, so no one touches them."

"That's horrifying, Heera." Connie breathes in deeply. It's as if everything I shared with her over email felt like fiction and is finally starting to feel real. "And you think Rosy is here now too?"

I want to say yes, that I feel it in my bones. But the truth is that I can't be completely certain. And I've been wrong before. "I don't know for sure, but I overheard the men who kidnapped me talking about sending her to the Taj Mahal. The same place Azra was told she was going. Whatever that means. And Manish seemed to think she was coming to the US. This is where they send their prize girls, and he heard them say that they had big plans for her."

"Yeah, only the best for your daughter, right?" Connie says, rolling her eyes.

"So, what do you think we should do?" I prod Connie.

"Well, we're supposed to pay a trip to Azra's shelter as part of the scholarship program," Connie says, unfolding the idea.

A spiderweb of nerves spreads through me. I nearly forgot that I agreed to talk at the shelter when we got there. I'd written the start of my speech on the plane—about how kung fu helped me fight off Gainul, about my life as part of the Nat community—but I haven't even been able to think about it since we started training.

"Do you think we'll have time to speak to Azra while we're there? Maybe try and find out more about the place she escaped from?" I ask.

Connie closes her eyes as if she's thinking hard. "We'll have to find a way to contact her to make sure she'll be there. There's also the chance that if we wait until then, it might be too late. But I don't know what other option we have."

"What do you have in mind? Do you have Azra's number?"

"No. But I'll think of something," Connie says with confidence.

CHAPTER TWENTY-FOUR

I wake up on edge, unable to even tell the difference between the pain and homesickness. My arms and legs ache with every step. The blisters on my feet throb from the chafing of the mat on my bare skin. No one can one accuse me of not trying my best, but somehow it just doesn't seem to be enough. Just as what I've tried to do in search of Rosy never seems to be enough.

For the past couple of days, I've been fighting through the pain, trying to keep up with my counterpart, Jack. Aiko's words echo in my brain. I choose to challenge my body. If Master Yi tells us to do ten snap kicks, I do twelve. But even so, every day, I'm reminded that my form and strength aren't up to scratch, not at this stage. I'm a guppy compared to the other four Shaolin competitors, and I'm lucky that they're all in different categories because I'd have no chance otherwise.

We work the longest on my core and on my speed. I feel the frustration deepen as we're forced to repeat the same move eight times, but I tell myself to stay calm. I slowly learn to concentrate my energy in different spots of my body, sometimes the tips of my toes and sometimes my fists. Master Yi is kind, but no matter how hard I try, he asks me to focus more.

Tomorrow, our masters are supposed to tell us where we stand before we begin training with a focus on our competition routine. After a week of camp, they've had time to assess our skills and identify the areas where we need work.

"You're a beginner. You can't compare yourself to people who've been learning for years," Connie keeps telling me. "If you weren't good, you wouldn't be here!"

But that's easy for her to say. She's the shining star of her group with just two years' training. She can run circles around boys twice her size. And whatever she says, it's true that Bornani and I *do* seem to have less experience than everyone else.

"Do you think we're only here because of this scholarship program for the shelters?" I ask Bornani at lunch.

She looks at me like I must have lost my mind. "Well, yes, of course. I know I'd never have been here otherwise."

"What I mean is, do you think they chose us because we were the best where we were or because we were at risk?" I watch her as she thinks the question through.

"As far as I know, there were kids from across the world up for this scholarship," she says finally. "We beat many people to be here, so, yes, I think we're good enough."

I hope she's right, but I'm not so sure. Last year, Nisha made it, and she is incredible. But I know I'm nowhere near up to her standard. Connie is also a part of the program, and she's undoubtedly talented. I don't know anything about jujitsu, so can't objectively assess Bornani's skills, but I know how I feel about my own.

"Either way," says Bornani, "we're here now, and I want to do as well as I can."

I wake up at my usual magic hour to power through my homesickness at the kwoon. But it doesn't seem to help. The silence feels too loud. The sense of calm never comes. Rini Di has left the camp until just the day before the competition to make a few other work stops in the States. She says she has to investigate the trafficking ring, meet some NGOs, FBI agents, and lawyers, as well as her donors, the ones who keep our Forbesganj hostel afloat. I just stood there as she told me, wanting so badly to tell her everything I've learned about Rosy. But here she was telling me about the lengths she goes to take care of all of us. How could I tell her then that I'd gone through her private files when I don't even know for certain that Rosy is here?

I'd been nervous about how I'd feel when the time came for her to leave me alone at the camp, but now that she's gone, I realize that I'm going to be okay. Because of her, I'll be able to get through anything.

I've made friends. I have the kwoon. There are no leery-eyed men waiting around the corner here.

Still, my heart aches for Mai, Sania, and Salman. Even Baba.

I go to the computer in the little room downstairs. No one is around at this hour.

Salman has been using the cybercafe near the hospital to email me. I picture him slumped over the machine, pressing each key with his pointer fingers. Perhaps Mai is hovering behind him, holding little Sania.

Hi Heera,

Connie sounds like a lot of fun. I hope you're eating enough to keep up with kung fu classes? That's from Mai, by the way. ☺

We all miss you, but we're doing well here. Baba isn't drinking or meeting his old friends. Sometimes his body twitches and then he goes away to sit on a bench in the railway station to sulk. He's still bossy and difficult. I've lined up one house after another and Baba finds problems with all of them. You'd think we live in a palace and not a bamboo hut between two brothels, the way he's acting. But he's begun to get a few odd jobs here and there. Sania jabbers away more and more. Mira Di's fever is gone. She sends her love. We're all rooting for you.

Yours,

Salman

PS Whatever you're thinking about doing about Rosy, stop. Remember why you're there.

Of course he still has to treat me like a child, even though he *has* just read me like a book. And of course he hasn't mentioned when he's going to the Siliguri school, or anything about what Baba actually does want. I live in perpetual fear that Baba will change his mind about everything—the house, Salman's school, my school, his own drinking and gambling. I write back and tell Salman to go to the Siliguri school before he does something stupid. At the very least, I know that the money from the school is in my bank account. And that gives us a power we've never had before.

While the rest of the house is still waking up, I go down to the small shop in the office to find the perfect postcards for Sadaf and Razia—I choose one that says *Yes We Can* with a picture of women flexing their muscles and pen them a few lines. For Mira Di, I choose a scene from *Enter the Dragon*. Bruce Lee is on a boat with some children who are holding out a rope to man in small raft. On the back, I write in Hindi:

> Namaste Mira Di,
>
> I miss you. I'm so happy to hear that your fever has passed. I'm learning a lot here. I chose this card because it's a photo of Bruce Lee sending a bad man adrift to sea. I wish we could do it to all the bad men we know. I hope you've thought about what we talked about. Remember what Uncle Darzi used to say? You've always had a gift.
>
> Love you,
>
> XXX Heera

That afternoon, Sue calls me for a meeting along with Connie and Bornani to discuss our visit to Sunshine House.

"This visit is a small but important part of the scholarship program," she explains. "Many of the students there are also learning martial arts, and all of them are either survivors themselves or were at risk before joining the program. And, as you already know, the three of you will each give a short talk as part of the session."

Sue must see the fear in my eyes because she shoots me a comforting smile. "It isn't a formal presentation, just a way to allow all the people there to hear your story. You can keep it simple. Follow a script if you prefer or just speak if that's what you're comfortable with."

"How long does it need to be?" I ask, though I know the answer already.

"Be ready to speak for about five minutes each, and there will be time for questions too."

"Will we get to ask them questions as well?" asks Connie.

"Of course," Sue says. "Aside from your talks, there will be an informal interaction at the home so you can get to know one another a little better before the talk. And last year, this continued after the talk as well."

Connie and I exchange glances. Hopefully we'll have a chance to talk to Azra.

"That's good," I say to Connie after we're dismissed. "Now if I could only rewrite this speech. Have you worked on yours?"

"Nah," she says with a shrug. "I might take some notes on my phone. But I'll probably just wing it."

"I'm terrified of forgetting everything I want to say," I confide to Connie.

"Don't worry," she says. "You're talking about your own life. You're the greatest living expert on it. You can't forget it even if you tried."

After lunch, Connie and I head to the room, as has become our custom, a routine of flopping down on our beds and either chatting or reading or sending emails home. Today, she rolls over onto her stomach, furiously typing away on her phone. I can't help but watch her with awe as she does this. I'm still fumbling around getting used to mine while she seems to use hers like a remote control to the universe.

"Yes," she says with a fist pump. "Got it!"

"What?" I say.

She shoots up in her bed. "The story about Azra's escape."

I sit up too.

"I found this article in the news, from a year ago. Listen to this." She begins to read.

> Seventeen-year-old Azra Tamang displayed extraordinary courage when she escaped from a brothel through the bathroom window, running five blocks in the snow in her bare feet to the nearest police station. Lured from her home in Nepal with the promise of work in the hospitality sector in the US, Azra found herself in a living nightmare, sold to a brothel keeper within hours of arrival in New York.
>
> "My passport was taken away as soon as I landed," explains Azra. "When I said I wanted to go home, I was told that I had been brought to the US at a huge expense and I would have to work to pay back my debts."

Azra said she was forced to have sex with multiple men a night.

"When I said I wanted to leave, I was told I was here illegally and that the police would arrest me if they found out I had overstayed my tourist visa."

About ten months into her ordeal, Azra was viciously attacked by a client. That was when she decided that even prison would be better than her current situation.

"I managed to steal a screwdriver when one of the pimps came to do some repairs in the house. There was only one window that I had access to when no one else was around, and that was in the bathroom. So, over a week, I loosened the screws in the bathroom grill, carefully replacing them so no one would notice. Then, when my captors left, I saw my opportunity. I removed the iron bars and jumped through the first-floor window and onto the pavement below. And then I ran."

Police say investigations are underway, but so far, no arrests have been made.

Connie looks at me, her eyes aglow. "When I met Azra, she said the guards were careful. She said she'd pretend to take the drugs they gave her, but she never actually did, and that helped her think clearly when she had the chance."

I'd heard about this. The girls get drugs and next to no food. It leaves them with no energy to fight. Just like they tried to do to me.

"I've seen what the drugs did to my mom. It was like she couldn't think about anything else," Connie says. "It makes it hard to imagine any other life."

I think about Mira Di and wonder if alcohol isn't the only thing she's taking. That maybe that's another reason she doesn't want to leave home, something else Rini Di couldn't share with me. "It's just so terrible . . ." I start to say, but Connie isn't listening. She's off scrolling on her phone again.

"Look—this has to be the same Azra!" She shows me a web page for the Survivors of Trafficking Network of New York. "Check this out—she's the secretary! I can send her a message through the site."

Connie taps away while a mixture of paranoia and guilt washes over me, Salman's words echoing in my brain—*remember why you're there.* But a whooshing sound escapes Connie's phone before I'm able to speak.

"There. Sent," Connie says. "Let's see if she replies."

That afternoon, Master Yi and the other instructors plan to sit us down one by one to give us our assessments and share how they plan to get us ready for the competition. Lucky for me, as a beginner, I'm up first.

I'm called into the kwoon, where Master Yi sits cross-legged on the floor.

"Heera, sit," he says.

I take my place before him, heart in my throat. He gives me a smile.

"Last year it was Nisha. This year it is Heera."

I would speak, but it's either that or keeping down my lunch.

"So much in common with each other, though you are quieter. It's a good thing in martial arts."

I smile at this.

"You came here as a bud, full of all you need to become a first-rate kung fu artist. And in just one week, I have seen you blossom."

I am not sure I have heard correctly.

"You move with the precision of one with years of training. And yet, you have been learning for less than a year?"

"Yes," I say with a nod.

"You may be the smallest in the batch, but your focus is like a razor. Your training—it is good. I know Rini Di well and understand now where your abilities come from. Control over body and mind are critical to what we do, and I have seen it from you in practice every day."

My smile widens. I wish Rini Di were here to hear this for herself. "Thank you," I say. "She'll be here before the competition."

"Wonderful. I can't wait to see her and congratulate her. You have shown me your old routine. We will need to change that for this competition, I am afraid. We will have ninety seconds to show off the full range of your abilities. I think we have the time to make you shine."

I nod.

"What we will have to really focus on with you is the second element of the competition—the forty-five-second weapon demonstration."

Master Yi has seen me with the bo staff. He *must* know just how far behind I am.

"Not to worry," he says, clearly sensing my unease. "You have the basics in place, though you must learn to free yourself from distraction, center your inner strength, and pace your speed. Now it is time to bring your practice to the next level. Your balance is good, and you are agile."

I smile to myself, imagining how Baba would feel to hear this—my balance and agility come from growing up in a Nat household. From walking a tightrope, learning somersaults, and jumping over high ropes with my cousins from an early age.

It's a much better assessment than I'd expected, and I silently thank Nisha for her crash course. But his words about freeing myself from distraction feel like a weight on my chest. "Thank you, Master Yi."

"You can stop thanking me. I am only bringing out what is within you. I believe I was told that you have fought off some pretty nasty people?"

I smile. "Yes."

"Then what is all this play fighting when you have already won the fight for your life?"

That night, Rini Di calls me to check in and I have the chance to tell her all about Master Yi's assessment—that he actually seems to think I'm in a good place. Somehow, she doesn't seem surprised by this.

"And do you feel set for the shelter visit?" she asks.

"To be honest, not really," I say. "I've never spoken in front of that many people in my life. I want to rewrite what I rehearsed with you."

"They want to hear your story. How you got here. The scholarship is about inspiring at-risk children. And you've done some pretty remarkable things so far."

"Have I really?" At the moment, all I can think about is what I *haven't* been able to do.

Rini Di laughs. "Well, of course you have. But even more than *what* you've done, they'd like to know *how* you've done it. And why. You're much more prepared than you think you are. And you can feel free to call anytime to run your speech by me. If you want to."

Her kindness twists into the guilt I feel in my chest. Now would be the perfect opportunity to tell her about the connection we've discovered between Rosy and Azra. But if I do, if I tell her about our plan to talk to Azra at Sunshine House and she decides it's a bad idea, then the one chance we have to learn more will be off the table. Somehow, it feels better not to tell her at all than to disobey her. But there is a question I *can* ask.

"Rini Di, I do have to know," I say, waiting to hear her attention on the other end of the line. "I wondered if you'd learned any more about Rosy. If you know whether she's still home, or if they've already taken her somewhere else."

Rini Di lets out a sigh. "I'm investigating all the leads I have, Heera. I promise you. I know what I'm asking is difficult, but please, until the competition, can you focus on your training? You have already put yourself in danger once trying to save Rosy. Suraj Sharma and Ravi Lala will be brought to account. But there is a way in which these matters must be handled. For the safety of everyone."

"Yes, but—"

"Heera, you need to listen to me. What have I told you? I don't give up."

"Okay," I agree. But if there's one thing I've learned about myself over this past year, it's that for better or for worse, I don't give up either.

CHAPTER TWENTY-FIVE

As soon as we arrive at Sunshine House, I'm struck at how different it is from our hostel back in Forbesganj. Nobody can see into any windows from outside behind the giant wall. Once we get out of the car and walk through the security check at the door, there's a well-kept garden with close-cropped grass. Finally, we see the gray building, three stories tall, with lines of windows. We walk straight through the glass doors and into the reception area. I'm too nervous to pay much attention to anything else, and it only gets worse as we pass through another door into a hall, with chairs lined up where people will be sitting, facing me as I speak.

Our host beckons us inside. "Your audience will be here shortly, but please make yourselves comfortable," she says.

"I bet no one comes," Connie says.

Sue laughs. "Last year it was a full house."

Sure enough, people do start trickling in. The first few take seats at the back and don't look at us.

"Yeah, they forced them to come," Connie says, and everyone laughs. But I'm not sure what she means. The kids might have a choice *not* to attend? There never seemed to be any choice for kids about anything back home.

"We are expecting at least one guest," I remind her. "Azra."

Connie nods. "Let's see if she shows."

Azra responded to Connie's email and told us she'd be here. But as the event begins, all I can think about is how to keep myself from blacking out.

The director introduces us and calls Bornani to speak first, which is a relief.

Hearing the musical lilt to her voice soothes me. Bornani talks about her life in Lagos, how she grew up with a mother who contracted HIV/AIDS after being prostituted by her husband, who then abandoned them. She didn't receive treatment in time and died when Bornani was just nine years old. And then she was sent to an orphanage that's been her home ever since.

I can hardly believe it. Bornani has never shared any of this before, and she talks about it all now without missing a beat. Everyone listens gravely and claps when she's finished. Looking around the room as they applaud, seeing people in the audience from everywhere, I almost lose my fear that my Indian-accented English will be incomprehensible to the listeners of Sunshine House.

But I'm still a trembling ball of nerves when my name is called next. Connie reaches out and gives my hand a squeeze. I give her a shaky smile as I stand up.

At the podium, I take my time spreading my notes out in front of me, adjusting the microphone down to my level.

"My name is Heera. I am from a town named Forbesganj, in a state called Bihar, in northern India, very close to Nepal," I begin. My voice is shaking, along with the rest of me. But I go on. "My brother and I are the first people in our family to ever go to school, and I have grown up believing that being sold for prostitution is my destiny. That there are few doors open to me as a child of an oppressed-caste family. Our people used to be wrestlers and performers, but overnight we were told we couldn't do those things anymore, that our entire way of life was illegal."

My voice is shaking less now, and I manage to look at the people in front of me.

"How do people survive when they aren't allowed to do the work they know and love? For my family of nomads, it meant asking people for a place to live, and then doing just about any job they told us we could do. One of these jobs was having sex with people for money.

"These children and women had no choice but to sell their bodies in exchange for a place to live, for food to eat, and for their husbands to be given work. And though people say that times have changed, they must not have changed everywhere, because I have been told since I was a little girl that selling my body was what I had to do to support myself and my family. And I believed it. Many in my family believed it too.

"Finally, earlier this year, it was my turn to be put up for sale. My family was in a tight spot, in debt to the wrong man. I grew up in a red-light area, so I knew what it meant, what it involved. There are no secrets kept from kids where I come from. So, I said no, and we tried to get around it.

"My mother paid back our loan, but the traffickers came for me anyhow. The first time, I got away. The second time, they got me, but I was rescued by my brother and teacher.

"When I was stuck in a tiny room, with my traffickers outside the door, I asked myself, why had they kept coming for me even when they had no claim? No right? And it wasn't until that happened that I fully realized that they believed that my body belonged to them, and I knew for certain that it did not. It was kung fu that helped me understand this. Because it is through kung fu that I learned that my body would do what I told it to. That my body listened to me—and only me." I take a breath. "There is power in my body. My body connects me to my cousin, my aunt, my grandmother, who were all sold for prostitution. But kung fu also connects my body to my ancestors, who were champion wrestlers. If both these things lived within me, could I choose which course I wanted to take?" I look up now, realizing that I've memorized the final words on the page. "For most of my life, I thought the answer to that was no. But suddenly, I felt that maybe there was another possibility. I didn't do it on my own: I needed my family to stand with me, and most importantly, a cheerleader who made me believe that safety could be mine. Rini Di taught me kung fu and opened the doors of the world to me. And that is how I have come to stand before you now."

I pause and there is a moment's silence. And then the audience bursts into applause. As I walk away from the podium, all I can think about is how I forgot to thank them at the end of my speech. I feel like my legs will give way, but I'm held up by the cloud I feel inside me until I reach my seat.

At the end of the talks there are a few questions from the audience, and then we wrap. Some of the teachers and caregivers in the home come forward to speak to me, but I don't have energy to do anything except nod and smile and say thank you. And then Sue is at my side, giving me a glass of juice and gently leading me into a seat.

"You were wonderful," she says.

"Thanks," I say, my heart still beating in my ears.

"Feeling exhausted?"

"Just like after a kung fu routine," I say.

"That's the adrenaline—it's what holds you up and then you come crashing down," Sue says, patting my shoulder. "I'll get you a plate of food."

A couple more of the adults come to congratulate me on my speech and wish me luck for the competition while Sue deposits some snacks in front of me, but I find that I have no appetite. A girl comes up to me then, older than the students but younger than the staff.

"That was very cool," she says. And immediately, I know who she is.

"Thank you," I say as my eyes scan the crowd in search of Connie. "I'm just glad I didn't faint onstage."

The girl offers a chuckle. "I grew up not very far from you. Just over the border in Nepal," she says, extending a hand. "I'm Azra, by the way."

"I—I think you know my friend," I manage to say, waving my hand above my head when I finally find Connie. She spots us and comes rushing over, abandoning her own crowd of admirers.

"Azra!" Connie exclaims, throwing her arms around the tiny girl. "You made it!"

"You girls were fantastic," Azra says before looking back and forth between the two of us, seemingly putting together the details of Connie's email. She looks at me. "So *you're* the one who's worried about your friend." She takes a quick look around. "It's too crowded here to talk properly, but I wanted to meet you and try and understand what you're trying to figure out."

I look around to make sure Sue isn't within earshot. The hall is sprinkled with groups of people huddled in their own conversations, but I keep my voice low.

"There's a girl from my school, a friend of mine, who we think is in danger," I say, reading the concern on Azra's face. "We think she might be in the same brothel where you were kept."

Azra's brow shoots down. "What makes you think that?" she asks.

"Because she was brought over here by the same gang that brought you." It's only then that I realize that Azra might have already met her. She's stayed in Rosy's house, after all. "The man with the Krishna tattoo. It's Suraj Sharma's daughter, Rosy."

Azra goes pale. "He brought his daughter here?"

"That's what her brother, Manish, told me," I reply.

"And you want to try to get her out?" Azra says skeptically.

Another wave of adrenaline shoots through me. "Yes," I say firmly.

Azra inhales deeply. "I'm not sure how you'd even track them down.

They don't stay in one place. They move around every few months. They had me for a year before I escaped, and I was in four different houses."

"Do you know any of the girls there still?" Connie asks.

Azra takes a moment to think. "It's been a while. I don't know if they'd talk to me even if I tried."

I try to think of other options as quickly as I can. "Did you talk to the police when you escaped? Are they going to arrest your traffickers now that you can testify against them?" I ask.

Azra bites her lip. "It's not simple. It takes time to build a case. Our support group has several lawyers who are following the case and gathering evidence, but there isn't a lot in the news. That happens when it's an active investigation."

"Do you think you can find out more?" I ask, desperate for any help we can get.

"I don't want to get your hopes up, but I do have one person I could ask." Azra looks at her watch anxiously, and I worry that we've asked too much of her. But when she speaks next, her voice is assured. "I'll be in touch."

CHAPTER TWENTY-SIX

I look for refuge in the kwoon. In my body. I waste no time. I set to work with a concentration that allows nothing else. I let nothing slip—from the curves of my fingers and toes to the bend of my back. Everything has to be precisely perfect. I note how one jab is slightly stiffer. It needs more fluidity. It has to be effortless. I wobble a little in the dragon stance. My hips pull my thighs back. I test my balance and change my position a little. I stretch like a cat and pounce like a tiger.

I do it again, over and over, first the right hand and left leg and then the left leg and right hand, until I have it as it should be. I listen intently to my body.

But again and again, I'm interrupted by thoughts of Rosy. How can I find peace in my body when my friend is out there in the dark, her nose pierced, her body invaded? I can't unsee the fear in her eyes as she looked out that window.

My technique gets better but my thoughts are in turmoil. After meeting Azra and the other girls at the Sunshine House shelter, the battle I've been fighting feels bigger and more powerful than I had ever imagined. It preys on little girls like us all over the world. Our small resistance in Girls Bazaar is like an ant standing up to an elephant.

For the next few days, we don't hear from Azra. Perhaps it's for the best. The kwoon leaves no time for anything else. We're approaching the halfway point of training, and there's no more room for mistakes. Our choreography is ready, and my routine is miles more advanced than what I did in Forbesganj. But as hard as I try, I can't seem to get the hang of my weapon, the bo staff. I will never get it right. Master Yi says I will control the bo when I control my thoughts. But my thoughts keep going to Rosy.

The longer we go without hearing from Azra, the more I feel as though I'm abandoning Rosy. And the longer I go without confiding in Rini Di, the more I feel as though I'm lying to her. The only thing I can do is go through the documents on my phone again and again, searching for a clue that I haven't yet noticed. I stare hard at the report about the girl from Nepal for hints that I may have missed, wishing I could ask Rini Di what some of these words in the police documents mean. Between the handwriting and strange English, they're hard to decipher. The only things I recognize are the names of Ravi Lala and Suraj Sharma.

But then my inbox dings. When I look at the sender's email address, my mouth nearly falls open.

Manish.

Heera,

I thought you should know that you were right. Well, we both were. I heard my father talking last night and it's true that Rosy is in the US, in New York. It's also true that she's gone to work at the Taj Mahal. But it's not a code word as you'd thought. Apparently, it's a restaurant. Don't get caught this time.

Manish

I can feel my heart beating in my ears. Finally, I understand.

That's why Ravi Lala's men were laughing.

I scold myself for not thinking of it sooner.

"Do you have any idea how many Indian restaurants there are in New York called Taj Mahal?" Connie says once I tell her. She scrolls through her phone feverishly. "I'm not sure what we would do even if we *could* figure out which one it is. We can't just call them up and ask for Rosy."

"We could tell Rini Di or Sue?" I say now that we know Rosy's really here. "What if we just tell them everything we know?"

"It's not that simple," Connie says, echoing what Azra told us. "They'll want to involve the police, who won't risk going right now because they're in the middle of an investigation. At the very least, they'll say it's too dangerous for us to get involved. And it'll be out of our hands."

"And they would be right," I admit.

"So? Do you want it to be out of our hands?" she asks.

As I let my eyelids close, allowing myself to think, it seems to all come flooding back—Mira Di's cigarette burns, the alcohol on her breath, the scraps of daylight that were able to creep through the wood as I lay trapped in that brothel. "No," I say. Even though I know it's dangerous. "Especially not after what happened to Azra."

"I don't either," Connie says. And somehow, I can tell that her own memories have come flooding back to her as well. "So, for now, let's just go to sleep, and tomorrow we can call Azra and tell her what we've learned. Maybe it'll mean more to her."

"So, I called one of the girls who I was in the brothel with," Azra says while Connie has her on speakerphone. "She got away too, but her boyfriend is a part of the gang, and they're still together. So I think she might be able to help us figure out where they've moved to now."

Connie and I look at each other.

"There's something else we've learned," I say. "Rosy's brother told me she's at a restaurant called the Taj Mahal. He overheard his father talking about it last night."

"But there are about a dozen Taj Mahal restaurants in New York," Connie adds. "We checked."

"She's at the Taj Mahal?" says Azra, panic in her voice. "Oh God, it must be the same place they took me when I first came. I know where it is," Azra says, her breath heavy. "It's a restaurant next to a hotel in Queens. It has an apartment above it. Some of the girls live there."

"In the restaurant?" I ask, confused.

"Above the restaurant," Azra says. "There's a small room with cubicled beds to cram in at least twenty girls. Most of the girls are Indian."

"So what now? Is that enough to go to the police?" I ask. "We could go to Sue? Rini Di is back in a couple of days too."

Connie looks at me then as if to say, *We've already discussed this.* Azra sighs. "That would be the right thing to do. But it'll take a long time to get the police to do anything here now that the investigation is active. They'll have moved by the time they're authorized to do anything."

"But it's better than nothing," I say.

"It might end up *being* nothing," Azra points out, the only one among us who might actually know what she's talking about. "What do we have so far? We know that Rosy has been trafficked out of your hometown. If she followed the same route as me, as her brother tells us, she is likely in New York, but we have no evidence. And we have a guess—it might be a good one, but it's still a guess—that she's at the Taj Mahal, which I know is definitely used for trafficking, but again, there is no proof outside of my saying so."

"Taj Mahal is not a guess. Her brother overheard Suraj Sharma say she is at Taj Mahal. I heard a snippet too," I say with some emphasis, hoping they won't back down now.

"And then there's the small matter of us being really, really busy," says Connie. "Between now and the competition, there's pretty much no time."

She's right; it's a tight schedule with no time to think, let alone stake out our own plan.

"So, we have a choice—take this to the people in charge, who may not be able to do anything. At least not quickly. Or risk everything and try ourselves," Azra says, her voice grim with determination. It's then that I truly understand—Azra isn't just doing this to help me. She wants to save Rosy from the fate she had to endure, just as much as I want to save her from the fate I've avoided. "How sure are you that Rosy is in there?" she asks me.

I look at Connie and see the same determination in her dark eyes, imagining what she had to witness her own mother go through. I take a deep breath. "Do I think she might be there? Yes. Am I sure she's there? No," I reply honestly.

"That's not a strong enough case to take to the police. But it's strong enough that we should try," Azra says. "I could take us. I just got my driver's license."

"Are you sure you want to help?" I falter. However much I want to find Rosy, I hear the reality of the evil these men can do in Azra's voice. I have doubts. I don't want to put my two new friends in danger for the sake of an old friend. I don't want to keep so much from Rini Di. I wish I never had to make this kind of choice.

"I got away from them once, didn't I? I want to do this for other girls from my village," Azra says gravely. But I can hear the worry in her voice. "Here's what I think we should do: We should try to get in, just to the restaurant. If it doesn't seem safe, we can wait outside, at a safe distance, and see if she comes or goes."

"We can't go there now—we're training all day and there will be no chance for us to slip out," Connie says. "But we have time over the weekend."

"All right. It's a plan, then. But I have to stress to you girls—this is dangerous, for all of us. I know I'm only nineteen, but that technically makes me the adult in charge and the one who will be in the most trouble if things go wrong. We need to be careful, and I need to know you'll listen to me if we do this."

"Yes," Connie and I both say in unison.

"Okay then. See you Saturday."

The first of our problems is the permission we need to leave the camp, and I'm almost certain we're not going to get it. But to my surprise, Connie returns with a smile less than five minutes after declaring she has it covered.

"Done," she says.

"What! How?"

"I told her about Azra, that she would be with us the whole day, and that we wanted to see some of the New York sites."

"That's it? So easy?"

Connie rolls her eyes. "This isn't jail, you know. It was nothing—she wants us to go out and have some fun, quiet our nerves before the big day. She told me they had to cut all the sightseeing stuff this year due to funding. Save the awe for when I do something really cool."

When Saturday finally arrives, I seem to be the only one who feels guilty about the lie, but this is soon forgotten in a fresh bout of uncertainty. We have set out on an errand that seems impossible in the light of day. It's too late to pull out, and Azra and Connie are both pretty much in this position because of me, so I can't buckle now.

It takes about an hour and forty-five minutes to get to the neighborhood called Queens. I look out the car window; we're on a busy road called Roosevelt Avenue full of delivery trucks, taxis, cars, and bikes. I hear the familiar sound of a train, but then I realize that the train is above us, raised on tracks. We drive past shops, restaurants, bars, and parlors. There are photographs of girls in bras and panties advertised under signs saying GENTLEMEN'S CLUB, different but also similar to the posters around the fair back home. The road is asphalted, and the sidewalks are cemented, but the avenue in Queens has begun to feel like the dirt stretch of Girls Bazaar. Banner photos of girls in various seductive poses offering relaxation, fun, happiness, and even heaven are stretched out above massage parlors and nail salons.

"This is the road," Connie says, pointing to the green road sign. We turn onto a street, shabbier than the avenue but equally crowded. Shoppers, vendors, deliverymen, people giving out handouts litter the sidewalks. "Those are chica cards," Azra explains. They have pictures of half-naked women with a phone number and the words FREE DELIVERY printed on top. "*Chica* means 'girl' in Spanish."

Near the upturned crates and overflowing garbage bags are women checking their cell phones, the same glazed look in their eyes as in Girls Bazaar. "They're scanning the street for anyone who wants a massage," Azra tells Connie and me, though we need no explanation. We are both all too familiar with this. One woman drags in a deep puff of smoke from a cigarette.

"This is where we get a lot of calls for help," says Azra. "A lot of girls here are stuck in hell."

The narrow storefronts are very close together with dim stairwells going up. Some of the street-level businesses are restaurants; others are beauty parlors, massage parlors, jewelry stores, bars, a grocery store, and lo and behold: a pawnshop. I gasp at the similarity to Girls Bazaar. There are about twenty or so buildings on either side of the street, three or four stories high—drab, narrow, and claustrophobic.

I can smell the earthy aromas of restaurant waste and fresh produce, and actually hear a Bollywood song from one of the restaurants as we drive past.

Azra knows this part of the city all too well.

And then we see it. The Taj Mahal is on a street that is even grayer and grimier than any of the streets we've driven through so far. I look out the window at people living in shanties, under bridges, and on the street, and I realize that there are poor people in America too.

We drive past the restaurant, as planned. It's poorly lit, too dark to see too far into it.

"Let's circle back one more time," Azra says. "Tell me what you see next time."

We circle back through a particularly grotty, narrow side street. We pass a sidewalk lined with dumpsters, a few boarded-up shops, and rats the size of mongooses rifling through litter. The boards have some nicely drawn graffiti in colored chalks with the words BELIEVE and LOVE FOREVER drawn on them.

"Narrow glass door covered in red plastic," Connie says. "There's a phone number. It says they deliver." Azra slows down as much as she can as Connie takes the number down on her cell phone. "What now?" Connie asks.

"Well, we can't just walk in and ask for Rosy on a hunch. But we can get closer. It is a restaurant, after all," Azra says.

Connie looks around outside. "Can we park on this road?"

"No, but we can a couple of blocks over."

Azra has to search for a while, but she does eventually find parking. She pulls into a space and turns to face us both, Connie in the passenger seat, me in the back. "I just have to make sure. Are we positive we want to do this?" she asks.

Connie turns to me. It's hard to believe I've only known her such a short time. "I know I do. We just have to promise we stick together, no matter what."

I think of Sadaf. What would I have done if she weren't with me the last time we went to find Rosy? If she hadn't thought to find Baba and Salman?

"It's a deal," I say, and Azra nods in agreement. "For now, let's just see if we can get a closer look," I suggest.

Before we get out of the car, Azra has some rules for us. "I need to get you back to the camp safe and sound, okay? Act normal. No speaking to anyone, anyone at all. And no obvious attempts to look around. But what we're looking for is any sign that there's a cleaning taking place." We both look at her, unsure what this means. "They do a deep cleaning some weekends in the apartment upstairs. Last thing they want is a sanitation violation. They hire a girl who has to use the sink in the restaurant's kitchen. If she's there, it means the doors upstairs are unlocked."

We nod in unison. As we begin to walk in the direction of the restaurant, Connie and Azra try to act casual, chatting about some movie they've both seen that I haven't even heard of. Which is fine with me because I have my eyes on the Taj Mahal down the road. No one is around at first. Then a woman turns the corner down the street and starts walking toward us. We continue as before, making one pass by the building. I stay between the two girls, taking a quick peek inside, but can't see much. It's too dim.

We get to the next crossroad and follow Azra's lead as she keeps walking. She stops outside a jewelry store where we can still see the restaurant.

"Did you guys see anything?" I ask.

"Nothing that would make anyone think it's anything other than a restaurant," Azra says. "You can hear music and some chatter. There're enough people inside that I feel comfortable getting a table."

We stand there for a moment as a white car pulls up outside the restaurant. A man steps out, built and tall. He walks with a slouch toward the door and then pauses outside to light a cigarette. The sun twinkles on the gold band with a red stone on his ring finger. A silver bracelet and bands of beads hang from his right wrist. He seems to wear some kind of gold chain around his neck as well. We take a few steps down the road to see his face more clearly and I notice the scar running down from his left ear to his chin.

Azra suddenly turns on her heel and starts walking in the opposite direction. "Oh God, oh God, oh God."

"What's the matter?" Connie asks.

"We have to get out of here," she says, her voice frantic. She's almost running down the road now, turning a corner so we can't see the restaurant any longer.

Azra bends over, hands on her knees, breath coming fast. She doesn't say anything.

"Are you okay?" I ask. "Do you need anything?"

She stands up straight, panic in her breath. "I know him. He was one of the worst ones. He would have killed me if I hadn't escaped." She crouches to the ground, her head in her hands.

We squat down beside her on our haunches. I feel sweat trickle down the back of my leg. My fingers dig into my palms. What have I done? All my fights for survival have been based around the idea of winning. In recent months I've begun to fight so hard for what I want that I've hardly given any regard to other people. I didn't even think what it might mean to Azra to come back to the place where she was exploited.

Connie puts a hand on Azra's sleeve. "We can leave right now," she says.

Azra lets out a ragged sigh. "I haven't seen him since I left. I just don't think I can go back there."

"I wish I'd never suggested this," I say fervently.

Worn out and remorseful, we try to think of what we should do next. But all I want is to help Azra feel okay again.

Finally, we go to a park by the river. There's a little stall there where Connie buys us snacks and drinks and we settle down on a bench.

"I'm so sorry," I say to Azra. "We should never have gone there. I didn't even think about what this would do to you . . ." I stammer, twisting my bracelet around my wrist. I wish I could knock on Jamila

Bua's door and have her come over with her tea leaves and sugar. I wish Mai were here to comfort her the way she's comforted Mira Di so many times.

"It's not your fault," she says, holding up her hand to stop me. "I knew the risks. I want to help her just as much as you do."

We all look out at the water for a while, eating our chips, all of us desperately fighting tears. Azra's cheeks are flushed. Slowly, the color on her face subsides. It's obvious that she's thinking hard. Her brow is creased, her eyes staring intently at the ducks in the river, her jaw clenched.

"It's okay. I'll be okay. That place is a fortress, but it's a fortress I know," Azra says, her breathing steadier. "We can't let her stay there. Not with him around."

CHAPTER TWENTY-SEVEN

When we return, the white car is gone. We wait as Azra parks her battered little car as close as she can to the restaurant. It's the car she uses for work, and she seems terrified that something bad will happen to it. "But we need it close so we can get away from here as fast as possible," Azra says.

"If I were her, I wouldn't worry too much about someone breaking into that old thing," Connie whispers to me. Her humor provides a small amount of relief to my nerves.

The bells on the front door to the Taj Mahal jangle as we push our way inside, my heart suddenly in my throat. The inside of the restaurant is no surprise after the pictures. It's cramped and ugly. The floor is sticky under my sneakers. But the smell still takes me home. I can see kebabs hanging from skewers over a tandoor through the glass window that gives a glimpse into the kitchen.

We're seated at a small table covered with a plastic tablecloth. Connie sits with her back to the kitchen. Azra and I sit across from her so she can keep an eye on the kitchen.

"I've never eaten any of this stuff," Connie mumbles, looking perplexedly at the menu.

"You've never had Indian food?" says Azra. "I'd say you're in for a treat, but I think we can find you a better introduction," she says, winking at me. But I swear I can feel her heartbeat vibrate through the table. Or perhaps it's mine.

There's a swinging door separating the dining area from the kitchen. From Azra's instructions, I know that the bathroom is right opposite the kitchen door, but I can't see it from where we are. There are enough tables with diners and waiters rushing about, and a great deal of noise coming from the kitchen for everyone to ignore us. We're all Asian and our brown skin blends in. But there are tables on either side of the kitchen door, so the passage in and out is quite cramped.

"This place is such a mess. I think we'll be able to walk straight out," Connie says.

"Don't make that mistake," Azra warns her. "It might look like chaos in here, but these people have an eye on everything."

The door swings open then, and I seem to see her at the same time Azra does—a woman with a mop. It could be anyone from the kitchen staff, but as the door is held open for a waiter to file through with an armful of plates, she heads for a door at the back of the kitchen.

Azra's eyes dart around nervously and I'm sure she must be worried that somebody might recognize her. That the man with the gold chain could come back. I know then what I have to do.

"I'll go," I say.

Azra's eyes widen. "What? Are you sure?"

"I'm sure. It's our only chance."

"You'll have to be quick," Azra says. "The longer you spend upstairs, the more likely you are to be caught."

"And if you're not back in five minutes, we're calling the police," Connie adds.

"Order the naan, kaali daal, and tandoori chicken," I say as I stand up. "You know the plan." I pick up my bag, slinging it over my shoulder as I head toward the door to the bathroom. I push it open and find the kitchen door is open too, with a waiter standing and shouting at someone inside. I get a quick look at the stairs to the back and then, as the waiter looks at me, I quickly turn my head away and push the door to the bathroom open. Once inside, I stand by the door, keeping it open just a crack.

The fight in the kitchen seems never-ending—they're shouting loudly in Hindi, the waiter defending himself against charges of breaking a plate, for which he'll have to pay. Finally, he shoves the doors to the dining area open. As the kitchen door swings shut, I bolt, sliding through the opening and turning in the direction of the back door, hoping with all my being that no one sees me. If they do, they seem too busy to care. I twist the knob. Behind the back door is a narrow set of stairs that I hope is empty.

And it seems like it is.

I press myself against the wall, creeping up each landing, heart pounding so loud that Connie and Azra can probably hear it from where they're sitting. I come to a halt as I hear more shouting behind me, but it's just the waiter going back into the kitchen.

I arrive on the first landing. Then the second. Each landing feels darker than the last. Finally, before me are two doors, one to the right of me and one directly in front of me. I look from one to the other, paralyzed. What if I knock on the wrong one? What if there are traffickers inside? Which one is it?

I take a few seconds to slow my breathing. The doors are identical, but underneath the one in front of me I can see a crack of light at the bottom. This must be it.

I hold my breath and wonder what to do.

There's rustling inside, the lock turning. The door opens a crack, and the woman from downstairs comes out holding her bucket and a mop. She looks cautious at first, frightened even, but then she gets a good look at me standing there and her expression turns suspicious.

"Please can you bring Rosy out here?" I ask, the words spilling out of my mouth.

"Who's asking?" she says.

"My name is Heera. You can tell her I'm from Forbesganj, her village."

She gives me a long, hard stare. There are no more words spoken between us, but I hope that my eyes tell her my story. That I mean her no harm. There's a pause between us that feels like a lifetime before she turns to go back inside, the door closing softly behind her again. I'm not sure what's happening inside. She could be getting Rosy. Or she could be alerting Rosy's captors.

As I wait, every one of my muscles tightens with terror. I hear what I think are soft voices behind the door and I remember what Azra said—there could be at least twenty girls in there, mostly Indian, trapped in the same nightmare. What will their fate be? Who's coming for them?

But then the door opens, just wide enough for one girl to fit through. In that moment, I catch a glimpse of the cubicled beds stacked up like shelves, just before the door is shut again.

The girl stands there wearing a short tight dress, so low in the neck that it makes her look slightly plump. I can hardly recognize her—her face is smudged with the remnants of makeup. But I do recognize her long black eyelashes, thicker because of the mascara. Her upturned eyes look dazed and I wonder if she's drugged. The sweet air about her has disappeared, replaced with a hard look. There is a red mark of a hand on the cheek above her dimple.

"Rosy," I say in an urgent whisper. "It's me. Heera."

She kind of nods. I hope she's not so out of it that my name doesn't register.

"What are you doing here?" she says languidly, as if she's talking to someone in her sleep.

I don't know why I'm thrown by this question. I wonder if the drugs make her talk like this or if she's imagined this scene so many times that she thinks it's a dream.

"I'm here to rescue you!" I say.

Her face hardens and her eyebrows shoot up. "Me? Why?"

The fear and despair on her face break my heart. She doesn't even look relieved. Or angry. I'd hoped that she would know I would never forsake her.

"Look," I say, with an impatient glance over my shoulder. The noise from the restaurant combined with the murmurs on the other side of the door feel loud enough to engulf our voices. "My friends are waiting downstairs. We can take you to safety, but you have to come now and come alone."

The cleaning lady opens the door then, her eyes darting all around us. "What's going on, Rosy? They'll be back soon."

"Nothing," Rosy says in a dull voice.

"You know this girl?"

"Yes, she's a neighbor from the village. She's looking for work."

My heart picks up a beat. Clearly, Rosy is alert enough to cook up a story. Maybe she's exaggerating her drugged demeanor enough to fool the traffickers as well.

The lady gives me another look, winks, and moves on.

I can hear the beginning of a commotion downstairs. It's Connie, as planned, with her distraction.

The clock has started.

"Are you coming?" I whisper urgently.

"How? I can't just walk out of here. They'll see me and beat me." Her voice is a hoarse whisper, trembling. She looks utterly panic-stricken. Her body sways a little and she leans against a wall to prop herself up. The drugs do seem to have a hold on her still.

I grit my teeth. We have to get out now or not at all.

I pull out a black burka from the plastic shopping bag that I have in my hands. Her eyes widen. "Put this on and make it fast."

Rosy's face lights up. Suddenly there's a hint of life and intelligence in it. Then, for a second, she hesitates, looking back at the room behind her. I can see her deciding, and I resist the urge to grab her by the arm and pull her out of here.

Then, finally, after what feels like an age, she steps forward.

I unfurl the garment and in seconds, the burka is over her frock, engulfing her arms and legs right down to her toes. I take a scarf out, wrap it around her head, and knot it at the back. All you can now see is her eyes.

I take her hand. "Ready?" I ask.

Another second. She nods.

We run down the stairs. I move her in front of me as we walk straight through the kitchen to the swinging door. There are a couple of pairs of eyes on us from the line cooks, but everyone's attention seems to be elsewhere.

Two waiters are huddled on the other side of the doorway, but they're looking out toward the restaurant at Connie as she throws a fit over a smooshed cockroach in her daal. "They'll be more afraid of the American girl than the Indian girl," Azra had said when she'd pulled the bug out of her bag and given it to Connie.

I close my eyes; we have no choice but to push ahead. As the waiters go over to help clean up the mess, I crane my head around the corner to ensure no one is looking in our direction.

I hear Rosy beginning to whimper and give her a nudge as we push past the waiters and back into the restaurant, alive with commotion. But as we get close to the exit, we have to pass by the cash counter. And a man, the owner it seems, sits there. As we pass, I see him giving Rosy a hard look. Somehow, I know it can't possibly be this easy.

Everyone's eyes are on Connie as she demands a comped meal while we walk quickly through the exit and onto the sidewalk outside, the bells on the door jingling as it shuts behind us. I don't let go of her elbow, afraid she'll slip through my fingers like sand.

And then I don't stop. I don't even look back for Azra or Connie. We're supposed to make it to the car and wait there until they can extricate themselves and join us. I even have the car key, and I know which button to press to open the door.

I push her. *Faster. Faster.* The car is there. I can see it, but I can hear the footsteps behind us, too hard on the pavement to be my friends, and I spin around.

The owner is there, lunging for Rosy. But I'm between them. He has to reach over my body in order to catch her. I push her hard, giving her a head start to run to the car.

I turn around and face him on the sidewalk in front of his restaurant. He's stocky and square, with rippling muscles, his tiny eyes close together. There are tattoos covering his arms, which are raised, poised to strike.

He stops for a second, taken aback when he sees that a fourteen-year-old girl is blocking his path. He laughs aloud, as if this is a joke. As if he can't believe that a girl half his size is poised and ready to fight him. He doesn't even bother to pull out a weapon. He simply puts out a hand to push me out of the way.

Size is never a true indication of muscular power and efficiency.

I'm too low for his hand to find me. I've already crouched down to center myself. He looks down when his hand hits air. In that split second, I punch him straight in the nose, my foot meeting the side of his head, hard, with a roundhouse kick. I may be smaller than him, but I kick high.

The smaller man usually makes up for the imbalance of power by his greater agility.

I see from the corner of my eye that Connie and Azra are out. Azra is shouting into her phone. Connie is with Rosy, screaming at her to get in the car.

Strive to keep him off balance, regardless of his size.

I feel a sharp pain shoot through my arm. He is falling to the ground but has yanked my wrist and pulled me down with him. I'm on him. He holds my face to push me away. But that leaves my arms, legs, and teeth free. I bite his finger as I thrust my right knee into his chin and jab my left elbow into his ribs.

Don't think. Feel.

I've never felt such total awareness as I feel right now, fighting for Rosy. I'm aware of my body, that it has performed perfectly. I'm aware of my friends out there protecting us. I'm aware of the gathering crowds. I'm aware of the sidewalk and the sky, but most of all I am aware of my opponent and his shortcomings.

Attack your opponent at his weakest points, applying leverage principles so that his body, and the limbs of his body, are used to work toward his own defeat.

He doesn't know how to control his body. He doesn't know how to control his mind. He has lost before he began because he was blinded by his size and strength. But I'm equally aware of my surroundings as of myself. I give and I take. I balance each move with a countermove. A forward knee thrust is matched with a backward knee jab. I don't waste an action or a moment.

As he groans in agony, I know I'll easily keep him down on the ground. But next I see that the white car has pulled back up outside the restaurant. Four men, including the man with the gold chain, spill out of the car. Rosy is screaming. I may have pinned the boss to the ground, but we can't take on so many people. Somebody is sure to have a gun. No one will help us here. And suddenly I feel trapped. One man tries to pull Connie away from the car. Another has grabbed hold of Rosy and suddenly, I can feel arms on me too. Connie spins and kicks the man in his chest before he can even turn around, but I feel someone strong hold me by my arms and pull me up . . .

And right then, a siren blares. One police car after another. The man's hold on me loosens and the sound of sprinting footsteps on pavement echoes through the streets.

The crowd quickly disperses and the four of us are standing there again, looking at one another with awe and wonder. All four men are gone. Azra holds up a hand in a salute. Connie and I exchange a look of victory.

But as the uniformed men come toward us, I watch as Rosy goes rigid with fear, crying and shaking, looking at us with suspicion.

"Not the police! Not the police!" Rosy screams in Hindi.

"Shh," I say, putting an arm around her. "It's okay! They're here to help."

Azra takes over, telling them that Rosy had been imprisoned and drugged, most likely raped. She shows them her ID. "We work with Survivors of Trafficking Network NGO. This girl is a survivor, and she needs medical attention."

Rosy's cries have not stopped. The medics lead her to the truck and do an examination. "We'll take her in," says the medic. "Only one of you can come with her."

"I'll go," I say. "I can translate for her. She doesn't speak much English."

He looks at me skeptically, but when Rosy's crying gets louder, he caves.

Azra is talking to the police officer. "Go," she says. "I'll meet you there."

I coax Rosy into the back of the ambulance, where they have her lie down. I sit beside her, holding her hand.

"They will kill my father," she howls. "You don't understand what you've done. They will kill him!"

At the hospital, Rosy is wheeled into an examination room. They find a nurse who speaks Hindi and make me wait outside. Soon, Connie and Azra arrive. We all get first aid. Our bruises are cleaned, antiseptic and ointments applied. Strangely, I just have a few scratches on my face and arms. We are given blankets to wrap around ourselves and asked to rest for a few hours in case we have any dizzy spells. My shoulder throbs. But some things are worth the hurt. Rosy is free.

"That was one hell of a kick, Heera," says Connie admiringly.

"Yours in that man's chest wasn't bad either," I say with a chuckle.

I tell them what happened upstairs—the cleaning lady, the burka, the drugged stupor that Rosy was in.

"How's she doing?" Connie asks.

"I don't know," I say. "They're still examining her. But she's really upset."

"Upset?" Connie asks, puzzled.

"She keeps saying they'll kill her father. I hope we did the right thing."

"Are you kidding? We just saved a girl's life," Azra says. "She's upset because these are the kinds of things traffickers say to control the girls, to keep them in fear. They do it all the time. I wish I knew kung fu. I would have broken a few teeth along the way."

I'm about to make my plea to Azra to get her to start training when Rini Di and Sue arrive, and suddenly it all becomes very real. Tears that I didn't know I was holding back rush out of me.

"Hush," Rini Di says, arms around me. "I was so worried about you two. You have no idea what those thugs are capable of. You put yourself in an extremely dangerous position." She hugs me again, then asks, "Where is Rosy?"

"She's still inside. They're examining her. I'm so sorry, Rini Di, I didn't listen to you," I say, my cheeks burning.

"There will be time to talk later," she says, looking at me keenly. "For now, you should know that while I'm proud of you for sticking up for your friend, against all odds, I'm disappointed that you didn't take me into confidence. We already had Taj Mahal under surveillance. That is why the police could reach you so quickly. We would have rescued Rosy without you getting hurt."

A wave of shame comes over me. I should have known I could always trust her.

Rini Di looks sad and then, as is her habit when worried, pushes her glasses up her nose. "It gave us all a big fright. Things could have gone either way. A trained adult would have made things easier. We could have gotten the police to go in and get Rosy out. There would have been no need for a kung fu fight on the sidewalk of Queens."

My lips quiver. I would have liked more praise from Rini Di. The last thing I ever want to do is disappoint her, but I felt I had to do something. And how could I believe that the police could help, if I go by the likes of Suraj Sharma?

So, stubbornly, I hold my own. "Rini Di, you know the police wouldn't go anywhere on a hunch. We had no proof. It was all just guesswork based on what Manish said and what Azra knew. Even Bruce Lee said, *There is no help but self-help.*"

"Perhaps," Rini Di concedes with a nod, "but that doesn't mean you should have kept me out of the loop. We have to work together like a team to bust the entire ring. They have many girls like Rosy. Now some traffickers may have escaped in the chaos, alerted their counterparts in India maybe. We were planning to swoop down on all of them together."

She doesn't say anything more. But I can picture the cubicled beds, the girls who I could have put in even more danger without realizing it. If I speak any more, I will cry again.

The doctor emerges and wants to know who is responsible for Rosy. Sue introduces herself and Rini Di. "She is dehydrated and is likely under the influence of narcotics," the doctor says. That's all I hear before Rini Di and Sue pull the doctor aside to discuss further, disappearing behind the door.

Azra and Connie come up to me then, their faces strained.

"She's okay," I say.

They're all smiles. Somebody has given them a candy bar and they give me a piece to nibble on. We never did eat that tandoori chicken and kaali daal at Taj Mahal.

Rini Di and Sue emerge from the room. I'm about to speak, but Rini Di puts her hand on my arm. "Not now, Heera. Let's finish here first."

Then she turns to face all of us. "Okay, look, they'll keep Rosy overnight. She is sedated, so they advise we go home and return in the morning to pick her up." We nod with relief, but Rini Di continues looking at Connie and me with concern. "But I'm worried about the two of you. The competition is tomorrow, and you two have been through quite an ordeal. The doctor says you are okay, but I'm not so sure that you should compete."

"We're fine, Rini Di! Please let us compete," Connie and I protest.

Rini Di let's out a breath. "Let's return to the camp now and we'll see how you feel in the morning. We'll talk about the rest after the competition is over." I can hear the note of finality in Rini Di's voice. She shakes Azra's hand. "Would you like to join us? And then we'd like to know exactly what happened."

Azra nods. "Of course. Don't be too hard on them, Rini Di. They were heroes today."

Rini Di and Sue both look at us, identical expressions on their faces: tiny smiles, lips pursed, eyebrows raised—a mix of something like pride and concern, perhaps some anger too. This thing is far from over.

On the way home Rini Di is silent while Sue reprimands Connie and me for the danger we put ourselves in. "You had the best of intentions, and you were able to do a good thing, but this could have been handled much more effectively by adults. By the authorities. Rescuing girls from brothels is not child's play."

We think these are her concluding words, but then she notices our woebegone expressions and drooping shoulders. "We're proud of your courage and loyalty but would have liked your trust as well. The important thing is that you're safe and we have Rosy," she adds. "We will celebrate with pizza and ice cream at home."

We turn to each other and smile. The day has ended well.

CHAPTER TWENTY-EIGHT

Wolves who look like Gainul are chasing me. I run to Rini Di's office in the library, but the door is shut. I wake up sweating.

A nightmare.

I sit up, exhausted after a fitful night thinking of how Rini Di must feel. I broke every rule in the book yesterday, but worse, I have smashed Rini Di's trust in the worst way possible. I resolve I will make her proud of me at the competition today.

The pain in my wrist that wields the staff is worse than it was last night. But I remind myself, I'm the boss of my pain; it's not the boss of me. I will prove to Rini Di that I am worthy of all the time and effort she has put in me. As I wash and dress, I tell myself that I will restore her faith in me. Still, it does nothing for the butterflies in my stomach as I head down to the breakfast room.

My gratitude and my guilt surface as I see that Rini Di has made me poha and boiled egg, the same meal that won me my last title. A surge of confidence flows through my body. Rini Di still loves me. Her first words are, "Are you okay?"

I respond with a grin. "Fighting fit, Rini Di," I say.

She smiles back.

The staff in my hand feels solid as I walk out the door. I know in my bones that whatever happens today, my life will never be the same again.

Rini Di tells us to do breathing exercises on the way to the venue in Sue's minivan. I'm not a big believer in yoga and meditation, but I know that she is. I breathe in and out fast.

"Breathe in for three seconds, hold it in for a second more, breathe out for six seconds," says Rini Di. "Repeat ten times. Do it slowly." I try, I really do, despite pointing out to Bornani that not everyone in India sits around meditating all the time. But it isn't working. Not only can I not meditate, I discover that it's in fact possible to forget how to breathe entirely.

Suddenly, I wish Mai were with me. I close my eyes, hoping to feel her calming presence, but the faces I see belong to Salman and Mira Di. The two humans who would be most aghast at just how close I am to giving up, reminding me just how much is riding on the next few hours. I think of the dreams that Salman sacrificed so that I could be here, how easily I could have been one of the girls in a back room just like Mira Di. And then we are about to arrive. I hurriedly open my eyes, knowing that if I let my mind travel down that path, there will be absolutely no way back.

Relief rushes over me when we finally reach the venue. The convention hall is smaller than I had imagined, around the same size as the stadium I last performed in back home. I look over at Connie and she flashes me a smile, but I can see that she's not with me; she's on that blue square already. I envy her focus.

Like a robot, I move with the team through the cold hallways to the locker room in the underbelly of the convention center. It's eerily quiet. I would have thought at least here there would be bustle. We walk past a gym where some kids are working out inside. Then we reach the locker room, buzzing with noise.

I follow Connie and Bornani, neither of whom show any outward signs of being nervous. I have nothing to put in a locker: Both Bornani and Connie have bags, but I'm wearing my uniform and carrying my bo staff and a bottle of water.

Connie sees some other kids she knows from past competitions, so I stand there absently until Bornani grabs my arm and makes me sit down.

"What's going on with you?" she hisses. Getting no response, she opens my bottle of water and hands it to me. "Drink," she says.

I do as I am told.

"Now take some water and put it on the back of your neck."

I do this too. And remarkably, I feel better.

"And now breathe with me," she says, her lyrical voice strangely soothing. I follow her. It's the same rhythm Rini Di suggested, but for some reason, it works now.

After what feels like forever, I open my eyes. I give Bornani a nod. A smile is still a step too far.

I wish I could get it over with now, in this moment that I'm finally feeling a little better. But I know there's still some time to go before my category is up.

The announcements begin in the arena, and the butterflies in my belly transform into a more violent sort of winged creature. I think I'm going to be sick.

Suddenly, I'm back on the pavement outside the Taj Mahal, hundreds of feet chasing me. I hear the roar in my ears as I get into position. I feel the hands pulling at me, someone knocking me on the back of my head.

I shake off the terror.

"You're going to be up soon," Connie says.

I nod. The beginners are always first.

She pauses her routine for a minute to throw her arms around me. "You've got this."

"So do you," I say.

She nods. "Yup. The only difference is that I know that. You don't."

Soon, Rini Di comes to call me. My stomach bottoms out when I see her standing in the doorway. I wonder if it's too late to bolt, but there's no way past her. And even if there were, I'd never be able to live with myself. I follow her out of the locker room and through the hallway. She's quiet all the way to the entrance to the arena. Then she turns to me.

"Walk through these doors. From there Master Yi will take over," she says. "I just want to say that whatever happens out there, you are already a star."

"Even after yesterday?" I ask, a knot forming in my throat. "Even though I betrayed you?"

She gives me a wry smile. "Yes, Heera. What you did was dangerous. But your intentions were good. I'm very proud of you. You stood up for your friend and used kung fu to fight off a man twice your size. We'll talk about the rest later. An adult who wasn't in charge of your welfare would probably agree that what happened yesterday was the true test, not what happens in there today."

Her words knock a million-pound weight off my shoulders. "But adults who *are* in charge of my welfare feel differently?"

She grins as she runs her hand over my arm in a gesture that is now as familiar as it is comforting. "We may *feel* the same way, but it is our job to *think* differently."

I walk out into the arena; the lights are blinding. There are individual competitions going on in different parts of the room. My eyes adjust and I see Master Yi. As I approach, it's clear that he's treated with deference by the other competitors, teachers, even judges. For a moment, I feel like the luckiest girl in the room with him in my corner. But when he looks at me, all that falls away.

"Heera, little diamond. You are up soon," he says.

I nod. Speech escapes me.

"You are ready. Ninety seconds for your forms demonstration, then sixty seconds off, and forty-five seconds with the staff. That's it. That's what all your hard work comes down to."

I nod again. He thinks I'm prepared. I disagree. He also doesn't know I hurt my arm yesterday.

I sit through several performances, massaging my wrist

absentmindedly. The Shaolin hand forms don't shake me. Yes, the competition is at a top level, but I've competed and won before. For the weapons display, I just don't know. I'm untested. One girl uses a saber as though she was born with it attached to her arm. Another uses a spear with equal grace. I wonder if my humble staff is a little *too* humble; it doesn't look as impressive as either of those weapons. And then my name is called. I'd thought once I stepped out onto the mat, it would be just like it had been back home, that everything else would fall away.

But now, the panic rises inside me as I look around, feeling just how much is at stake—the prize money itself is enough to change the trajectory of my entire family, maybe even enough to get Mira Di out of the line. Enough to keep Sania from getting anywhere near it. There's the prospect and the hope of future camps, my new friends and mentors, my own future course in life. Standing here at all feels surreal. If I win, I promise myself that I'll keep going. If I don't win, I'll keep going. I could be an English teacher, a kung fu teacher, anything . . .

"Heera," Master Yi says. "Go on."

I try to move my feet, but they're cemented to the spot.

"Heera?" he repeats, more urgently.

I bring myself to look at him somehow.

"Master, I—"

He gives my hand a squeeze, kind eyes sparkling. "One foot in front of the other, Heera. It's now or never."

I search the audience for someone, anyone, who might bring me back into the moment. I find Rini Di, and she smiles her warmest smile. I see the pride in her eyes behind those round metal glasses. I think of what she said. That I had already passed the actual test yesterday. This should be nothing by comparison.

"Be like water," I whisper, closing my eyes.

I take a step, and then another, and another. Before I know it, I am in the center of that blue mat. I take my position.

Later, I know I won't remember a thing that happens out here in the arena—only the feeling of oneness, as though my body, the floor, the surrounding air are all made of the same stuff. I don't have to think about my next move. My body knows what to do. As I move from stance to stance, it comes to me like a heartbeat.

But the forms demonstration was always going to be the easy part. As I walk off to applause, I'm focused on Master Yi's face. It is inscrutable. He won't be distracting me with talk of what is already done. He's thinking only of what lies ahead. As I approach the sidelines, he hands me my staff and rests a hand on my shoulder. "The staff is you; you are the staff," he says in a grand voice. "But the elbow," he adds in a conspiratorial whisper. "Remember to tuck in your elbow."

I'm floating on a cloud as I go back out to the center, staff held proud in front of me. All the fears have now subsided, and I feel only the mat and the weapon in my hand. I begin with the meditative breath, left hand rising and falling in harmony with it. And then I shift gears as I complete the forward stance sequence, swinging the staff to strike, spinning, twirling, as if I am alone in my earthy kwoon in Forbesganj and the staff is nothing more than the bamboo pole that I held as a child when I learned to walk on a tightrope. I am me—the past and the present and the future.

With no time to think, I move into the sequence that has tripped me up since the beginning—the under-the-leg spin—and for once, I encounter no resistance. With a surge of adrenaline, I complete the sequence and then, finally, thrust the staff forward as I crouch down, balancing just inches above the ground. I drive it into the air, ignoring the pain in my arm as I hold position to bring my routine to a close.

And then it's as though the volume has suddenly been turned up again. I hear the applause of the audience; my name being shouted by someone out there. I bow and step out of the arena. I still don't know how I've done; they won't reveal the scores until the end of the competition, but I know how I feel, and it couldn't be better.

I collapse into a chair as Master Yi finally flashes me his impish grin. "You have finally conquered your greatest opponent."

"Who?" I ask, out of breath and feeling the gazes of my competitors seated all around the blue square.

"Yourself, Heera. It is always yourself."

My eyes widen. And then, as usual, I realize that he's right and has been right all along. Because I am done so early in the day, I can watch Connie as she goes up. She will win something—she's magnificent out there, every move full of power and confidence. She's just as cool as she was during practice at the camp. I leave the bench once she's done and wait by the doorway that leads to the locker rooms.

She throws her arms around me, and only then do I realize something is wrong.

"Connie! You're trembling!"

She smiles, her teeth on the verge of chattering. "You think you were the only one who was afraid? I just pretend they don't exist until it's over. Fake it till you make it, baby!"

Both ravenous, we find Bornani and hunt down Sue, who gives us money to buy what we want at the cafeteria, settling down for a long wait until we can finally hear the results at the end of the day's events.

At long last, all the categories are complete. The fifteen of us from the camp huddle together with our teachers. "What's the prediction, Coach?" Steve, one of the older boys, asks.

"I don't make predictions," Master Yi says.

A howl of protest goes up.

"But if I were to try," he continues with a smile, "our medal tally was nine out of fifteen last year. This year, twelve at least."

There are hoots of approval.

And then Steve turns to me. We've barely exchanged five words until today, and they've all been either "hi" or "bye," so this is strange.

"Are the rumors true?" he asks.

I look around nervously. "What rumors?"

"That you two busted a group of girls out of some slave camp?"

"You bet we did," Connie says, flashing me a cheeky grin. "But it wasn't a slave camp. It was a brothel."

"And it wasn't a group," I say, nudging Connie with my shoulder. "Just one girl."

"Cool," Steve says, turning away.

"That's it?" Connie whispers to me. "Cool? When was the last time he saved another human?"

Is there any reason Shaolin has to come at the very end of all the announcements?

Jujitsu, judo, and karate are all done, and so far, Master Yi's prediction looks like it might just come true. Loud cheers go up each time one of us wins, and there are encouraging words for those who don't. Finally, it's Connie's category—intermediate kung fu. She grabs my hand and presses down on it so hard that I think she's going to break my fingers. Luckily, she has my left hand, so it will soon match with my right, which is aching even more now after my performance.

The announcements begin—the booming voice of the man on the mike is too loud, too final.

Once those are out of the way, Connie lets go of my hand and squeezes her eyes shut.

First comes bronze . . . and it's not her.

Next comes silver . . . once again, someone else.

She opens her eyes, deflated. I grab her arm.

"And in first position is Connie Wright!"

Her eyes widen, and for a second, she freezes. Then she lets out a roar, pumps her fist, and leaps into the air. She's about to run off before she turns back to throw her arms around me in a fierce hug, high-fives her laughing instructors, and then zooms to the podium.

At least Connie won. The day is good regardless of what happens next.

But despite my efforts to slow down my racing heart, I know I didn't come so far to lose.

Finally, the moment of truth has arrived: Beginners are up, the last remaining category of the day. I stand there, with Connie to one side, shiny new jewelry around her neck, Rini Di to the other.

"Look who's here," Rini Di says in my ear. She holds out her phone and I see Salman's face in extreme close-up, before he focuses out and turns the phone to Mai with Sania on her hip. And behind them, Baba stands tall with a proud smile on his face. They all wave out to me, looking slightly confused. I wave back, shooting Rini Di a look of utter amazement.

"How did you do this?" I ask.

"Someone went over from the hostel with a phone and got them on a call."

It's the new house; I can tell from the bright pink of the wall behind them. Sania immediately makes silly faces at me. Mai is crying and waving. For a moment, I feel I've already won.

"They're on mute for a reason," Rini Di says with a smile.

The announcements begin. In third place is the girl with the spear. Figures. She was great.

I breathe in as deeply as I can, bracing myself for disappointment.

"In second place, all the way from India, is Heera Kumari!"

Everything becomes a bit blurry and it's as though I'm flying. Then I realize that I'm upright, thanks to Connie and Rini Di, who have propped me up. Master Yi crushes me to his chest, laughing as he lets me go. My family is no longer on mute, and I know I'm not dreaming when I hear Salman's piercing whistle. I don't hear who comes in first; it doesn't matter. Somehow, someway, I get to the podium on jelly legs.

I raise my hands in a namaste.

"I'm not sure where to begin," I say, staring into my lap. Azra and Connie sit beside me on a couch in Sue's office.

I'm more afraid of this moment than I was of standing before hundreds of people yesterday, with everything on the line. This is Rini Di, and even though she was there for me yesterday, I know I've let her down. Not because I rescued Rosy and not because I didn't tell her the when, how, what, and where of our operation, but because I didn't trust her enough. I might not trust the police, but I have had no reason not to trust her.

"At the beginning is usually a good place," she says gently.

I steal a glance at her face, but I can't read anything from her expression.

"I know you told me to forget about it, to concentrate on the competition. But I just couldn't. Because whatever happened to Rosy and me started in Forbesganj. When they took me, they were planning to send us both off together. If you hadn't rescued me, it would have been me in that room above the restaurant. Instead, I'm here, having the time of my life." A load lifts off me as I get the words out. I look up at last. "Still, if it was only that, I may have been able to let it go. But through Connie, and Azra, we started to figure some things out. We finally put it all together when I got an email from Manish saying she was at a restaurant in New York."

I look at Azra, my eyes pleading for her to step in.

"I had been there before when I was imprisoned by them," she says. "I knew where it was, and a way we could get her out."

Rini Di gives Azra a piercing look. "How did you meet these girls?"

Connie clears her throat. "That was kind of my doing. I met Azra at the shelter a few weeks ago. I wrote to Heera about it, and we worked out that she was from Nepal, just over the border from Forbesganj. And then we started putting together that she was trafficked by Suraj Sharma, and that it sounded like Rosy might have been following the same route."

"We met Azra after the speeches at Sunshine House," I tell her, but I trail off. I can't bring myself to confess to breaking into Rini Di's office. I just can't. But somehow, I know that she already knows.

"Once we figured out where she was, it seemed that unless we got Rosy out of there, we'd lose her," Azra says.

Sue sighs. "So that's how you figured out where she was. But how did you even get her out of there?"

Connie, Azra, and I all lean in. We tell the story, trying not to sound like we're having too much fun as we do it, when we actually do want to crow a little in front of our teachers—the people who have taught us to be brave and fearless. Their mouths hang open just a little.

Rini Di gives her head an incredulous shake. "That is really some story." She pauses, begins again, stops once more. Then, finally, after a deep breath, she speaks. "I know you tried to tell me about this, Heera. There was nothing I felt we could do. And I'm sorry if I didn't hear you properly or share what I was doing more. Sometimes adults feel helpless, and we don't know what to do either, without risking the safety of innocent children. But you—all of you—put yourselves at risk in a way that could have had a disastrous outcome. Heera, you are my responsibility here, so far away from home."

"I didn't mean to—"

Rini Di puts her hand up. "I know. Your intentions were good. By some miracle, the result was excellent too. But we should also consider the process, the risks, and the limits of our ability before we act."

"I was the adult in the room," says Azra. "I'm the one you should blame."

Rini Di turns to her. "How old are you, Azra? Eighteen?"

"Just turned nineteen."

Rini Di shakes her head again. "This isn't about appointing blame. It's about ensuring that nothing like this happens again. You can't put yourself in harm's way when the stakes are so high. These traffickers are killers, which none of you need to be told. All three of you could have been easily captured and seriously hurt."

Rini Di and Sue look at each other.

"But you weren't," says Sue. "So now that the lecture is over—and please know that we were serious about every word—we want to let you know that Rosy is safe at Sunshine House and that we will work with her until her case is resolved."

"Will she make a statement?" I ask.

"She doesn't need to for the FBI to take action," Sue says. "Her traffickers have broken so many laws that the prosecution will continue with or without her. If she chooses to testify, our partner organization will guide her through it."

Connie grabs my hand, and we can't help ourselves; the smiles are wide across our faces. Rini Di looks like she would smile if she weren't trying to be stern.

"And her father?" I ask. "What will happen to him?"

"Well, that's a different story," Rini Di says slowly. "You know that Suraj Sharma has trafficked many girls in the past, including Azra. Including Rosy herself. One of the reasons I couldn't intervene with Rosy is because there is already an investigation into him back in India. This will hopefully lead to his arrest."

"And Ravi Lala?"

"He's part of the same investigation," Rini Di assures me.

I close my eyes and let out a breath I didn't know I was holding. "So, Suraj Sharma won't be killed by his boss?"

"Killed? Probably not," Rini Di says. "But when you make your living trafficking children, you give up the right to have others consider your safety before they take action. You are not responsible for what happens to Suraj Sharma. And neither is Rosy."

"You'd think what we did might even be a good thing, wouldn't you?" says Connie with a grin. I marvel at her courage.

"You'd think, but don't let it get to your head," Sue says with a laugh. "Particularly with what we're going to tell you next."

They exchange a look again.

Finally, it's Rini Di who speaks. "The Martial Arts Foundation would like to award you both with scholarships for a continued training camp here for one full year, along with admission to the local school." Finally, the grin she has been holding back spreads from ear to ear.

Connie and I look at each other, gaping holes where our mouths once were. Then Connie lets out a shout as she leaps to her feet and does a dance of joy. Rini Di and Sue laugh. I sit there like a statue until Connie pulls me off the sofa and twirls me around. She puts me down, and now my world is literally spinning.

Rini Di gives me a reassuring smile. "Celebrate, by all means, but you need to get to work immediately. It's even harder than the camp you just completed. And you'll still be working with Master Yi." She points a finger at us to make sure we're listening. "And this time, don't give us reason to put locks on your doors."

Azra, Connie, and I leave the room. I'm relieved, excited, and exhausted. I collapse onto the warm sofa in the living room and don't think I'll ever move again.

"That worked out better than either of you expected, didn't it?" Azra says with a smile.

"So much better," Connie says, eyes dancing.

"I still can't believe it," I say.

"You girls are amazing," Azra says. "And you really deserve it."

Connie gives her a hug. "Thank you for everything. Are you staying for the party tonight?"

"After everything you girls put me through, of course I am! I have some work to do first, but I'll be back later." Azra gives me a hug too—I'm still getting used to this business of embracing randomly. I suppose there's a lot I'm still getting used to.

"So," Connie says to me. "What's next?"

"I think I'm going to sleep for the next three days," I say.

I go to my room to be by myself, pulling out the Bruce Lee book and opening it to a random page. *I am that which sees the world, and the world is that which is seen by me. I exist for the world, and the world exists for me. If there were no things to be seen, thought about, and imagined, I would not see, think, or imagine.*

I smile as I think of the months of practice before me, and a year of adventure with Connie. I think of my family in the pink house. I think of Salman in the Siliguri school. I think of Rosy in Sunshine House and Suraj Sharma and Ravi Lala in jail, no longer on the prowl in Girls Bazaar. It is like a whole new world awaits me.

One in which we are not just safe, but unstoppable.

CHAPTER TWENTY-NINE

In my dream, a year has gone by. Rini Di drops me near the hospital. I want to walk to Girls Bazaar by myself. My mouth waters as I think of Jamila Bua's samosa and chai. I can't wait to see Mai's expression when she sees I'm an inch taller. I can't wait to go with Salman to the highway and chat under the stars. I wonder what Mira Di will look like now that she's stopped drinking. If Baba's work at the station as a railway porter keeps him away from the gambling den. I hear that little Sania talks nineteen to the dozen now.

The street beneath my feet has changed, now made of asphalt. The usual stench of booze and filth is missing. I can't hear the brawling, the yelling, the crying. The loudspeakers are off. There is no garbage or litter scattered everywhere. Instead, I see rows of rain-washed pink and blue brick houses sparkling in the late-morning sun. Some have pots with flowers outside the doors. Many of the walls are painted with beautiful patterns in white, yellow, green, and red.

My eyes follow the tune of a woman's voice as she dries clothes on the balcony of Ravi Lala's house. The balcony where he used to stand and watch me. It finally hits home that Ravi Lala is really in jail.

I walk toward Chacha's house. There is no smell of liquor brewing. Some marigold flowers in a pot flank the door of the hut. The walls are painted blue with a border of red and white flowers. A yellow-and-green three-wheeled auto-rickshaw stands where the brewery was. On the back of it is painted SHAUKAT'S TUK-TUK.

I look toward where my home used to be, wondering who owns it now. My family has built a pink brick three-roomed house somewhere. I've seen pictures of it. But this home looks pretty. It's a pink brick structure too. The new owners have a small bamboo stall leaning against the front of one wall—a betel paan leaf shop, lined neatly with jars of nuts, spices, and pastes. Some betel leaves soak in a steel bowl on a small table. Packets of tobacco, chips, and sweets hang from a bamboo pole above the raised platform. There is no loose litter on the floor, but a proper garbage can in front of the shop.

Realization dawns.

It can't be, but it is. Mai's dream. Her betel paan leaf shop.

I look more closely. My family has not moved.

The other pink wall on the other side of the door has a flowerpot with a hibiscus flower in it. The wall is painted by my mother, her signature white flowers painted with rice powder.

Next door, I hear the whirring and clanking of a sewing machine. I pause. My eyes pop. There is a sign outside: **MIRA'S SEWING CENTER.** *We take orders for pants, shirts, salwar kameezes, sari blouses, and petticoats.*

I look down the lane. There are no girls sitting on benches.

I'm afraid to move a muscle. I close my eyes and inhale the scent of wet earth. I open my eyes and look toward Jamila Bua's tea shop. I'm a little early. They don't know I'm here.

I linger in the shadow of the wall. And then, there they all are. Those closest and dearest to me. Salman, in long brown pants and a white shirt, with a little stubble and more flesh on his bones. He's taken a couple of days off from his boarding school in Siliguri. He is playing with baby Sania, who leans on his knee in a green polka-dotted dress. I stare harder. She is twice the size I left her. All her baby fat is gone and she's grown several inches. Baba is in a blue-checked cotton lungi and brown shirt. His bandanna is gone and so are his glasses. He is holding a cup of tea in his hands as he jokes with Shaukat and Chacha. They are laughing at something. Both are in clean T-shirts and pants. For once, Shaukat's hair is cut and combed neatly. Jamila Bua is frying pakoras. At last, I see Mai, chopping onions for Jamila Bua. Her hair is tied back in a bun as usual, but her lime-green sari is stiffly starched and ironed. It looks brand-new. There are no stains, tears, or creases. Chachi too has a new orange sari. They are all smiling. But where is Mira Di?

I knew it was too perfect to be true. My throat constricts, my fist clenches as I look toward Chacha's back room. The whirring and clanking have stopped. Suddenly a figure in a yellow salwar kameez rushes out and engulfs me in a hug.

I can't remember what happens next. Salman takes my bags. Mai buries me in an embrace. Her sari smells different, but her skin is still the same. Sania is a little shy, but as soon as I pull out a chocolate, she jumps into my arms. Baba smiles at us from afar, observing it all. I blink. Once, twice, three times.

It's not a dream.

A Letter from the Author

I started writing this story when a fourteen-year-old girl just like Heera won a gold medal in a karate competition in Forbesganj. She was being groomed for prostitution along with other girls in her lane. A lane just like Girls Bazaar.

Her journey was not easy. Her achievement was heroic. I saw how she and her friends overcame hunger, fought off their fear, and stood up to traffickers with grace and gusto.

An annual cattle fair used to claim girls from that lane every year. When my NGO, Apne Aap, opened a community center and hostel there, we were constantly attacked by men like Gainul and Ravi Lala. They would stalk the mothers, their daughters, and me, hurling abuses, throwing stones, stealing from our offices, and even kidnapping girls.

We built higher walls around the hostel to prevent traffickers from jumping over. I posted guards outside my home, hired lawyers, filed police complaints and cases in court. Just like Mai, some mothers in the lane disobeyed their husbands, even though they were beaten up. Their daughters were the first batch of girls in our hostel.

Most of the events in this book are inspired by real people, places, and events.

I still remember it was early morning and I was fast asleep when a boy and his mother came to my home asking for help. The boy's sister and cousin were locked up by traffickers who wanted to stop the girls from returning to our hostel. We had to mobilize the police to get them out. I noticed then that the girls were badly bruised, while the traffickers were unscathed. I wished that the girls had been able to fight back. Our Apne Aap women's group met that afternoon at the center. Everyone was scared that they would be beaten in retaliation for the police raid. That's when I suggested martial arts classes.

The women loved the idea. Someone knew a local karate teacher who taught in a private boys' school. We hired him and the classes began. The bullying at school stopped. When the girls began to win competitions, something changed. The very townspeople who had asked the school principal to expel our red-light children began to respect them. Fathers in the community began to value their daughters.

The biggest change was in the girls themselves. They began to own their bodies and respect themselves. Their grades improved along with their self-confidence. Hundreds of girls from the lane have since finished school. Many are college graduates. They have jobs as animation artists, teachers, doctors, lawyers, chefs, and managers of pizza parlors and gas stations.

Our NGO's community has become a safe space to hold meetings, share stories, get food, do homework, and plot against traffickers. Women very much like Mai and Mira Di still meet regularly in the center to solve their own problems. They fill out forms, with the help of Apne Aap social workers, to access government entitlements like low-cost food, housing, and loans. They go collectively to speak to authorities when there are delays. There is a real Jamila Bua who was the first president of our first women's group.

Apne Aap's legal team helps victims file police complaints, testify in court, and get traffickers convicted. The real Gainul and the real Ravi Lala are convicted and in jail. In 2013, Apne Aap survivor leaders and I testified to Indian Parliament for the passage of Section 370 IPC, a law that punishes traffickers and allocates budgets for services to the prostituted and vulnerable.

There were seventy-two home-based brothels in the lane when Apne Aap started. Today there are two. Girls no longer sit outside huts waiting for customers. The two sisters who were locked up in the hut have finished school. One is a chef, and the other is a teacher. The girl who was kidnapped is a karate trainer. Someone like Mai really has a betel paan leaf shop and someone like Mira Di is a seamstress. The cattle fair is no longer allowed to bring dance or orchestra groups.

I had no magic wand, no experience or knowledge on how to stop the kidnapping of girls or put traffickers in jail. I was an English literature student who was a journalist. But I resolved to do something, invented ways, and moved forward.

Most importantly I listened. Apne Aap's business plan was based on four dreams that the women had. They were: school for their children; a room of their own; an office job; and punishment of those who bought and sold them.

I learned that the best solutions come from those who experience the problem. The idea for the hostel, the idea of food in the community center, and even the idea of karate came when we sat in a circle in the mud hut that is our community center.

It evolved into a grassroots approach we call asset-based community development (ABCD). Every woman or girl who becomes an Apne

Aap member gains ten assets. These are both tangible and intangible—a safe space, education, self-confidence, the ability to speak to authorities, government IDs and documents, low-cost food and housing, savings and loans, livelihood linkages, legal knowledge and support, and a circle of at least nine friends.

Each asset is a building block in an unfolding story of personal and community change. I wrote this story because I wanted to share with you that change is possible.

You will want to know why I started Apne Aap. As I have already told you, I was a journalist. I was researching another story in the hills of Nepal when I came across rows of villages with missing girls. I followed the trail and found that a smooth supply chain existed from these remote hamlets to the brothels of India. Little girls as young as twelve were locked up in tiny rooms in Kolkata, Delhi, and Mumbai for years and sold for a few cents every night.

All the girls were from poor farming families. Many, like Heera, were from nomadic indigenous communities or marginalized castes. Like her, they were either not sent to school, bullied until they dropped out, or pulled out by their fathers and sold into prostitution.

I was sad, then angry, and finally determined to do something about it. I decided to expose the horror in a documentary, *The Selling of Innocents*, and won an Emmy for it.

As I stood on a stage in Broadway, I saw beyond the glittering lights, the faces of the women in India. They had told their stories in my documentary because they wanted their daughters to have a different future. I knew then that I wanted to use the Emmy, not to get another job, but to make a difference.

I did two things. I traveled with *The Selling of Innocents* across the world. I dubbed it into six languages and screened it in villages to show parents what the brothels were like. I also showed it to the UN and the US Senate, when I testified against the crime of human trafficking. It contributed to a global push by activists that finally led to a new UN protocol to end trafficking and the first US anti-trafficking law, the Trafficking Victims Protection Act (TVPA).

At the same time, I started Apne Aap with the women who had bravely spoken up in my documentary. Something had happened while I was making the documentary. A pimp had stuck a knife at my throat while I was filming. I was in a small room. There was nowhere to run away. Suddenly I was encircled by the twenty-two women I was interviewing. They told the pimp that he would have to kill them first. He knew it would be too much trouble to kill so many women, so he slunk away. I was saved. That moment changed my life.

I learned in a very practical way the power of women's collective action and the importance of sticking by one another. I promised myself I would never give up on the women's dreams. Today thousands of girls have exited prostitution systems from brothels across the country, there is more awareness about sex trafficking globally, and there are better laws and services for victims like Mira Di in over a hundred countries.

The truth is that there is not one, but many Heeras. Girls Bazaars still exist in many parts of our world, including the US. The brothel in Queens is real. A trafficking survivor from Indonesia told me the story of how she was locked up there and escaped by disguising herself in a burka. She is now a global leader in the struggle against trafficking.

The International Labour Organization estimates that there are over 40 million victims of human trafficking globally, with hundreds of thousands of victims in the United States. Human trafficking is the second-largest organized crime in the world, involving billions of dollars, according to the United Nations Office for Drugs and Crime (UNODC).

Thank you so much for reading *I Kick and I Fly*. I wrote this story because I wanted to share with you that someone somewhere of your age fought back and won. I wanted you to know that change is possible. I have witnessed it in my own lifetime.

Heera's story is a story of hope in spite of great odds. It's about our bodies—who they belong to and the command they can give us. It is the story of a community that resolves to make change contagious and succeeds. I hope you find a friend in Heera who will give you some clues to making the changes you would like in your own life.

The martial arts classes continue in Forbesganj.

Ruchira Gupta

Acknowledgments

I'd like to begin by thanking Gloria Steinem. Your brilliance is only matched by your sensitivity and fierce commitment to a fairer world. I still remember a day in Forbesganj, when you told a little girl like Heera, "your body belongs to you." And that meant the world to her. Thank you for being an example and thank you for the contribution you have made to our world. You made us realize our voice matters.

Boundless, bottomless thanks to Samantha Palazzi, my editor at Scholastic, who pushed me, believed in me, and chiseled my words with her heart. You got it right every time. I am so grateful for your professional expertise and personal friendship.

A most important thank-you to David Levithan, my publisher, for matching us and seeing the truth and hope in the book. I could not have followed better footsteps in fearless writing or found a better home than Scholastic.

Thank you to my husband, Sunil; my parents, Vidyasagar and Rajni Gupta; and my sister, Chikoo, who have constantly created a safe space for me in the middle of my activist adventures. To my first readers—my fourteen-year-old nephew and niece, Aanya and Anav Gupta, and nineteen-year-old Pia Haykel. This book was vastly improved thanks to your insights.

To my agents, Samantha Heywood and Laura Cameron at Transatlantic, for helping me navigate the world of a debut author.

To Shuyun Sun and Madhumita Bhattacharyya for steadily pointing my story in the right direction. To the early lovers of the story, Alice Walker, Sujata Prasad, Suzanne Goldenberg, Mona Sen, Kanishka Gupta, Tinku Khanna, Karthika VK, Amitava Kumar, Nandana Sen, and John Makinson.

I am grateful to my activist family of choice—Ashley Judd, Catharine A. MacKinnon, Dorchen Leidholdt, Taina Bien-Aimé, Purna Sen, Malini Bhattacharya, Rachel Moran, Tatiana Kotlyarenko, Simone Monasebian, Per-Anders Sunesson, Grégoire Thiery, and Anne Ostby for your leadership, for visiting Forbesganj, and for joining our struggle against sex trafficking.

A loving hug to my friends Irena Medavoy, Sybil Orr, and Rosanna Arquette, for their staunch support every step of the way.

Most significantly, my deepest gratitude to Shandra Woworuntu, for your leadership of survivors and for sharing your own journey from survivor to leader. You continue to inspire me.

But there is no one I'd like to thank more than the young girls and boys and the women whose lives I portrayed in the book, the real Heeras, Miras, Salmans, Jamila Buas, and Mais. It is because of you the book is written. Your strength and determination is what created the story.

You are standing up to sexism, racism, casteism, poverty, and marginalization. I was lucky that I could be part of your lives, witness your heroic struggles, and celebrate your achievements.

Finally, I want to thank all of you who are now reading the book. You are the generation that will set us free from fear, shame, and guilt. You are the generation that will not concede to a world where someone your age is bought or sold.

Additional Resources

What is child sex trafficking?[1]

Per the US Trafficking Victim Protection Act, "child sex trafficking is a form of child abuse that occurs when any child under eighteen years of age is advertised, solicited, or exploited through commercial sex where something of value—such as money, drugs, or a place to stay—is exchanged for sexual activity. The item of value can be given to or received by any person, including the child."[2]

It is important to know that human trafficking differs from smuggling and forced migration. In migration and smuggling, there is always movement, and the purpose is not exploitation.

Who are the victims of human trafficking?[3]

Traffickers around the world frequently prey on individuals who are poor, vulnerable, living in an unsafe or unstable situation, marginalized, and in search of a better life. According to research[4] out of the University of Pennsylvania School of Social Policy and Practice, nationally, 95 percent of "prostituted teens" were victims of earlier childhood sexual abuse. Homeless, runaway/throwaway, and foster children are the most vulnerable population of kids that are at risk for sex trafficking.

What can I do?

You can take concrete actions that include gathering information, reading, watching films, organizing activities in your community, advocating, and

---

1 National Center for Missing and Exploited Children. Definition based on US Trafficking Victims Protection Act (TVPA). https://www.missingkids.org/content/dam/missingkids/pdfs/CSTinAmerica_Professionals.pdf
2 https://www.state.gov/what-is-trafficking-in-persons/
3 https://www.unodc.org/unodc/en/human-trafficking/faqs.html
4 https://repository.upenn.edu/cgi/viewcontent.cgi?article=1131&context=edissertations_sp2

supporting anti-trafficking NGOs.

LEARN

- Find out if your city/state has a human trafficking task force. Sign up for updates and attend a meeting.

- Research human trafficking in one country not your own.

- Watch a human trafficking film. Watching with a group of people is a natural way to open a discussion among your community.

RAISE AWARENESS

- Write a blog or an op-ed to your school, community, or city paper related to human trafficking.

- Organize a book, movie, or arts-based awareness campaign in your community, public library or faith community, school, or campus.

- Include human trafficking in a classroom presentation, term paper, or report.

- Celebrate July 30 as World Day Against Trafficking in Persons to raise awareness about the growing issue of human trafficking and the protection of victims and their rights. In 2013, the United Nations passed a resolution designating this day.

- Invite a representative from a local anti-trafficking organization to a Q and A session.

VOLUNTEER

- Identify two or three anti-trafficking organizations and reach out to their volunteer coordinator or executive director. Set a goal to start volunteering by a specific date!

- Sign up to receive newsletters of two organizations whose mission you believe in.

- Share your commitment to these organizations on social media.

- Inquire about internships.

- Collect gently used professional women's clothing and back-to-school supplies from your friends and neighbors for survivors.

ADVOCATE
- Advocate for laws to protect minors from exploitative practices.
- Send an email to your local elected officials urging them to keep traffickers and trafficking victims top of mind.

DONATE
- Sponsor a child in a part of the world you know little about and educate yourself about human trafficking in that area.
- Make a regular contribution. Even ten dollars a month can make a big difference. Most organizations let you do this online.
- Donate to an anti-trafficking organization.
- Raise funds for the organizations by holding a community yard sale or a party, or in lieu of birthday or holiday gifts ask family members or friends to donate to your crowdfunder.

REPORT

What to do if a child in care goes missing?
There are people and resources available to help.
- The Childhelp National Child Abuse Hotline—Professional crisis counselors will connect you with a local number to report abuse. Call 1-800-4-A-CHILD (1-800-422-4453) or visit childhelphotline.org.
- The National Center for Missing and Exploited Children (NCMEC)—Aimed at preventing child abduction and exploitation, locating missing children, and assisting victims of child abduction and sexual exploitation. Call 1-800-THE-LOST (1-800-843-5678) or visit missingkids.org.
- National Human Trafficking Hotline—A twenty-four-hour hotline, open all day, every day, that helps identify, protect, and serve victims

of trafficking. Call 1-800-373-7888 or visit humantraffickinghot line.org.

The following are survivor and/or BIPOC-led programs offering comprehensive services to sex trafficking survivors. This list is not exhaustive but groups I have seen in action. It's a starting point.

- Apne Aap (New York and India)
- Asian Women for Equality (Canada)
- Breaking Free (St. Paul, MN)
- Courtney's House (Washington, DC)
- EVA Center (Boston)
- GEMS (Girls Educational & Mentoring Services) (New York, NY)
- LIFT (Living in Freedom Together) (Worcester, MA)
- Mentari (Queens, NY)
- MISSSEY (Oakland, CA)
- More Too Life, Inc. (Miami, FL)
- My Life My Choice (Boston, MA)
- OPS (Organization for Prostitution Survivors) (Seattle, WA)
- Stop Trafficking Us (Maine)
- Thistle Farms (Nashville, TN)
- YouthSpark (Atlanta, GA)

In addition, there are intergovernmental agencies like UNODC, UNICEF, and OSCE (Organization for Security and Co-operation in Europe) ODIHR (Office for Democratic Institutions and Human Rights); outstanding aid groups such as International Rescue Committee, Save the Children, and Mercy Corps; and NGOs working in countries across the world like CATW (Coalition Against Trafficking in Women) Asia-Pacific, CAP International, Kvinnefronten, Embrace Dignity, and others that are not listed.